This Time Next Year

This Time

New York   The
Vanguard
Press
Inc.

Next Year

a novel by Anne Nall Stallworth

Manufactured in the United States of America

Designer: Ernst Reichl

Library of Congress Catalogue Card Number: 74–155672

Standard Book Number 8149–0729–6

To My Mother and Father

This Time Next Year

✝✝✝✝✝✝ 1

There was a storm coming up, so I went to bed with my clothes on, even my shoes. There would be no time to dress later, no time to come awake slowly, for the storm would be almost on us.

Mama was terrified of storms, and her mother before her, and her grandmother and her great-grandmother. It was a family trait, passed down through the generations like a string of rare pearls, spoken of not with embarrassment but with pride. Mama often said, "My family has been scared of storms as far back as anybody can remember."

Daddy and I got sleepy and went to bed and left Mama sitting on the front porch steps watching the clouds. Sometimes a storm would go around after threatening for a while and spilling a few drops of rain, but tonight the wind had risen strong enough to bend the huge mountain oak tree in our front yard.

Mama came to my bed, shook me awake, and said, "There's a cyclone coming, Florrie, the sky's as black as coal and I think the oak tree is going to blow away. Go tell Toliver we're going to Mira's."

Then she went back to the front porch and stood, still watching the sky, the night turned into white, electric day. She was illuminated briefly in the flashes of light, while the wind tore at her, pulling her dress tight around her legs.

"Hurry, before we're blown away," she called, her voice rising in duet with the wind.

I went through the kitchen to Daddy's room, off the back porch, and the wind was so strong that it took all my strength to pull open his door.

"Hurry, Daddy, Mama says there's a cyclone coming."

He sat up, dressed just as I had been, except for his shoes. He rubbed his hand across his uncombed hair, then leaned over and began to pull on his shoes without putting on any socks. He looked around at me; his eyes were puffy from sleep.

"This house has been standing here for more than twenty-five years, and it wasn't until your mama came here to live that there was ever any thought about it being blown away by a cyclone." He shook his head.

"Don't tie the strings, Daddy, your shoes will stay on without tying the shoestrings."

He tied them slowly and carefully. "She's making a nervous wreck out of you," he said. "You should have seen us when we had to run from a storm over in Georgia. It was farther than Mrs. Kirk's house. We had to run about a mile to a colored family's house. Seems like anybody's house is safer than the one your mama's in at the time. I guess if she lived at her sister's, this is where she'd run to."

Daddy and I went to the front porch. Mama took my arm and we fled from the house, the lightning striking over in the cemetery as we crossed the road into the lane.

Dust flew in the air and got in our teeth, and every now and then one of us would spit into the grass along the lane. When we left the house the clock on the mantel in the living room said it was ten-thirty. Mama started to trot, pulling at me. "Let's try to make it to Mira Gray's before the rain."

"This is nothing in the world but damn foolishness," Daddy said. "Running from a little thunder cloud. You're making a nervous wreck out of Florrie."

Mama answered, "Mister, you don't have sense enough to know a bad cloud when you see one. You can sit there and get blown away, but don't expect me and Florrie to."

"I don't think going to Mrs. Kirk's will keep you from being blown away," he said. "If anything, I think the Lord will pick her house especially to blow away."

Then he told us the same story he told every time we ran from a storm. Sometimes the thunder drowned out his words completely, but Mama and I knew the story by heart and could fill in the missing words.

"Papa went to sit on the porch just to watch the storm," he said, finishing the story. "Then lightning struck him and ran up his pants leg, making a blue streak. 'Isn't the work of the Lord beautiful,' Papa said, and he wasn't hurt at all. People still tell that story around Tolbertville."

Daddy took long steps, striding along in his Army walk to keep up with our trot. He still walked as he had when he drilled as a soldier, holding his right arm close to his side and swinging his left arm.

"Joining the Army was the only way I could think of to have some fun," he told me once. He left his mule standing in the field, still hitched to the plow, and went to join the Army one hot July day in 1915.

"I didn't even tell Papa I was going, and that was wrong of me, but I couldn't stand the thought of plowing another furrow and I knew he'd try to argue me out of it. So I just waited and wrote him a letter from Brownville, Texas. That's the first he

9

knew where I was. I saw other boys around Tolbertville joining the Army, and I didn't see why I had to stay home and farm, with them going away and seeing something besides Georgia."

He was in the Cavalry for two years, and every now and then I took out the fading brown pictures of Daddy in brown khaki shirt and jodphurs, standing by his horse. I looked at them and thought how handsome he was, so tall with his coal-black hair.

We walked up on Aunt Mira's porch just as the rain began to fall. Daddy sat down on the front porch glider, refusing to go in. He had not been inside Aunt's Mira's house since the first time she sprinkled us with holy water to protect us from the storm. Daddy came from a long line of primitive Baptists. "Goddamn heathenistic Catholic," he said. "Thinks a little water blessed by the pope has some kind of magic power."

Mama and I went inside. The living room was warm and smelled musty. Aunt Mira kept the windows closed in the living room and the draperies pulled to keep the pale blue brocade chairs and couch from fading and mildew from setting into the rug.

Ralph Junior sat in one of the brocade chairs reading the paper. He was now what people in Gray's Chapel called an Old Bachelor, because he was past thirty. On his last birthday he was thirty-five, and already his straight blond hair was thinning the same way that Uncle Ralph's had, and a paunch pushed out beneath his belt buckle.

Dink, Aunt Mira's youngest boy, was sixteen and away at a Catholic boys' school, to be with the priests in hopes that he would take his school work more seriously. He was also my best friend. He was one year older than me, and we had played to-gether for as long as I could remember.

Mama and I sat down, Mama in the other brocade chair and me on the couch. Aunt Mira sprinkled each one of us with holy water, crossing herself each time she shook the glass bottle and the drops fell to bless our heads.

When she sprinkled Ralph Junior, he said with his English accent, "Thank you, Mother." Ralph Junior had gone away to school in Virginia, and when he came home he had an English accent. When I asked Mama how come he talked like that, she said that as far as she knew, people in Virginia talked the same way we did. "Maybe he was ashamed of the way he talked and wanted to change," Mama said.

Outside the storm broke and raged, and inside the lights flickered and went out and then came back on again. Each time I held my breath, wondering if they would come back on.

Mama sat dozing unafraid in the brocade chair. The storm didn't seem so close to you in here; the sounds came dimmer through the thick walls and the tight windows and doors, and because the house was set among the trees, the wind could not rush through open spaces to push at Aunt Mira's house, like it did ours. When a storm came up after we had gone to sleep at night, I would wake to feel our house trembling on its four stone pillars.

I leaned my head back. We sat there not talking, bound together for a while by the storm and blessed by the holy water that had dampened our hair. Sleepily, I watched Aunt Mira, short and plump at the other end of the couch, her feet barely touching the dark red rug.

She was the only Catholic in the family. She had married a traveling shoe salesman who came to Stillwater, where she and Mama and Aunt Marcy and Uncle Wilbur were born. Stillwater had a thousand people and was bounded on one side by the Coosa River and on the other by the Southern Railway tracks.

Uncle Ralph rode into Stillwater on the train one Saturday morning, carrying his sample case of shoes. He came to Uncle Wilbur's dry goods store, where Aunt Mira was working, his brown derby hat tucked under his arm; during the seven days he was in town, he and Aunt Mira were seen almost every day, arm in arm, walking toward the river. Uncle Ralph rode out of Stillwater the next Saturday morning taking with him not only his sample shoe case but Aunt Mira as well. They were married in Mobile, Uncle Ralph's next scheduled stop.

It mattered not at all to the rest of the family that the poor Catholic shoe salesman later owned a chain of shoe stores and became a rich man. Aunt Marcy said that Aunt Mira's love of money came from her changing to a Catholic, but Mama said that wasn't so. Mama said Aunt Mira had loved money all her life.

Grandmother Lee died without seeing Aunt Mira ever again, after she left on the train that Saturday afternoon. Aunt Mira cried at her funeral, begging her mother's forgiveness for not coming back to see her.

"It's too late for tears after somebody's dead," Mama said.

Wealth set well with Aunt Mira and Uncle Ralph, and they lived at the end of the lane in the white two-story house that Uncle Ralph had built for them. They collected rent or mortgage money from just about everybody that lived in Gray's Chapel. If they didn't own all the land now, they had owned it once upon a time.

Uncle Ralph named our community Gray's Chapel, Gray being Grandmother Lee's maiden name. Aunt Mira told him to name it for her. Aunt Marcy said Aunt Mira was pouring balm on her conscience.

Gray's Chapel was mostly a community of dirt farmers. Some of the people owned their farms, and others, like Daddy, tenant-farmed somebody else's land. A few, like Mr. Patton, a quarter-mile up the road, worked at the powder plant in Coal Town, five miles over the big hill.

There were no more than fifteen families, and if you walked

three miles in any direction, you were out of Gray's Chapel. Huxley was four miles away past the cemetery and through the woods, and Pitilla's, the Italian store there, was where we went for the things we couldn't grow at home. There was a barbershop and a drugstore and a café. And Huxley High School. A two-room grammar school was set among the trees on the same grounds as the high school.

Uncle Ralph bought Aunt Mira the cemetery next door to the white frame Methodist church, telling her all the money from the cemetery was hers to spend as she wanted to. She drove a hard bargain for the lots, and cash was all the payment she wanted, most times turning down pigs and chicken and corn. "I don't need anything to eat," she said one time. "It's money I want."

I thought we were lucky to live next door to the cemetery and the church. Most of the social life of Gray's Chapel centered around the church, and if I couldn't go to a funeral, I could at least watch from the window or the yard.

Dink was born in 1921. He was named David Nathaniel, but when Mama saw his initials embroidered on his clothes, she called him Dink. Aunt Mira fussed and called him David and told us to do the same, but the nickname stuck. Mama said Dink was a change-of-life baby, sick a lot of the time. He kept Aunt Mira from seeing to the land Uncle Ralph had bought all over Alabama, and from collecting the rent from her tenant farms as often as she would like.

The same year Dink was born, Uncle Ralph dropped dead of a heart attack in a lawyer's office in Rome, Georgia. He was closing a deal for another shoe store. Aunt Mira buried him in the big cemetery in Birmingham. She finally hired a trained nurse to come and look after Dink, and then she was able to spend all her time seeing to the money and land Uncle Ralph had left her.

*　　*　　*

The storm was over. Mama motioned to me and I stood up, warm and sleepy. We said good night to Aunt Mira and Ralph Junior. I wished they would ask us to spend the night, but even if they had, I knew, Mama would rather go home and sleep in her own bed.

Daddy still sat on the porch glider, and when we came out he stood up and stretched.

"Next time you'll have to come in, Mr. Birdsong," Aunt Mira said.

"Mrs. Kirk," Daddy answered, "I'm not a Catholic, and even if I were, I'd have a hard time believing a little water blessed by the pope could keep the lightning from striking me."

Aunt Mira turned and went back in the house without answering. Mama pulled at Daddy's arm. "How come every time you see Mira you have to throw up to her about being a Catholic! She could put us out of her house, you know."

Daddy didn't answer and we walked back home through the lane. I was so tired I ached with longing at how good the bed was going to feel. It was twelve o'clock. Aunt Mira's clock in the upstairs hall had chimed twelve times right before we left.

The wind was fresh, carrying the smell of rain; beyond the trees lightning still flashed now and then, but the faint rumble of thunder said it was far away. The clouds ran before the wind, and the sky was almost clear; you could see the stars. There would be sunshine tomorrow.

We passed through the dark of the woods, and when we got to the fields we could see the lights of our house across the road. I started to run, reaching the house before Mama or Daddy. I climbed the front steps and went through the front door, heading straight for the sleeping porch. I fell across my bed and kicked off my shoes while lying down. Mama came in

14

and kissed me good night and told me to get up and put on my gown, but I didn't even answer.

I was almost asleep when I heard Daddy tell Mama, "See, the house didn't blow away, Mrs. Birdsong. It's still here."

When I woke up the next morning, I could tell it was late from the slant of the sun coming through my windows. Two of my walls each had three windows, going from the floor to the ceiling. The windows opened shutter-like, and in the summer with all of them open, it was almost as good as sleeping outdoors. There were two trees outside the screens, one a black gum and the other a pine. I had pushed my bed close to the windows, and when I lay on my back and hung my head off the side of the bed, I could see the sky.

I stretched and yawned, knowing I ought to get up, but school had ended last week and the summer lay ahead. Then I remembered Dink away at school, and mourned the loss of my playmate.

Aunt Mira said sixteen was too old for him to be running wild in the woods with me, and fifteen was not a bit too young for me to start acting like a lady. She didn't approve of me, and she especially didn't approve of me talking Dink into going to revival with me one hot summer night last summer.

Dink and I got to the church, laughing and acting silly, and while the invitational song was sung I talked Dink into going up front and pretending to accept Jesus Christ as his saviour. Aunt Mira got the word from the neighbors the next day about how Dink stood up in front of the congregation laughing when people came around to shake hands with him. Aunt Mira had him to the priest for confession that same afternoon to ask forgiveness for going into a Protestant church, especially a Protestant church revival.

I sat up on the side of the bed. After a long, shuddering yawn, I pulled at my overalls and smoothed my shirt. It wasn't half bad to be dressed when you got up. I stood up and pushed through my bedroom door into the kitchen. It was empty. Dishes were still on the table, where Mama and Daddy had eaten breakfast. A pan half full of biscuits and a pot of coffee sat on the back of the wood-burning stove in the corner; a puddle of water in the kitchen fireplace ran down onto the hearth in sooty streams. Mama's window box had already begun to steam, the pink and white petunias lying sodden in the mud. The kitchen was hot, but the wood floor was cool under my bare feet.

The kitchen was the biggest room in our four-room house—four rooms if you didn't count Daddy's room off the back porch. Daddy called his room the shed room, because it was built on after the rest of the house was finished, jutting out at the far end of the back porch.

I got a cup that was draining on the white enamel worktable by the kitchen window and poured a cup of coffee. I sat down at Mama's round dining room table and sipped the coffee black, sucking it through my teeth to cool it.

Grandmother Lee told Mama when she was a little girl that this table and six chairs could be hers when Mama got married or when Grandmother Lee died, whichever came first. Grandmother Lee died first. She died from typhoid fever at the two-story house in Stillwater. Two men carried her down the stairs lying on a cot mattress, and when they saw Mama standing there, they shook their heads and smiled sadly at her. Her mother was dead. Mama, only eight years old, reached up and touched her, and she was so warm, Mama thought they were wrong.

But they took her out the back door and lay her gently in the back of a wagon, covered her over with a quilt, then climbed on the wagon and drove away, slapping the reins softly across the

16

horse's back. Mama watched until they were out of sight, then she went to play with the boy next door.

They squealed and chased each other, throwing water on each other from a bucket until the boy's mother called and fussed at them for being so wet. Mama went home, and Aunt Mira was sitting at the kitchen table dressed in black. It was only then she believed her mother was really dead.

She hid in a closet, pulling the clothes close around her, and when they brought her mother back to the house that night and lay her once again in her bed, Aunt Marcy came to the closet. She begged Mama to come out and see their mother one last time. But she would not. And she would not go to the funeral the next day.

Mama was the youngest of the four children and, like Dink, a change-of-life baby, born ten years after Aunt Marcy. Uncle Wilbur was the oldest, then Aunt Mira, Aunt Marcy and Mama.

Mama's father was a doctor, going all over St. Helen's County in a horse and buggy. He died when she was three years old, and she didn't remember him at all. People around the county said a young doctor in Stillwater, who was having trouble getting his practice started, poisoned Grandfather Lee. They said he put arsenic in the bottle of whiskey that he kept in his medicine bag. But that was only a story.

After Grandmother Lee's funeral was over, Mama was called to the living room, where Aunt Mira, Aunt Marcy, and Uncle Wilbur sat. Uncle Wilbur's wife, Ruby, was there, too. They were all dressed in black. The shades were drawn, and from the gloom they watched Mama with their long faces and sad eyes, wondering aloud to each other what would happen to Julia now that she was an orphan.

"I will be her guardian," Uncle Wilbur said. "Julia will live with Ruby and me."

Mama went to Aunt Marcy. "Marcy," she begged, "I want to live with you," but Aunt Marcy said, "I have my own little girl to raise. You must do what Wilbur says."

So Aunt Marcy and Aunt Mira went back to Birmingham to their families and Mama stayed with Wilbur and meek, scared Ruby, and they all lived together in the family home.

Mama worked in Uncle Wilbur's store after school, and if sometimes she forgot and went home to play, he whipped her. Aunt Ruby tried to comfort her when Uncle Wilbur wasn't looking, but Mama said Ruby made her sick with her nervous attentions and fear of Uncle Wilbur.

Aunt Marcy, in a fit of conscience, Mama said, returned once to Stillwater to take Mama back to Birmingham with her. Uncle Wilbur grabbed a butcher knife from the kitchen and chased Aunt Marcy from the house and told her never to come back. She never did.

One summer afternoon, when Mama was eighteen, she was sitting on the front porch swing with a boy she had known all her life, named James Miller. Uncle Wilbur, home early from the store, came up the front porch steps and walked over to them, pulling his gold watch from his pocket. Their whispering and soft laughter stopped as they watched him. After he looked at the watch for a long time, he said, "It's time for you to go home, James," and he put the watch back in his pocket, the chain hanging in a curve over his large stomach.

"I just got here, Mr. Lee," James said. "I'd like to stay a while longer, sir."

"Get," Uncle Wilbur said, watching him so coldly that James ran from the porch.

That night, Mama said, she lay awake in bed for a long time, then got up and went downstairs to Uncle Wilbur's bed. She hit him with her fists, crying and saying over and over,

"You'll never do that to me again, you'll never do that to me again."

Uncle Wilbur lay there, saying nothing, while the blows fell on his head and body. Ruby sobbed beside him. Mama went back upstairs, packed her suitcase, and left the house. She climbed the long hill to the railroad track and flagged the midnight train to Birmingham.

"I never saw him again," Mama said, "and I never wanted to."

Uncle Wilbur died on my eighth birthday, and Mama didn't go to the funeral. My birthday celebration went on as planned, and as far as I could tell, Mama's gaiety was real.

I turned up the cup and drank the last swallow of lukewarm coffee, leaving only the undissolved sugar in the bottom of the cup. I went to the back porch and leaned over the bannister.

"Yoda-la-*dee*-heeeeee," I yodled, calling Mama.

"Whoo," she answered from far away.

I went in the yard and stood in the June sun, looking toward the woods. She came from among the trees, pulling a log.

"Mama, wait," I called. "Wait and I'll help you." I ran to meet her and she dropped the log and waited. When I reached her, I sat down on the log, panting.

"You ran too fast," she said, laughing.

"I want to help you bring the log," I said. "It's too heavy for you by yourself."

She sat down next to me on the log and stretched out her legs. She wore a pair of Daddy's khaki pants and one of his khaki shirts. She wore an old pair of Ralph Junior's shoes.

I watched the dappled shade moving on her face and on her dark auburn hair, which waved softly to a bun on her neck. A hairpin had come loose, and I reached to push it back in place for her. Strangely, the men's clothes and the heavy men's shoes emphasized the curvings of her body, pointed out the slender bones of her ankles and the narrow slope of her shoulders.

I thought she must have really been beautiful when she married Daddy twenty years ago. But she was getting old now, forty-five on her birthday the nineteenth of July.

Mama had told me many times about her gray wedding suit and the silk blouse with the lace jabot she wore with it. Daddy came over from Atlanta to see an Army buddy in 1918. He met Mama the first night he was in Birmingham, at a party. It took him three weeks to talk Mama into going back to Tolbertville with him, writing her letters and coming to see her at Aunt Marcy's house. But Daddy didn't like to talk about that now, and if you wanted to make him mad, all you had to do was mention something in the letters he wrote to Mama those many years ago. Mama still saved his letters.

"He kept writing me about the little white bungalow we were going to live in," Mama said. "I guess that's what finally decided me, knowing finally I'd have a home of my own after all those years of living with Wilbur and Ruby."

She was as far from a home of her own now as she had ever been in those twenty years, I thought. Mama and Daddy came to live in Aunt Mira's house two months before I was born, and that made it fifteen years last February. They came because Daddy had lost the farm in Chaffee, Missouri, when he could not pay the taxes. They stayed because the Depression swept the land and there was no place else for them to go.

We lived in Aunt Mira's tenant house, next door to Aunt Mira's cemetery, and Daddy hated her but he loved her land. He farmed it with tenderness, but if one year it turned whore, the corn knubby and the potatoes small and hard like stones, why, this time next year it would be different, the crops bountiful. We'd have money left over in our pockets to spend on foolishness, Daddy said.

Mama sighed. "What are you thinking about, Florrie?"

"Nothing, just drowsing," I said.

"You're glad school's out, aren't you?"

"You just don't know how glad."

"I was sitting here thinking about when we move to town, you'll be going to a good city school. And we'll have a furnace and a basement in our house and won't have to pull in logs for stove wood any more."

I moved off the log and lay on my back in the grass, while Mama began her daydream of how it would be when we moved to town, and gradually I didn't hear her words anymore because I had heard them so many times before. I only heard the gentle cadence of her voice droning softly in the morning sunshine.

With Dink away at school, I thought, there won't be any reason for me to go to Aunt Mira's house so much. Not that I liked to go to see Aunt Mira, but because I would miss playing croquet on the smooth lawn and swimming in the concrete pool.

But I could go when Aunt Mira and Ralph Junior were gone. Last summer, when I saw them drive through the big iron gates and head for Huxley, I walked down the lane, the fields on either side of me. But when I came to the woods I ran, because they were full of bootleggers. My heart pounded and I pressed my hand against the pain in my side as I ran.

Everybody in Gray's Chapel knew bootleggers were in there. Daddy said they were. There was always a knocking deep in the woods, and everytime I passed through, I knew this was the time a bootlegger would step into the lane. He would be wearing faded bibbed overalls and a worn-out felt hat, and carrying a hammer, to account for the knocking. He would stand facing me, and then he would hit me in the head and step back into the woods to finish making the white whiskey that almost every man in Gray's Chapel drank. Including Daddy.

Daddy said the revenue agents were cracking down and that one of these days they would run the bootleggers out of there. Somtimes the sheriff came from Huxley and parked his car on the road and went into the woods, trying to catch them. But Daddy said he wasn't doing anything of the sort, he was sitting in there drinking with them. Daddy must have been right, because he never caught anybody.

After I passed the woods, I would go down the hill and turn the curve. Then I was at Aunt Mira's. I sat on her front porch, swinging in the glider and pretending Mama and Daddy and I lived in the white two-story house with the porch that went on three sides. When Uncle Ralph was living, Aunt Mira used to give parties and the people danced to the music from the Victrola on the front porch.

I would look toward the garden in front and imagine I saw Mama walking there among the roses, dressed in a blue print voile dress and wearing white shoes like Aunt Mira's. I walked beside her, dressed in white organdy, and every now and then Mama would stroke my long, silky blond hair, which hung in waves over my shoulders. I tossed my head, shaking back my hair from my face like Dr. Fairfax's daughter Lucille did. I dreamed of long hair, yearning for the day when I would no longer be sent to the barber in Huxley to have my hair shingled in the back and bangs cut.

Daddy was hard to imagine. Every time I put him in a white suit like Ralph Junior's, it turned wrinkled and threadbare, so I kept Daddy a shadowy figure in the background.

On days when Aunt Mira was home, I stayed close to the woods, picking blackberries and eating them as I walked along. Always, I went to the springhouse at the edge of the woods behind Aunt Mira's, to sit in the dim light and cool my feet among the watermelons that were lying in the pool of spring water.

Sometimes I stayed so long that when it was time to go home, the hot, bright outdoors seemed unreal, and I had to force myself to leave, keeping close to the edge of the woods so no one would see me.

🌲🌲🌲🌲🌲🌲 2

The pick hit the packed dirt with a heavy thud. Again and again, Daddy brought the pick down hard, until finally I saw the shape of the grave. It was a tiny rectangle, a grave for a child. The pick rose and fell rhythmically, its curved shaft sinking deep. Daddy grunted as he tore loose the wet, black earth.

Aunt Mira would pay him five dollars for digging the grave, enough money to pay for all the seeds he planted this year. I wished that I could have a dollar of it to buy the white pumps I had seen in the store window in Birmingham.

I sat down cross-legged under a tree near Daddy and thought about Goo-Goo Barfield, the four-year-old boy that would be buried in this grave tomorrow afternoon. He was born in 1933, eleven years after his sister, Nell, born long after Sharon and Clyde Barfield had given up hope of ever having another child. And given up hope for the boy that Clyde dreamed of.

Sean was born when they were in their forties. People smiled fondly at Mr. Barfield's joy in his son, smiled to see that big man holding so gently that little baby in the crook of his arm. "He's more the mama than Sharon is," they said, and for a year it was true. He bathed and dressed Sean and took him to the fields with him and kept him all morning, laying him on a pillow under a tree. He took him home at noon to his mother.

Daddy said, "That boy means that Clyde will have a strong back to help him in the fields and someone to pass the farm to when he gets old," and I was sad that Daddy had no strong boy's back to help him in the fields.

Clyde Barfield took care of that baby son so much and talked to him so much that the baby could tell his step when he came into the room. The baby would stretch his neck and roll his round eyes trying to find his father, and people would laugh and say, "Look at those goo-goo eyes." So that's what everybody called him.

Goo-Goo did fine the first year. He was plump and happy, but the second year he stayed sick most of the time, and Clyde didn't know how to take care of the fretful, unhappy child. He gave his son back to Sharon and he went to the fields by himself and stayed until after dark.

Nell came up to the house and we talked, being the same age and in the same room at school. But we didn't have much in common, because she was going out so much with boys and I wasn't, and she was so pretty with her white skin and black hair. Nell said it was gloomy around her house and she stayed gone as much as she could.

"They just sit around talking about Goo-Goo," Nell said. "We used to laugh and tell jokes but since Goo-Goo's been sick,

Papa thinks it's a crime to joke. Sometimes I wish Goo-Goo had never been born." She put her hand across her mouth, horrified at what she'd said.

Goo-Goo had tonsilitis one whole winter, but in the summer he seemed better. But the third winter was the worst of all, and the doctor in Huxley said Goo-Goo's heart was bad and the only hope for him was to take out his tonsils in the spring when he was better. Goo-Goo had bled to death yesterday in the operating room of the hospital in Birmingham.

I looked over the tombstones toward the road and saw Ralph Junior's shiny black Plymouth wobbling through the gates. He got out of the car, his white suit luminous in the noonday sun. He took off his wide-brimmed Panama straw hat and stood there fanning himself, then shaded his eyes with his hand and looked toward our house. His gaze moved slowly to the cemetery and stopped when he saw Daddy and me. He waved his arm and motioned, and as sullenly as I could from that distance, I yelled, "What?"

With a jerk of his arm, he motioned again. I stood up and brushed the grass carefully off my overalls before I began to walk slowly down the hill. I stood at the cemetery fence that ran along the road and waited.

Ralph Junior picked his way carefully through the dust, stooping in the middle of the road to rub his handkerchief across his white buckskin shoes. He glared at me over the fence, his face red and angry.

"You knew durn well what I wanted, Florrie Birdsong. You go tell that old daddy of yours to get on down here and fix that flat tire of mine. He needs to do something around here to pay for you all living in our house."

"You shut your goddamn mouth, Ralph *Junior* Kirk. Fix your own flat tire with your pretty hands."

I turned and ran back up the hill before he could see me

crying, and he yelled after me, "I'm telling Julia how you cursed me, and I hope she beats the hell out of you," his voice rising louder as I got farther away.

I reached the far side of the cemetery, where there were no graves, only trees and shade and grass. I dropped to the ground and lay back in the shade of a live oak tree and gave myself to the wind, a lover who held me and comforted me, who cooled the dampness on my neck, caressed my face and bathed it with his sweet breath; then, rising, rattled the leaves above, moved on to top the hill, flattened the grass as he rushed down its slope, and in a final frenzy spent himself among a stand of trees.

I sat up and saw Ralph Junior on the hill talking to Daddy. He jerked his head toward his car; then Daddy stepped out of the hole and followed him down the hill.

I stood up to go home, looking toward the road. Daddy was kneeling in the lane, bent toward the tire. I imagined for a moment that Daddy would take the tire iron and hit Ralph Junior in the head and he would fall, his blood splashing in the warm dust. Then I went home.

I stopped at the stone well that stood at the end of our back porch and got a drink of water from the bucket, filling the dipper twice before my thirst was quenched. Then I went in the house and stopped inside the door, blind from the sunlight. The kitchen smelled of cold biscuits and grease hardening in the skillet.

I went to find Mama. I stopped at the mantel in the living room and looked at the clock. Quarter to one. I was starved, and wondered if Mama had eaten lunch. I had seen no signs of lunch in the kitchen.

I tiptoed to Mama's room and looked in. She was standing in front of her dresser mirror, dressed in her good clothes, even to gloves.

26

"Mama, where're you going?" I asked, leaning in the door.

She whirled around, her hand flying to her heart. "You like to have scared me to death, Florrie. Don't slip up on me like that," and she turned back to the mirror, fluffing up the white lace jabot on the front of her dark blue eyelet dress.

"I'm not going anywhere. I'm just trying to find something decent to wear to town when we go," she said.

"When are we going to town?"

"One day next week, to see about something I've been keeping a secret."

I looked at her with horror. "You're going to have a baby," I said, my voice flat.

"Florrie," Mama said in a whisper, her hands clasped. "How can you talk like that? I'm ashamed of you."

I shrugged. "Everybody seems to keep having change-of-life babies. You were one yourself, you said. And Dink. And Goo-Goo Barfield."

"I knew it. I knew you've been talking too much to Nell Barfield. What else has she told you?"

"Nothing I didn't already know, Mama," I said. "I've known for a long time where babies come from, and that husbands and wives sleep together to get them."

She pulled off her gloves, blowing into them to make them puff out. Then she smoothed them and put them in her dresser drawer.

"I have my room and Toliver has his. There's not likely to be any change-of-life baby, or any other kind. And if you're so wise and grown up, why don't you start wearing a brassiere?"

Our eyes met in the dresser mirror, held, and then I looked away. "If we're going to talk about my wearing a brassiere, I'd just as soon not stay," and I turned to leave the room.

"Wait a minute, Florrie, don't go. I really do have a secret. Sit down on the side of the bed and I'll tell you."

I sat down on her blue hobnail bedspread and waited.

"Do you promise you won't tell?" she said.

I nodded, and she pulled open her bottom dresser drawer. She reached under the neatly folded clothes and pulled out a candy box. The box was red and square and had a picture of an old-fashioned girl dressed all in white and wearing pantaloons. An open umbrella rested on her shoulder, and she smiled at us. Mama saved pretty candy boxes; this was the one I had given her on Mother's Day two years ago. It came from the drugstore in Huxley.

Mama sat down next to me on the bed and put both hands, palms down, on top of the candy box.

"I've got something I'm going to show you, Florrie, but promise me once again that you won't tell."

"I promise, Mama, I promise," I said, impatient now to know what was in the box.

"First, let me tell you something else. You remember those times I went to Birmingham by myself and stayed all day long? You remember I told Toliver I was window-shopping?"

"Yes," I said.

"I wasn't window-shopping, I was looking at houses. I was looking at houses for the day we move to town."

She was watching me. I smiled at her.

"That's not all I've done. I've looked for a job, too, and I found one. I've got a job selling shoes in the basement at Davis's in Birmingham," she ended triumphantly.

I looked at her, and had the same feeling I had the day we went to Birmingham to see President Roosevelt ride through on the train. He waved and smiled from the observation platform of the train, but he had a look of far places and important matters to attend to. Mama seemed that way to me now. Imagine having the nerve to ask somebody in the biggest store in Birmingham for a job.

28

"Well, I'll be damned," I said.

"Will you please stop cursing, Florrie? Just because Toliver curses is no sign you have to. It's not refined."

"Mama, what's in the box?" I begged.

She pulled the lid off slowly, and when it was finally off, there was money inside. There was paper money, and a lot of coins. I saw a ten-dollar bill and a five-dollar bill and some ones.

"Mama, where did you get that?" I asked.

"From the getting place," Mama laughed.

"I mean *really*, Mama. Quit acting silly. Where did you get it?"

"I've been saving for a year," she said. "I set myself a goal of fifty dollars in a year, and I made it."

"I don't understand where you got money to save. You wouldn't even let me have a dollar for the white pumps at Davis's," I accused.

"The money's not for white shoes. It's for a house in town. I saved it out of Toliver's Army disability, and I got fifteen dollars for the black pig."

"You mean Daddy's black pig?" I asked.

"I mean Daddy's black pig," she answered.

"You mean you stole Daddy's black pig?"

"No, I didn't steal Daddy's black pig," she said irritably. "It was as much my pig as it was his."

"But Daddy fattened that pig up for six months. He was planning on taking it to the stock auction in Birmingham and selling it for a hundred dollars at least, he said. Mama, you ought not to have stolen Daddy's pig."

"Will you please quit saying I stole it, Florrie?"

"How did you slip that big, fat thing away, anyway, Mama?"

"I didn't slip it away," she said. "One day last summer when Toliver was working in the far field, I was out hoeing in the

29

garden and that thing kept on grunting down there in the pig pen. I went back down there and looked at him for a long time and then I decided I'd do it."

"Do what?"

"Sell him and keep the money. I walked up the road right then to Howard Beeton's. I asked him if he wanted the pig for fifteen dollars if he promised not to tell Toliver. I knew if Toliver sold it, I never would see any of the money. He'd just keep on pouring it back into Mira's land, for all the good that'll ever do us."

"You sold Daddy's pig to one of those old Beetons?"

"The Beetons' money spends just like anybody else's." She picked the paper money up, riffling the bills. "This money goes for our house in town," she said. "This time next year, God willing, that's where we'll be."

"How did you keep Daddy from seeing Howard leave with the pig?"

"That wasn't hard. Howard put a rope around the pig's neck and led it off through the woods. He didn't go home down the road."

The Beetons were our closest neighbors, except for the Gogginses next door. The Beetons lived about a half a mile down the road. I shook my head. I had to hand it to her. That pig was Daddy's pride and joy, and when he came home to milk our cow, Beautiful Eyes (named by Mama because of her round deep brown eyes), and feed the pigs, late that afternoon, and found his fattening hog gone, he went to Huxley for the sheriff. The sheriff went all over Gray's Chapel, asking if anybody had seen Daddy's pig. Howard must have kept it hidden down in the woods. Looking back on it now, I remember how quiet Mama was, never saying a word the whole time. And that wasn't like Mama. She usually had a lot to say about anything that happened in our family.

"I told Mira two months in a row, Florrie, that I couldn't pay the rent, so that was eight dollars a month I was able to keep out of the fifteen dollars Army disability. Then I saved a dollar here and a dollar there, and it got to be fifty. That's when I decided to tell you."

"When do you start work?"

"Not until after school starts."

She put the lid back on the candy box and knelt to put it back in the dresser drawer. She turned to look at me before she put it back under the clothes.

"I wanted you to know I had it and where it was, Florrie. If anything happened to me, you'd know where it was and could take the money."

"Nothing will ever happen to you, Mama," I said.

Mama put the box away and closed the drawer and came to sit on the bed beside me. "Do you think it's a sin, the things I've done for money, Florrie?"

"No. I don't think there's any such thing as sin. Or heaven or hell either."

"I believe there's a heaven," Mama said. "I believe there's a place you go and find out what all the things that happened to you meant."

Tears rolled down her face and dropped on the dark blue eyelet dress, darkening and spreading out. I put my arm around her shoulders, and I cried, too.

"I always thought that if Mama hadn't died with me so young, things would have been different. Mama wouldn't have let Wilbur treat me like he did, and I would have gotten some of the money and land that went to all the rest. Wilbur took all the land that was supposed to have been mine and later sold it to Mira Gray. Sold it to his own sister."

We sat for a long time without moving, Mama's finger idly pushing at the damp spots on her dress. I was cramped and hot.

I heard the sleepy sound of a rooster crowing far away.

Daddy came up on the back porch stamping his feet; then we heard the rope on the wheel unwind as he let the water bucket down into the well. Daddy was drawing water to wash up.

"Hush crying, Florrie, you'll make yourself sick," Mama said, and kissed me. She stood up and left the room then, but I lay on her bed until the room was almost dark, unwilling to leave the velvet comfort of its womb. I stayed until supper noises were coming from the kitchen, and then I stretched and stood up, thinking, "I wonder whether Billy Paul would notice me if I wore a brassiere," and I went to help Mama finish cooking supper.

🌲🌲🌲🌲🌲🌲 3

I sat at the kitchen table with Mama, drinking coffee and listening to Aunt Mira's voice, muffled and angry through the closed living-room door. A man's voice, tearful and pleading, answered. The funeral bell rang from the belfry of the white frame Methodist church.

From the kitchen window I could see mourners already gathered at the grave Daddy dug yesterday under the cedar tree. It was an ordinary summer day, its fabric much like that of all other summer days, except today there was a funeral, so it was a day to be remembered, a day that would later be plucked from the others and mulled over.

Summer was the right time for a funeral, because life was abundant all around you, and it was easy to believe that there was a God after all, and that when we died, we lived again and grew in heaven.

The door to the living room opened and Aunt Mira and Mr. Barfield came into the kitchen. Mr. Barfield's eyes were red from crying, and he was holding his straw hat in both hands, rolling the brim back and forth.

He wore black pants and a blue check sport shirt, neatly closed at the neck with a black tie. He was big, with bright blue eyes and blond hair.

Daddy farmed on halves with him last summer. Daddy said together they could raise more than either one of them could alone, and he asked Aunt Mira if it was all right with her. She said it was. Not only was it all right, she said, but she wouldn't ask for anything they grew that year for herself. But when harvest time came, she drove to the field late one September afternoon, motioning Daddy to the road.

He came to face her over the fence.

"Mr. Birdsong, half that corn is mine," she said.

"Mrs. Kirk," Daddy said, "you said you didn't want any corn this year because I was farming on halves."

"I didn't say any such thing, Mr. Birdsong. I said that after I got my half, you and Mr. Barfield could divide it any way you wanted."

Mr. Barfield had come up behind Daddy; he stood listening. "There's a place she'll go some day, Tol," he said, nodding his head toward Aunt Mira. "When she dies, she'll have to leave the corn and the big house and stand before her maker just like you and me will have to. I don't believe if every priest in the world prayed for her, it would keep her soul out of hell."

Aunt Mira was polishing her glasses and dropped them on the ground. When she bent to pick them up, a big foot came down and crushed them, grinding them into the ground. The three of them stared at the broken glass, and when a dog burst into the field yelping and chasing a rabbit, they watched the chase like friendly neighbors gathered to discuss the quality of this year's crop.

"I'm sorry, Mrs. Kirk," Mr. Barfield said. "I've got to have my half of the corn this year because my boy is sick and . . ."

Aunt Mira turned and walked away, climbed in her car and drove slowly away. They harvested the corn three ways, and Daddy took hers on the wagon and dumped it on the croquet court.

"Please, Mrs. Kirk," Mr. Barfield was saying now, "please don't make me wait any longer to bury my son. You'll get your money when my brother gets here. My brother's going to let me have the money to finish paying for the lot. He's on his way here from Jackson."

Aunt Mira shook her head. "This is business, Mr. Barfield. You know I'm a widow woman with two sons. I make my living from the cemetery. I've got to have my money now."

Mama left the kitchen and in a minute came back with money in her hand. "How much does he owe you, Mira Gray?"

"Where did you get that money, Julia?" Aunt Mira asked.

"None of your business. How much does he owe you?" Mama said.

Mr. Barfield went to Mama and put his hand on her shoulder. "God bless you, Julia, but I can't take your money. You people need money just as bad as we do."

"How much do you owe her, Clyde?"

34

"Thirty-five more," he said.

Mama counted out the money and pushed it into his hand.

"If you've got money like that, Julia," Aunt Mira said, "how come you can't pay rent?"

Mr. Barfield threw the money at Aunt Mira, and it fluttered down around her feet. She picked it up, making sure each bill faced the same way, then put it in her purse. She left the room, and we were quiet until the sound of her car had died away.

"Florrie," Mama said, "you planned on going to the funeral, didn't you?"

I looked at her and felt sorry for her that she had lost most of the money it had taken a year to save.

"Yes, Ma'am, I'm going," I said.

"Walk with Mr. Barfield to the cemetery, and try to be some comfort to the family. I hear from Mrs. Goggins that Sharon is taking this hard."

Mr. Barfield nodded his agreement, and we left the kitchen and started for the cemetery. Mama had never been to a funeral in Aunt Mira's cemetery, and though she didn't mind me going, when I asked her to go with me, she wouldn't. Sometimes she would stand in the yard, one hand on her hip, and stare toward the cemetery for a long time.

"If I die before Toliver, and you all put me in that cemetery, I swear I'll come back here to haunt you," she told Daddy and me.

Mr. Barfield took my hand as we walked up the path toward the cemetery gate. His feet dragged, drawing wide lines in the dust. He stumbled and caught himself. A red bird whistled overhead.

As we went through the gate, the heart-shaped wreath of red and white roses came into focus at the head of the grave; the women's sunbonnets could be matched to faces, and Mrs. Barfield's keening blended with the organ music floating out the church windows. Effie Johnson would play hymns until Brother Gridley began the funeral sermon. Then someone would go to get her.

Mr. Barfield turned loose my hand, and we stepped into the circle of mourners. There were chairs set in a row by the side of the grave, and he sat down with Mrs. Barfield and Nell. His brother was not there. The tiny casket was covered with a blanket of white carnations and lay on straps that were stretched across the grave.

Mrs. Barfield was quiet now, her hands folded in her lap. She wore Sunday clothes that were no more becoming than her housedresses. She was small, her skin brown and coarse. She looked like pictures I had seen of the women who went west with the wagons.

She had worked side by side with Mr. Barfield in the fields before Goo-Goo was born. Her hair was straight and cut short, and she wore it pulled back from her face. Her white crepe dress had thick shoulder pads, making her shoulders too square for her small body.

And then you saw her eyes. They were dark blue and deep-set, outlined with thick black lashes. From them looked the young girl trapped forever inside. Mama said when Mr. Barfield brought her here a bride, she was the prettiest little thing you ever saw, and Clyde would hug her and say, "She brought the blue of the Irish sea in her eyes so she could never forget her home."

He had met her when she came from Ireland to work in a canteen in England in 1918. Mama said Nell was the spitting image of Sharon fifteen years ago.

Aunt Mira tried for a long time to get Sharon Barfield to go to Mass with her, but she never would. Sharon fondled her rosary when she visited the Ladies Missionary Society meetings, but last summer she joined the Methodist church during revival.

Brother Gridley cried with joy that night and said that bringing a Catholic into the fold was a triumph over the devil. He often pointed his finger at her during church service to remind us of the lost sheep he had saved from hell fire. People shuffled and murmured as they turned to look at Sharon Barfield, nodding their heads in approval as they looked in the direction of the pointing finger.

One Sunday her place was empty on the third bench down from the front. And the next. And the next. Brother Gridley's sheep had slipped from the fold.

Little Ben Mizell was sent to the church after Mrs. Johnson, and the music stopped when he hollered through the window: "Come on, Mrs. Johnson, Brother Gridley's starting the service now."

A stillness settled over the people who had gathered there to say good-bye to Goo-Goo and to tell when they went back home how the family was taking it. Mama would be watching for me from the window, and when the funeral was over I would sit at the kitchen table with her and tell her all that had happened.

Ben and Mrs. Johnson trotted across the grass toward us, holding hands. As the sun climbed higher in the sky, the carnations on Goo-Goo's casket wilted, their warm, sweet smell hanging in the air. Every time I smell a carnation, whether growing in a garden or in a corsage on a girl's dress, I see a funeral. For me they will always be funeral flowers.

I watched Daddy across the cemetery, his arms rising high to bring the swing blade down hard on the tall grass. He was clearing new ground in the cemetery. Aunt Mira was opening up a new section; tomorrow she would begin selling lots in it.

Most of the time Daddy would quit whatever he was doing if he was in the cemetery on the day of a funeral and come and stand beside me. But he wouldn't today. He never came to a child's funeral. "A child is the only really good thing on earth," he said, "and I can't stand to see it put away."

The wind brought the smell of the fresh-cut grass to blend with the smell of the carnations. The sun was straight up in the sky, and our shadows lay on our feet as Brother Gridley raised his arms to begin. Mrs. Johnson and Ben were here.

Brother Gridley held a Bible in one of his upstretched hands, and he wore the long black coat and string tie that he used both for weddings and funerals. He was short, with wavy brown hair, and his cheeks were red from tiny blood vessels that lay just under the skin.

Brother Gridley had been the preacher at the Methodist church for ten years. He believed that the end of the world was due any day now, and he sat on a straight chair on the church pulpit, his chest heaving with emotion after one of his hell-fire sermons. He scared me when I was little, and I ran home to tell Daddy that the end of the world was coming that night.

"Brother Gridley's full of prunes," Daddy said, and I climbed on his lap, happy to know it was prunes and not truth.

Now Brother Gridley was praying for Goo-Goo, but he called him "this child Sean." I couldn't put "Sean" on Goo-Goo's face. He asked God to forgive Sharon Barfield for being a backslidden Methodist, and he finished the prayer by saying, "Open wide the door of heaven for their innocent son, who, had You in Your infinite wisdom allowed him to live and choose, he would have chosen the true, Protestant church of the Lord. Allow this child, oh Lord, to push open Thy gates of pearl and walk down Thy streets of gold to be with Thee forever. Show this mother and father the terrible wrath of the Lord. Bless us all gathered here today, and if it be Thy holy will, let this be the year the church pays off the mortgage. Amen."

He read from the Bible. "In my house are many mansions, if it were not so I would have told you. I go to prepare a place for you."

Clyde Barfield broke a carnation off Goo-Goo's casket and handed it to Sharon. She began rocking back and forth, wailing, her hands clasped across her stomach.

Brother Gridley nodded to Brother Lowrey, one of the church deacons, to lower the casket into the grave. The handle's joint creaked as Brother Lowrey unwound the straps that lowered Goo-Goo into eternity. Mrs. Johnson had gone back to the church organ, and once again music came from the windows.

Two men on each side of the grave stepped to the edge and dropped in bits of fern they had been holding during the sermon. Children broke flowers from the wreaths and threw them on the casket. Mrs. Barfield fell across the grave, sobbing.

"I can't let my baby go, I can't let my baby go," she cried.

Mr. Barfield and Nell pulled at her. Nell was crying. Mr. Barfield said, "Sean's not really in there, Mother, come and sit down."

She pulled herself up, black dirt on the side of her face and on the white dress, and knelt by the side of the grave. She pulled a handkerchief from her pocket and unfolded it. Inside was her rosary, and she took it out and held it, touching each bead, her lips moving silently. Jesus hung from the cross on the end of her rosary, and she kissed the blood that was a ruby stone over his heart. "I want to see my baby," she said.

Mr. Barfield shook his head, and with his voice breaking said, "No, Mother."

Nell sat down in the chair and covered her face with her hands. Mrs. Barfield said again, "I have to see my baby one last time."

Mr. Barfield nodded his head to Brother Lowrey, and the

casket rose out of the grave as he turned the handle back the other way. Brother Gridley raised the casket lid, and the flowers and fern slid off into the dirt.

Noon sun streamed onto the body lying on the white satin mattress, and shone on the head lying on the satin pillow. Goo-Goo looked shrunken, drawn into himself and unready to walk the streets of heaven in his white suit and shirt with the black tie.

Mrs. Barfield leaned over and kissed the marble forehead. She raised his hand and put the rosary under it. Then she fainted, Mr. Barfield catching her as she fell. People moved the chairs close together and stretched her out. Mr. Barfield fanned her with his hat.

Brother Gridley closed the casket and told the men to hurry and get it into the ground and covered with the dirt that lay piled to one side.

I turned and walked from the cemetery back home, singing along softly with the organ music:

> "Abide with me, fast falls the even tide,
> The darkness deepens,
> Lord with me abide."

I never stayed when the men shoveled the dirt back into the grave. I would come back at dusk, to look at the flowers and take a walk in the twilight, to read the tombstones, and to touch the stone lambs and angels, still warm from the heat of the sun.

✝✝✝✝✝✝ 4

I lay deep in the grave, while the choir of women's voices held the same high note. When the sound ended, I could move and come out of the grave, but until then I was frozen with terror. A hand gripped my shoulder and shook me, and I moaned and opened my eyes. Mama's worried face was close to mine.

"Wake up, Florrie, you're having a bad dream."

Night was almost gone from the room, the sleeping-porch windows gray with dawn and summer rain. Mama got in bed with me and put her arm over my shoulder, fitting her body to mine. I lay for a while, watching the rain run down the windows, and finally my fear began to fade. I wished Mama would go back to her own room, but she was asleep, her breath coming in gentle puffs.

I stretched and moved to my side of the bed, but Mama slept on. Today was Saturday, tomorrow Sunday, and a thrill of joy streaked through my stomach. Billy Paul. Tomorrow I would sit in church and watch Billy Paul lead the congregation in singing.

Billy Paul went with a girl named Elaine Parish. Elaine had

41

round hips and large breasts. One Sunday morning Billy Paul smiled at me as he passed my bench. I blushed and looked away. I cursed myself and went home and sat under the tree and dreamed of him.

Next Sunday, I vowed sitting there, when the young people were gathered around the piano singing before church service, I would walk down the aisle toward Billy Paul. He would turn, a smile breaking on his face, and walk to me, putting his arm lightly around my waist to escort me to the group. But I had gone to church at my usual time and worshipped Billy Paul from afar.

He sat with Elaine, his arm draped carelessly across the seat behind her shoulders. Brother Gridley stomped his foot and shouted from the pulpit that the end of time was at hand.

"Oh Lord," I prayed, "please don't let the end of time come before I've known Billy Paul's touch."

I told Nell Barfield one time how I loved Billy Paul, but that I knew it was hopeless because how could I ever hope to take him away from somebody like Elaine Parish.

Nell said, "Why don't you just picture him straining over the toilet and then you won't care anything about him at all."

I was horrified, and told her that was like trying to imagine Jesus in the bathroom.

"Well, I know Billy Paul's just like everybody else," she said. "He's not Jesus, that's for sure, because I saw him peeing on a tree at the school picnic last year."

I quit talking to her about Billy Paul.

The springs squeaked as Mama got out of bed. "Florrie, you can't sleep all day," she said. "You've got to come and help me with breakfast so Toliver can get back out to the field. The Ladies Missionary Society meets here today."

Oh God, I thought. I had forgotten. All those old hens sitting around in our living room with their eyes darting around. They didn't miss a thing that they could talk about later, that's for sure. This was the first time they had met here in a long time, and I could tell Mama was all up in the air.

When Mama left Stillwater those many years ago, she took Grandpa Lee's surgical case with her. She said it was as much hers as anybody else's, and she wouldn't give it back to Uncle Wilbur even when Aunt Mira told her that would be the Christian thing to do.

When the Ladies Missionary Society met here, it was displayed on the mantel in the living room. Mama would call the ladies' attention to it, would remind them that, when she was a young girl in Stillwater, her father was a doctor and that her family had lived a genteel life. The ladies would nod and murmur approval, but Nell said when they met at her house, they really talked bad about Mama.

"She's not living so good now," they said, "in spite of her having a rich sister living down the lane. They don't even have an indoor toilet."

An indoor toilet. We certainly didn't have an indoor toilet. And what was worse than that, we didn't even have an outhouse. We had a chamber pot. Mama had partitioned off one end of the back porch with orange curtains. Inside sat the chamber pot. Daddy had built a shelf onto the wall, braced with boards. A tin pan was placed on this and, next to the pan, a bar of soap. This was our bathroom.

Every evening, just at dark, Mama went into the woods behind our house. She carried the chamber pot in one hand, and in the other a long-handled shovel. She was going to flush the toilet.

The ladies of the Missionary Society never forgot to ask

Mama when Mrs. Kirk was going to put indoor plumbing in our house. "We're doing fine just as we are," Mama always told them.

Aunt Mira would never put a bathroom in our house, because it was something Daddy could use, too. Besides, I thought, chamber pots were better than outhouses, anyway. At least, on cold winter nights we only had to go as far as the back porch, and we never had to chase the chickens away to keep from being pecked.

Mama was rattling dishes in the kitchen. She had told me to get up and make my bed, but still I lay there, watching the rain. It was a slow rain that would last all day, I knew. In the winter, I could go behind the stove and read; nothing much was expected of me when it rained. Today, it meant I would have to stay inside for the whole Missionary Society meeting, unable to slip away down the lane or go to the woods with my library books.

I got up and made my bed, then went to the kitchen to help Mama. She was kneading dough for biscuits, flour almost up to her elbows and dusted across the front of her dress. She never wore an apron. I made her one in sewing class, and she said, "Florrie, I'm surprised you sew so well," then folded it and put it in her dresser drawer. When someone knocked on the door, she took the apron and wore it until they left, then it went back in the drawer again. I once sewed pearl buttons about the size of a quarter on Mama's blue eyelet dress. She said the dress looked beautiful, but the next time she wore it, the old buttons were back on again.

"You took long enough to get up," Mama said when she saw me standing in the doorway. "Start slicing the white meat and get it to frying, then set the table and call Toliver."

Mama was leaning over the table, pushing hard at the dough with the heels of her hands. When I got behind her, I put my hand on her leg under her dress. She screamed and jumped, mad until she saw me bent with laughter. Then she laughed, too. "I swear, Florrie, one of these days you're going to give me a heart attack. Go on now and slice the white meat so Toliver can get back out to the field."

"I have to go to the bathroom first," I said, starting for the back porch.

"Don't forget and use the pot," Mama said.

"Well, hell!"

Mama turned, bracing one hand on her hip, breathing hard. She always breathed hard when she thought somebody was hearing something she didn't want them to hear. "Mrs. Goggins is out in the back yard, feeding the dogs," Mama said. "Don't let her hear you cursing."

I went out the door to the back porch. Sure enough, Mrs. Goggins was feeding the dogs, all seventeen of them. She was walking around the yard, passing out plates, skillets, and boilers. The dogs ate out of the same dishes the family did.

Mama said she'd die of starvation before she'd ever eat over at Mrs. Goggins's house. Sometimes Mrs. Goggins gave Mama a bowl of butter beans she'd cooked that day, handing them over the fence. "These are for you all's supper, Mrs. Birdsong," she'd say.

Mama thanked her and took them in the house, but at dark, when she made her daily trip to the woods with the chamber pot, the beans went, too. The next day, Mama passed the washed bowl back across the fence to Mrs. Goggins. "We sure did enjoy the beans, Mrs. Goggins. Nobody can cook beans like you!"

I went down the steps into the back yard, hunched against the rain. I bunched my nightgown and held it up out of the puddles and headed for the back of the yard. Our bathroom was behind the barn until the Missionary Society meeting was

45

over. It was awful, stooping down in the rain, the wet grass rubbing your behind, the bush you hid behind shaking drops of water on your head.

But Mama said that the ladies, upon arriving, must find an absolutely clean chamber pot. No matter that it was not clean after it was used the first time by one of the ladies. The first one who went to the bathroom would report to the others that the pot was clean and unused.

I waved to Mrs. Goggins as I passed, and she looked up from separating two dogs fighting over the same dish. "Where're you going in the rain, Florrie?"

She knew damn well where I was going, so I answered, "How's Daisy and Small Fry?"

Daisy was Mrs. Goggins's orange-haired old-maid daughter, and Small Fry was Daisy's small black dog. Daisy had an unnatural attachment to the dog, and everybody in Gray's Chapel laughed at her. Daisy slept with Small Fry, and bought him a white satin pillow to sit on, and she held him on her lap and fed him. She combed his hair, nestling ribbons among the curls. She held the little dog up to her face, making kissing sounds. "Who do you love, darling, who do you love?" she simpered. Small Fry wriggled and barked and strained to lick her face. Daisy hugged him to her triumphantly. *She* was the one he loved.

Mrs. Goggins went back to feeding the dogs and didn't answer my question. Besides the dogs, the Gogginses had indoor plumbing. They also had an electric iron, and a car. They didn't have to ride the big blue-and-white bus that came through Gray's Chapel twice a day.

I found a bush behind the barn and heard Mama calling. "Florrie, come on," she yelled.

I tried to hurry, wiping the rain away as fast as I could, and ran back to the house. When I got to the back porch, I could smell the white meat frying, and my mouth began to water. I was glad that Mama had gone ahead with it, because I hated to touch the slick, rubbery meat before it was cooked.

I stopped and watched Daddy come across the field toward the road. He didn't wait for us to call him, I thought. I waved my arm but he didn't see me, his hat pulled low over his face against the rain. I waited for him, the drizzle turning to warm rain that ran down my face and neck, soaking my nightgown and making it cling across my breasts.

I rubbed my hands over my chest and longed for some boy—no, not some boy, Billy Paul—to be here with me in the summer rain, and to have his hand, not mine, touching my breasts.

Daddy was coming in the gate of the yard, and for the first time in my life I was embarrassed in front of him, knew that he shouldn't see the wet gown sticking to my body.

I held up my gown as I went back up the steps. Mama had the table set, and was spooning sweet milk gravy into a bowl. She didn't turn from the stove when I came in. But she said, "Go change your wet clothes." She was mad.

"I'm sorry I didn't help you, Mama. I was having fun in the rain and forgot."

She turned and looked at me, her eyes moving over the thin nightgown that clung to my body. "When we go to town next week, either you buy a brassiere, or you go no place else except to school, when it starts. I bet everybody in Gray's Chapel is talking about you behind your back." She turned away, spooning the gravy so hard into the bowl that it splattered, sizzling on the hot stove. "You ought to be ashamed of yourself," she said. "I know I'm ashamed to have a daughter who won't wear a brassiere when the time comes."

Anger stung my eyes with tears, and then Daddy came onto the back porch, making a great racket, stamping the mud off his feet.

"And that's another thing," Mama said. "The way you act around Toliver. You're a big strapping girl and yet you show no modesty at all around him. He's your father, but he's a man too. You go get dry clothes on before he comes in here."

"You're just jealous because he loves me more than he loves you," I said.

She set the bowl of gravy on the table and left the kitchen. I heard the door to her room close. At once I was sorry. Daddy came in, rubbing his hands dry. I had forgotten to hang up the day's towel.

"What smells so good, sugar pie?" he asked, sitting down at the table.

"Sweet milk gravy and biscuits," I said.

"Let's eat before it gets cold. Where's your mother, anyway?"

"I have to go change clothes," I said, not answering. I pulled at the front of my gown and shook it to make it hang straight. I hunched my shoulders, and as I left the room, he said, "I'm going ahead and eat. I have to get back to the fields and see if I can't finish thinning those watermelon vines. That's about all I can do in the rain."

"All right," I called from the sleeping porch.

"Where's Mama?" he called.

"She's coming in a minute," I yelled back.

I zipped up the front of the gray striped coveralls and went to Mama's room. I opened the door and looked in. She was lying across the bed on her back, her eyes closed. She looked dead.

"Mama?"

"What is it?" she said, not moving.

I lay down beside her and put my arm across her chest.

"I'm sorry for what I said, Mama."

"One of these days, you're going to regret how you talk to

48

me. One of these days, when you pass by my coffin and look down on my dead face, you'll remember this."

"I'm sorry, Mama."

"We ought to be careful how we talk to each other," she said. "We ought to be good to each other while we're still living."

"I know it, Mama. Come on and let's eat breakfast, then I'll clean up the living room for you while you make the tea cakes."

"I tell you one thing, if my mother was living, I'd be good to her. You don't have your mother with you always, you know."

"Come on," I said, pulling at her arm.

We got off the bed and went to the kitchen. "What time will they be here?" I asked.

"It's always around two o'clock," she said.

Daddy had gone back to the field, his plate still holding a piece of uneaten meat, streaked with dried gravy. His knife lay in a straight line across the top of the plate, his fork beside it, upside down. There were dried coffee rings on the red checkered oil cloth where he had set his cup. Some essence of him was still here; there was a feeling that he was still about.

Loneliness welled up in me, and I walked to the kitchen window in time to see him disappear through the gates of the lane. I pressed my forehead against the cool glass and closed my eyes. I longed to be in the field with Daddy, bent to the vines, the rain on my back.

When I turned, Mama was watching me. "He'll be back in a little while, Florrie. You know I love you, don't you?"

"Yes, and I love you."

We agreed that all we really wanted for breakfast was a cup of coffee; the important thing was to get ready for the meeting. Over coffee, we talked about who would probably be there. Then Mama got out the flour and the sugar and butter and the milk to make the teacakes, and I went to the living room.

I stood at the mantel and wondered how I could make the

room look more presentable to the ladies of the Methodist Missionary Society.

The brown paint was gone from the pine floor, except around the edges, where nobody ever walked. The white wicker love seat and two chairs looked good, except that the green flowered cushions were worn on the edges.

Our one light was a crook-necked floor lamp that had a pink silk shade with brown fringe. Its light threw one bright spot on the ceiling and one on the floor, leaving the rest of the room in half darkness, the furniture crouching in the shadows.

I pulled the chairs close to the lamp and brought our one small end table from next to the wall, placing it between the two chairs. I dusted the table and arranged our year-old copy of *Pictorial Review* at an inviting angle. The lucky ones who got here first would get these seats.

I went to the kitchen to get the chairs from around Mama's dining room table. I watched her for a minute rolling out tea-cake dough. Then I reached around her and pinched off a corner of the raw cake, savoring its grainy sweetness. Mama's rolling pin never lost its rhythm of swooping and flattening, but only changed direction to smooth the gap in the edge of the dough.

I took the chairs, all six of them, and set them here and there in the living room. Some of the ladies would have to sit straight during the meeting. I lowered the tan window shades, making the room almost as dark as if it were night. The room looked better in the dark.

I went to Mama's room and opened the cedar chest at the foot of her bed. The surgical case lay between two blankets, but I didn't dare touch it. Nobody touched that but Mama.

I took out the white linen doily edged with pink embroidered roses that went on the mantel. I looked at the pink roses set into the yellowing linen, and thought about Grandmother Lee embroidering them. I looked at the small, even stitches and thought, "Her hand pushed the needle through to make these roses," and I was caught up in a feeling of the past, a feeling for the things that people leave behind them.

Mama did not wash the doily; it was so old, she was afraid it would go to pieces. She sponged it gently with a wet cloth, and pressed it with a warm iron.

I took the doily into the living room, but just as I was about to put it on the mantel, Mama called, "Don't put the doily on the mantel until I wipe it off, Florrie."

"How did she know?" I wondered.

I dragged my finger along the mantel; it came away dark with soot. Idly, I licked off the dirt, then rubbed my finger against the side of my coveralls. Mama came in with a wet dish-rag, her face red from the heat of the stove, and from excitement.

"I've got the tea cakes in," she said. "Let me hurry and get through in here and get back, so they won't burn. The stove's roaring hot. Looks like you could have thought of this, Florrie, you know you don't put a clean doily on a dirty mantel." She wiped the rag along the mantel, stopping every few inches to fold the rag over when it got dirty. "Hand me the doily," she said when she finished. She spread it carefully in the center of the mantel, one embroidered side hanging over the edge. It really did look pretty, I thought.

"Mama, how does the living room look?" I said, sitting down on the wicker settee.

She came and sat down next to me. She looked around the room. "It looks nice," she said. "One of these days, Florrie, when you're grown up, you'll have a pretty house with pretty things in it. When we get out of here and get to town, you'll see how people live. We might even get us a house on the streetcar line and go downtown every day." She laughed and clapped her hands, like a child over a birthday cake, and looked at me. "How does that sound to you?" she asked.

"I like it fine right here," I said.

She stood up, angry. "Well, I guess I just might as well accept it. You're on Toliver's side and always have been. You always take up for him."

"I'm not taking up for anybody, Mama. You asked me how I liked the sound of living in town and I said I liked it fine here. That's all."

"You just better remember one thing," she said. "You better not ever let me catch you going around with any of these country boys. When we get to town, you can meet some city boys, some boys like Papa was, or Ralph Kirk."

"I don't have anything to say to you about country boys, Mama. Daddy was a country boy and you married him. And I love him. I wouldn't love Daddy any more if he was a city boy."

I left her standing in the living room and went and lay down across my bed and listened to the rain. I went to sleep, and when I woke up, it seemed that I had been asleep for a long time. It was raining harder, water pouring off the roof in wide streams. I went to find Mama.

She was sitting in the wicker rocker in the living room. She wore her dark blue eyelet dress and her good black lace-up shoes. She wore the pearl earrings Aunt Marcy had given her at least ten Christmases ago. She sat outside the circle of lamplight, her hands folded in her lap and her eyes closed.

I walked over to her, touching her lightly on the knee. "Mama?"

Without opening her eyes, she said, "What time does the clock say?"

The clock said five minutes after three. "It's five after three, Mama."

"I guess they're not coming," she said.

"They know today's the day, don't they?"

She nodded her head and began to rock, slowly.

"Let's wait a few more minutes before we decide they're not coming," I said.

I sat down in the chair by the window and looked out at the rain. I could hardly see the cemetery, it came down so hard, running in streams down the window panes. I looked at Mama. She had stopped rocking and I thought she was dozing, her chin resting now on her hand. Daddy was on the back porch. The rain ran him in from the field, I thought.

Mama stood up. "I think it's time to give up on them," she said.

"It was the rain, Mama," I said.

She started for her room.

"Mama, wait a minute."

"What is it?"

"We didn't eat breakfast or lunch, and I'm starving. Could I have some tea cakes?"

She nodded. "I'll bring them to the living room," she said.

Soon she came back with a tray. On it were two steaming cups of coffee with milk and sugar, and a plate full of tea cakes. With a look of merriment, she stood in front of me, bowed low, and said, "Would Madam care for a cup of coffee and some tea cakes?"

"Yes, thank you, I would," I said, bowing from the chair.

We pulled our chairs around to the end table and set our coffee cups on the *Pictorial Review*. We ate the still-warm tea cakes and drank the scalding coffee, listening to the rain. Then we heard Daddy come into the kitchen and Mama said, "Come on Florrie, and help me fix Toliver some supper. He wouldn't be satisfied with tea cakes."

🌲🌲🌲🌲🌲🌲 5

I knelt and pulled the white ribbon with the gold letters free from the dirt. Stretching it out flat on the ground, I read the words "From Mother." The wreath it belonged to lay on its back, and I picked it up and stood it on its three wire legs at the head of Goo-Goo's grave. I tied the ribbon and stuck it with its wooden pin back among the wilted roses along the bottom of the wreath.

I stood back and looked. It was a rag-tail wreath, the petals fallen from most of the roses. No one from Goo-Goo's family had been back since the day after the funeral. Mrs. Barfield had taken Nell and gone home to Ireland, and some said they wouldn't be back. Mr. Barfield had gone to his brother's in Mississippi.

One night, about two weeks after the funeral, we were all sitting on the front porch. We heard footsteps on the gravel walk, and Mr. Barfield appeared out of the darkness. He took off his hat and walked to each of us.

"Evening, Julia, evening, Toliver, evening, Florrie."

He sat down on our top step and leaned back against the post, waving away the offer of my rocking chair. He and Daddy

54

talked a while about the weather and then he said, "Sharon's very bad since Goo-Goo died. Very bad." He gazed into the darkness and we sat there in silence while we thought about Sharon.

Then Mama said, "I guess I know how Sharon feels."

"Thank you, Julia," Mr. Barfield said. "And something else. I want you to know I'll never forget what you did for me the day of the funeral. I'm sorry, but I've got to beg you to wait a while on the money you let me have."

Mama didn't say anything, but kept on rocking.

"Clyde," Daddy said, "you were a lucky man to get that money. I didn't even know she had it or even where she got it. Just goes to show the things a man doesn't know about his wife."

Mr. Barfield cleared his throat and shifted his feet, but didn't say anything.

"Lord," I prayed silently, "please don't let Mama and Daddy start fussing. Amen."

Daddy pulled his chair close to the bannister and propped up his feet.

"You've got a fine wife, Toliver," Mr. Barfield said. "I don't know anything about the money, except if it hadn't been for Julia that day, I don't know what I would have done."

"From what I've heard, Clyde, you're not the only man in Gray's Chapel that thinks she's a fine woman."

Daddy was talking about Frank Sadler. Frank drove the bus that took us to town, and he had a crush on Mama. I looked down into my lap and squeezed my hands. Mama would really get mad now, Daddy talking like that in front of Mr. Barfield. I waited, and when she didn't say anything, I opened my eyes and peered at her in the darkness. She seemed undisturbed.

Mama was rocking and singing her one-line song. It was a song she sang under her breath as she went to see who was knocking on the door and when she stepped up on the bus going to town. I had heard her sing it for as long as I could remember. It went, "and to the day." She sang it now about every third rock of the chair. Rock, rock, "and to the day," rock, rock, "and to the day."

"Sharon's gone home to Ireland to visit her mother," Mr. Barfield said, "and Nell's gone with her. I'm going to my brother's in Jackson for a while. It'll do us all a world of good to get away, and when we come back we'll start fresh. I'll beg you, Toliver, to look after my land while I'm gone."

Daddy told him he would, and I listened to Mr. Barfield's voice droning in the dark, giving Daddy instructions about his crops. I didn't see how Daddy could take care of his crops and Mr. Barfield's, too, but I knew that if he told him he would, then Daddy would be true to his word.

At last Mr. Barfield stood up to go. "I know Nell is missing you, Florrie. She thinks a mighty lot of you."

"I think a mighty lot of her, too," I said.

He leaned over Mama's chair and took her hand. "Thank you again, Julia," he said. "You'll have your money back one of these days, I promise."

"I'm sure I will, Clyde, I'm sure I will. I always thought that people are more important than money."

I was sleepy, and suddenly wished that I could climb on Mama's lap, lay my head against her chest, and go to sleep. But I had found that the older you get, the lonelier you get, and knew that I was far too old to look for comfort on Mama's lap.

"I promised Mrs. Barfield I'd ask you to look after Goo-Goo's grave, Florrie," Mr. Barfield said.

"I will," I promised.

He took each of our hands by turn and held them clasped in his. "God bless you, Julia, God bless you, Toliver, God bless

56

you, Florrie," he said, and then walked down our front steps and disappeared into the night.

I sat still as I listened to his footsteps fade away, and thought that terrible things took a long time to happen and that you could see them coming. But that was wrong, because two weeks ago Mr. Barfield had a family and was planning the future, just like we were. Now he was all alone, and I believed that we would never see him again, that he would never come back to Gray's Chapel. Tomorrow I would talk with Daddy about it and see if that was what he thought, too.

On this bright June day, though, I would decorate Goo-Goo's grave. Tomorrow I was going to Aunt Mira's for a week. Aunt Marcy was sick, and Mama was going to take care of her. Mama said she owed it to Marcy for all the help she and Uncle Joel had given us.

I was not allowed to stay in the house overnight with Daddy when Mama was gone. It began last summer when Aunt Mira told Mama that it was wrong to let Daddy and me stay by ourselves at night.

"Julia, you don't go away and leave Florrie and Mr. Birdsong by themselves, do you? He's her father, I know, but you know how country people are, don't you?"

Mama didn't tell Daddy what Aunt Mira said, but she told me. "You know how people around here talk, Florrie. Mira's right, it's better if you don't stay by yourself at night with Toliver anymore."

I understood only in a vague way what she and Aunt Mira were talking about, and it made me ashamed. I was ashamed of the intense love I felt sometimes for Daddy, and when he touched me or patted me on the head, I turned away from him coldly. After a while he stopped touching me, and I was glad.

I began clearing away the dead flowers and the wreaths from

Goo-Goo's grave, stacking them next to the fence. I dug up a paper pot of dark red crepe tulips, throwing the fading, garish flowers on top of the wreaths. The tulips spilled from the pot, falling onto the grass like clots of blood.

I knelt and smoothed the dirt with my hands. There was a tiny stone marker at the foot of his grave, with the initials S.E.B. I wondered what the letter E stood for. Finally, the grave was clean and bare, ready for decoration. I was determined that every detail of Goo-Goo's grave be perfect.

I walked among the other graves, looking for Mason jars. There were bound to be some, I thought, bound to be some with dried, brittle flowers that would be all right to take and use on Goo-Goo's grave. There was a large quart-size one on Mrs. Hobson's grave, empty except for the fetid water in the bottom. I pulled it from the dirt, leaving a round, smooth hole.

I had destroyed the ground bugs' homes and the earth worms', sending them scurrying and wriggling frantically, going nowhere. I took a stick and poked at the sides of the hole, making the dirt fall in on them. Some surfaced, more frantic than before, and tried to climb the sides of the hole.

"Well, little animals," I said. "You thought God was a great big boy bug, or a big boy worm, didn't you? All the time your God was a great big human girl, but you didn't know it."

I took the stick and punched at the sides of the hole until the dirt fell in and filled it up again. I waited, but no more came to the top.

"I'll bet none of you stupid bugs believed that smart bug that went around preaching that God wasn't what you thought it was. I've destroyed your world, and since I'm God, I could put it back, but I won't. Death to unbelievers."

I stood up to look for another jar. I needed at least two. There was an empty one lying on its side next to a grave, so I took it, too. I walked across the cemetery to the spring that ran along by the church. A water oak tree grew next to the spring, and farmers came from all around to cool their hands and arms and wash their heads and faces. They brought their lunches in bread wrappers and grease-spotted newspapers and sat on the bank under the tree, eating their sausage-and-biscuit sandwiches and drinking the cold water.

On the night of church suppers, the spring was an ice box for watermelons and for jars of lemonade braced against rocks. At the end of summer sermons, children ran for the door, grownups hurrying behind them to gather at the spring to drink. The children lay on their stomachs and drank while grown people made cups from church bulletins, the ink blurring and finally erasing Brother Gridley's sermon topic as they filled the cups over and over.

Many years ago Brother Gridley had built a sign himself and put it next to the spring. He put it facing the road so people could see it as they passed, painted white and with a carefully lettered message:

"WHOSOEVER DRINKETH OF THIS WATER SHALL THIRST AGAIN: BUT WHOSOEVER DRINKETH OF THE WATER THAT I SHALL GIVE HIM SHALL NEVER THIRST. JOHN 4:13–14."

I sat down by the spring and pushed the jars under the cold water, leaving them there until they filled up. Then I shook the water in them, holding my hand over the opening, until the dried dirt began to wash loose. Then I heard voices inside the church. I looked up and saw the side window raised about halfway. The doors of the church were locked every day except Sunday, and Wednesday night prayer meeting.

Someone was in there. They were stealing the church organ. But how could they get it through the window, I thought. They would open the door from the inside and bring it out. But in broad daylight? A small wood crate was pushed under the window. Somebody had stood on the crate and crawled in the window.

I tiptoed to the window and stood listening. The gravel was hot on my bare feet, and I stood first on one foot and then on the other. I heard nothing but the lilting song of a mockingbird in a tree across the road. I climbed up on the box and looked in. It was dark inside the church, with the dry smell of last Sunday's yellow roses, still in a vase on the pulpit, hanging in the air.

At first I saw nothing, but then there was a girl's laughter, and I turned toward the sound. Through the gloom, I saw the pale shape of someone lying on the first bench.

"Who's there, who's in the church?" I called, leaning in through the window.

A male voice cursed as the figure rolled off the bench and hit the floor, and then I saw there were two people on the bench.

"Who's at the window?" a girl's voice asked.

"Who's in there?" I demanded.

The boy walked close to the window looking up at me. It was Billy Paul. "It's Florrie Birdsong," he said to the girl on the bench.

She came and stood with him, putting her arm around his waist. It was Elaine Parish. Both of them smiled at me.

"Florrie, what are you doing peeping in church windows, anyhow," Billy Paul said, tucking in his shirt. "You like to have scared me to death."

Elaine smoothed her hair and straightened her skirt. "Paw sent me here to get his Bible," she said. "He left it on the bench at prayer meeting Wednesday night."

"It's none of *my* business, Elaine, what you're doing in the church. I thought somebody was stealing the organ. How come you didn't just get the key from Brother Gridley and come in the front door?"

60

"Brother Gridley's in Coal Town," Billy Paul said. "There was a cave-in in the mines last night."

"Oh, that's terrible," I said. "I'll read about it in the evening paper, I suppose. Well, see you all Sunday at church," and I stepped down off the box and went back to the spring to finish washing the jars.

I knelt down and got the jars out of the water and picked at the dried mud with my fingernails. Billy Paul had come with Elaine to get her Paw's Bible, and they had stayed to smooch. I sat back on my heels, rubbing idly at the slippery mud and wished that it was me instead of Elaine in the church with Billy Paul. I closed my eyes, so delicious was the thought.

"Good-bye, Florrie," Billy Paul said.

I looked around, and Billy Paul and Elaine were standing in front of the church. Billy Paul held up Elaine's father's Bible, and I nodded and smiled. "Good-bye, Billy Paul, Elaine."

They left, and I watched them run down the bank and walk across the picnic ground. I watched until they went in the woods and were out of sight. I looked at the open window of the church, and I was lonesome. I turned back to the spring and sank the jar once again in the water and began to hum, my voice running up and down the scale, looking for a song. I finally hit on "When They Ring those Golden Bells."

I sang and washed, and when the jars were clean I went back to the cemetery and spent the rest of the morning picking wild cornflowers and daisies. I put them in one of the jars at the foot of his grave, and then picked red roses off the bush that grew next to old man Baker's grave. Goo-Goo had to have red roses, because red roses meant you were remembered. I pushed the jar full of roses into the dirt at the head of the grave.

Then I stood back to look. The roses nodded in the breeze, and the wildflowers were still fresh. After a while the wildflowers would know they had been picked and they would droop and die, but that was after a while, and I would not see them withered. I would leave before then.

I went back to the church. All was quiet. The wood crate was still under the window, so I sat down on it and leaned back against the warm boards of the church and closed my eyes. The afternoon pressed down around me, warm and heavy.

A bobwhite called from the tall grass behind the church, sweet and questioning; a car sputtered along the road, and I opened my eyes in time to see Aunt Mira's gray Plymouth turn in at the gate of the lane. Coming home from where, I wondered. White, feathery clouds floated high in the sky. Cirrus. Clouds shouldn't have names. I closed my eyes and slept.

When I woke up, my back was aching and cramped, and I was sitting in the wide angle of the church's shadow.

"Florrie," Mama's voice came faintly across the cemetery.

I stood up and headed for home. I skirted the cemetery and took the road, and when I passed the field I waved to Daddy. I wished that Mama loved it here like Daddy and I did; long ago I tried to get her to come and walk in the fields with me and in the woods. But she wouldn't, and I had given up trying to get her to.

I turned onto the path that led to our back gate and saw Mama wave to me from the back porch steps. I waved back and climbed over the gate and ran to the steps and grabbed her. I kissed Mama, spinning her around. "Florrie, stop," she begged. "I'm falling off the steps," but she was laughing.

We went in the kitchen, and I got the plates and began to set the table for supper. Tonight, when I went to bed and the house was quiet, I would lie in the dark and think about Billy Paul.

🌲🌲🌲🌲🌲 6

In the first light of morning, it was hard to tell what the weather was like. I lay on my back and looked through the upstairs windows, but I could not tell if it was cloudy or fair, so I pulled the covers up around my neck and looked around the room. It had been a long time since I had spent the night at Aunt Mira's, but it was no different from the last time. I pushed deeper into the feather mattress.

The bedroom wall was covered with tan wallpaper, printed with a dark brown trellis. Through the trellis were threaded rose-colored roses, and I thought, how funny, rose-colored roses. There was a crucifix on the wall next to the windows; it was the first thing I saw when I woke up this morning. A bleeding, suffering Jesus hung on the cross, His head sunk against His chest.

A pink china wash bowl and pitcher were on the night stand next to my bed. A large, framed picture of Uncle Ralph hung over the dresser. He survived in oils, his gray suit neat, his bald head shining, to gaze sorrowfully at me when I looked at him. I could not meet those sad eyes for long, and I tried not to look his way.

On the dresser, under Uncle Ralph's picture, were smaller framed pictures of men and women and laughing children frozen in time.

I slept in Aunt Mira's guest room. My windows were over the front door of the house, facing toward the tennis court. Beyond the tennis court were the woods. Next to the guest bedroom was Aunt Mira's room, and across the hall from her was Dink's room. There was one bedroom downstairs, and that was Ralph Junior's.

The bathroom was off the upstairs hall, and last night I had lain in the bathtub with the claw feet and soaked until Aunt Mira knocked on the door. "Come out of there, Florrie. Somebody else in this house has to bathe, too, you know."

Yesterday morning, Uncle Joel, the tic in his jaw twitching, had picked up Mama and me in the black Packard. Uncle Joel was short and fat and didn't talk much. Years ago, I had loved him. And he had loved me. He and Aunt Marcy came to see us in Gray's Chapel and he sat on the porch for as long as I wanted him to and talked to me.

"It's a marvel the way that man talks to Florrie," Daddy said once. "He's never said more than ten words to me in all the years I've known him, but he talks his head off when he's with Florrie."

Aunt Marcy cried. "It's because she reminds him of little Janie, Mr. Birdsong," she said. "Janie was blond like Florrie, and just about her size when she died." Janie was the only child Aunt Marcy and Uncle Joel ever had, and she died of colitis when she was five years old.

When I was in second grade a car hit me. I wasn't hurt bad, but I looked awful with my black eyes and swollen, blue lips. Aunt Marcy and Uncle Joel came to see me, even though Uncle Joel couldn't stand to be around sick people. He gave me a big bakery box tied with pink ribbon; inside was a solid chocolate swan. After he gave it to me, he kept his hands in his pockets as if he was afraid he would touch me, but he smiled at me and said, no, I musn't break off a piece for him, see, he was too fat already. He patted his stomach. "Keep it until you're well, Florrie, and then you can eat it," he said.

I don't remember the exact day he quit talking to me, or when he quit bringing me presents. But he did quit, and I thought it was because I no longer looked like Janie with my long legs and dark blond hair. For a while I still took his hand or sat on the arm of his chair, but he was embarrassed, so I stopped, though I was sad to lose my friend.

When Aunt Marcy and Uncle Joel came to see us, Mama always asked Uncle Joel for money. We sat in the living room laughing and talking, and sometimes I told the latest "knock, knock" joke. When they stood up to leave, Mama cleared her throat and looked nervous. "Joel, do you have a little money you can spare?"

Aunt Marcy answered for him. "Daddy, you've got some change, haven't you?"

Uncle Joel reached deep in his pocket and brought up a handful of coins and poured them into Mama's hand. It was never more than two or three dollars, but when Mama thanked him, Uncle Joel's face turned red with embarrassment.

I hated for Mama to ask him for money. "Mama, we ought to have more pride than to ask him for money," I said.

"That money goes in the candy box to build up for the down payment on our house in town. You can't buy a house without a down payment, Florrie. There's such a thing as false pride, and you ought to know that, going to church as much as you do."

And that was another reason she'd gone to Aunt Marcy's. She really did think she ought to help Aunt Marcy, her being sick, but there was another reason. The night before she left for Aunt Marcy's and I left for Aunt Mira's, Mama came and sat on the side of my bed.

"Wake up, Florrie."

I sat up in bed, asking what was wrong.

"Nothing," she said. "I just want to tell you that I'll miss you this coming week and for you to behave and try not to make Mira Gray mad. While I'm at Marcy's I'm going to look for houses. I might not find the exact one we'll buy, but I can at least decide on a neighborhood."

She kissed me good night and went back to her room, and I got out of bed and went to stand in my window. Our back yard, steeped in moonlight, was strange and unfamiliar. Ghosts lurked in the shadows of the bushes and trees; Mrs. Goggins's dogs knew they were there; they paced back and forth in the yard, stopping now and then to point their nose at the full moon and howl.

I tried not to look at the moon shining through the branches of the tree outside my window; that was bad luck. I got back into bed, lying on top of the spread. Moonlight spilled through the windows and flowed over me, making leaf patterns that moved restlessly on my wall. When I awoke the next morning, my room was filled with sunlight.

Downstairs, Aunt Mira tinkled the breakfast bell, and I kicked back the covers and stretched. I got up and pulled at the covers, making my bed. This was what Aunt Mira expected me to do, even though the Negro maid, Dorothy, came to clean house for her every day.

Dorothy was the only Negro I had ever known to talk to. There were no Negro families in Gray's Chapel; Dorothy lived in Huxley and came on Frank's bus every morning to work for

Aunt Mira. I used to talk to Dorothy a lot before Aunt Mira made me stop. "Darkies don't understand when you're too friendly, Florrie," she said. "They take friendliness to mean they can be lazy and steal. She's a servant, so stay away from her and let her get her work done."

After that, I'd smile and wave to her, but I didn't stop to talk. I missed talking to her, though, and thought Dorothy was pretty, with her brown eyes and long black eyelashes. She was coffee-colored, and when she laughed she threw back her head, and the gold on her front teeth flashed.

I pushed at the lumps in the mattress, but when I smoothed here, a lump appeared there. I pulled the white chenille spread over the pillows and patted them into shape. It was passable enough so Aunt Mira won't complain, I decided.

I pulled my gown over my head, and the breakfast bell rang again.

"Damn," I said, my mouth full of gown. I yanked free and yelled, "I'm *coming*, Aunt Mira!"

I pulled on blue denim overalls, deciding to wear my blouse on the outside, rather than tucked under the straps. The metal grippers were cold on my chest, and I thought, what if I just didn't wear my shirt and went down to breakfast the way I used to when I was little. I laughed aloud when I thought how shocked Aunt Mira would be. She would probably grab her rosary and start to pray.

The breakfast bell rang again. Aunt Mira was the only person I knew who could make a delicate silver bell sound irritable. I left the room and started down the stairs, stopping on the landing, where the telephone sat on a small table. I lifted the bell-shaped receiver gently from the hook and put it to my ear. There was a low hum. My finger itched to dial the phone, to ring someone. After a while I would call Mama.

I finished buttoning my blouse as I went down the rest of the stairs. Then I walked through the living room and dining room, finally pushing the swinging door open into the kitchen.

Aunt Mira was washing her hands at the sink, her diamond rings lying on the counter. Dorothy stood next to her wearing a red dress, her hair bound up in a white turban. Aunt Mira turned and looked at me as I came into the kitchen.

"Go on to the breakfast table, Florrie. You're the slowest girl I know. Julia needs to get square in behind you."

Dorothy winked at me and turned down her lips behind Aunt Mira, and I turned away before I laughed and made Aunt Mira mad. Then I stopped in my tracks and stared, slack-jawed. Dink sat at the table grinning at me. I rushed and threw my arms around him, upsetting glasses and knocking forks and spoons to the floor.

"Stop it, Florrie," Dink shouted, but it was too late. His chair turned over sideways, and Dink lay on the floor, still sitting in it.

"Here, now," Aunt Mira said, grabbing my shoulder. "Get up off that floor Dink, and Florrie, you stop that boisterousness, you're entirely too big to act that way. What you need is a year at school with the nuns. They'd get you straightened out in a hurry."

Dink stood up and picked his chair up off the floor, and I knelt and began to pick up the scattered silver, my joy gone in the face of her anger. Dink knelt to help me and our faces met under the table. He crossed his eyes and waggled his tongue, and I sat back on the floor and laughed and laughed. I couldn't quit laughing. I laughed until the tears came and flowed down my face. I started hiccuping.

Aunt Mira was alarmed and told Dorothy to get some ice from the refrigerator and put it on my neck. Dink pounded me on the back, and at last I quit laughing. We sat down to eat and

Aunt Mira prayed: "Bless us, O Lord, for these Thy gifts which we are about to receive." Crossing herself, she said, "In the name of the Father and the Son and the Holy Ghost."

Dorothy put the cold scrambled eggs and cold biscuits on our plates. Aunt Mira fussed. "Florrie, you'll be here for a week. I'll expect you from now on to be at the table at the first ring of the breakfast bell."

Dorothy sang in the kitchen, and I told Aunt Mira I would be on time from now on. I had promised Mama faithfully I would not make Aunt Mira mad. Nothing was impossible with Dink here. He was home for two weeks' summer vacation from the Catholic boys' school.

"Ralph Junior picked me up at the bus station at six o'clock this morning," Dink said as we ate. I remembered waking up when Ralph Junior backed his car out of the garage when it was still almost dark and wondered where he was going so early. I had not waked up when he came back with Dink.

I watched Dink taking big bites of eggs and biscuits and thought how much bigger he was now than when he was home for Christmas. His shoulders were broader, and his arms in the white polo shirt had the look of a man's arms. His hair was the same, blond and wavy, his eyelashes pale. I decided he would be handsome when the pimples cleared up. He looked up and saw me watching him, and I smiled at him.

Aunt Mira said she was going to Greenbriar to collect rent from her tenants. "Dorothy's here to look after you," she said. "I've got the card table set up on the porch so you can play Monopoly."

Dink's toe nudged me under the table. I nudged him back. The nudges said, Imagine, Monopoly on a day like this, when we have so much to tell each other. And when there are fields and woods to roam, flowers to pick, and grassy shade to lie in.

But it was natural that Monopoly was Aunt Mira's idea of fun. It involved money, and money was Aunt Mira's grassy shade, her fields and woods.

After breakfast she settled Dink and me at the card table on the front porch, and then she got in her car and drove away up the lane. We sat there and watched her out of sight, and then Dink grabbed my hand and we ran down the hill toward the springhouse.

"Come back here, you, Dink, and you, Florrie," Dorothy shouted from the side porch steps.

We walked back to the porch.

"Mrs. Kirk's left me to see you all don't get in no mischief," Dorothy said. "You all sit on that porch and play that game like she told you."

Dink pushed his hands down in his jeans pockets and walked up close to her. "If you try to stop us from leaving, I'll tell Mama when she comes back that you've been stealing. I'll tell her you took money out of my room."

Dorothy's chin jerked up and she leaned close to him, whispering. "You know you ain't going to tell Mrs. Kirk nothing like that."

"He certainly isn't, Dorothy," I said, walking up to stand by Dink. "Dink, you ought to be ashamed, talking like that to Dorothy. She's just doing what Aunt Mira told her to do."

"I'm sorry, Dorothy," Dink said. "If you won't tell Mama we left, we promise to be back before she gets home. And we won't get in any trouble. I promise."

She nodded her head curtly, and we walked down the hill. When I looked back she still stood there on the steps watching us, her hands folded underneath her apron.

When we got to the springhouse, Dink took a watermelon and smashed it on the ground. It broke open, the black seeds

70

spilling on the ground. We dug out the heart with our hands and ate it as we walked along, throwing down the rind when we finished.

Deep in the woods, we climbed a blackgum tree and sat among its highest branches, talking. Dink said the Catholic school was hell. "We pray a lot, and when we're not praying, we're studying the catechism, and when we're not studying the catechism, one of the priests is lecturing us about the sin of the flesh."

"I don't understand," I said.

"You know," Dink said, breaking off a leaf and shredding it, letting the pieces flutter to the ground.

"I don't know what you're talking about, 'the sin of the flesh.' "

"Lust," he said. "Lust. Like a man lusting after a woman."

"You mean sex."

"I suppose so, but the priests don't call it that."

I told him about seeing Billy Paul and Elaine smooching in the church. Dink was interested, and pressed for details. I exaggerated some, making it more interesting, and he forgot to hold on and almost fell out of the tree.

"You mean they really didn't have on any clothes?" he asked.

"That's right."

"Could you see, uh, details?"

"What details do you mean, Dink? I could see everything, if that's what you mean."

"Wow!" he said.

We climbed down and walked in the lane, picking daisies. We sat down under a tree and made a chain, and when we were finished I wore it around my neck. Then we went to the corn field and pulled tassels and put them under our noses, our mouths scrunched up, for mustaches. We ran Mrs. Johnson's dog through the corn, shouting and hollering at him until he disappeared into the woods.

We went all the way up the lane to the iron gates and sat in the shade of the rock pillars. I saw Daddy plowing with the mule, far across the field, his arm rising and falling as he slapped the leather strap across Dixie's back. Then Dink asked me to sit closer to him.

I moved next to him, my knees drawn up, our shoulders touching. He put his arm around my waist and kissed me softly on the cheek. Then he put both his arms around me and kissed me on the mouth.

"I love you, Florrie," he said.

"I love you, too, Dink."

Then he took my hand and pulled me up, and down the road we saw Aunt Mira's car coming. Hand in hand we ran down the lane, laughing, our lungs nearly bursting. I stopped once to look back, but her car was not in sight.

When Aunt Mira got out of the car and came up the walk to the porch, we were sitting hunched over the Monopoly board. Dink was frowning, undecided whether he should buy the New York Railroad.

🌲🌲🌲🌲🌲🌲 7

Dink and I sat in the dark on the side steps of the porch, planning the next day. Aunt Mira and Ralph Junior sat with their chairs pulled close to the radio, listening to Major Bowes tell them that round and round she goes, and where she stops, nobody knows.

"Did you all hear that?" Aunt Mira called to Dink and me. "With a voice like that, that boy will be rich one of these days."

We didn't answer, and after a while the program ended and Ralph Junior came out and went down the front steps.

"Where're you going?" Dink asked.

"Out," Ralph Junior said. We watched him as he got in the car and drove away.

"Let's face it, Florrie," Dink said. "My big brother's an ass."

"Lordy, that's the truth," I said.

Ralph Junior never bothered me, because I pretended he wasn't there when I had to be around him. But when Dink was little he had worshipped Ralph Junior and wanted to go places with him and be like him. But Ralph had no time for Dink, and

I was glad when Dink stopped liking him and started despising him. I couldn't imagine Dink with an English accent.

"Know what I'd like to do tomorrow?" Dink asked.

"No."

"I'd like to go up the lane and go in those woods and look for bootleggers."

"You're kidding," I said.

"No, I'm not, I mean it."

I didn't know what to say. I stood up and pulled Dink by the arm, and we went to sit in the glider, propping our feet up on the bannister. We pushed slowly back and forth. I was ashamed to tell him how scared I was of those woods. Usually, I was brave and he was scared. If he wanted to go in those woods, then I would go with him.

The week was almost gone; in two days I would be going home. And next week Dink would be gone until Christmas. The memory of this week would have to last a long time.

The porch was dark except for the dim light coming through the living room window. The waning moon gave enough light to show the dark outline of the trees where the woods began. Deep within that darkness an owl screeched as it captured some little woods animal. I shuddered.

"Dink," I whispered, "what would it take to get you to go by yourself, without even a flashlight, into the woods right now?"

"Are you crazy? I wouldn't go in those woods at night even with a flashlight."

That was the right answer, and I was happy. He was honest, not needing to puff himself up, at least not to me. He was different from the boys at school, different from the ones who carried a comb in their shirt pocket. When they were talking to a girl, they would take it out and comb the long forelock, swirling their hair to make it wave. They strutted and swaggered, and the girls in their tight dresses smiled at their preening.

74

We talked about the still in the woods, and we talked about Dink going back to school, and promised to write every chance we got. But I knew he wouldn't, and he knew I wouldn't. We quit talking after a while and sat there with our heads resting on the back of the glider. Dink gave a long, groaning yawn. "I'm going to bed, Florrie, so I'll feel like slipping up on those bootleggers tomorrow."

I caught his yawn. We laughed, went inside. Aunt Mira was asleep in her chair, her chin drooping onto her chest. There was music on the radio. Dink touched her on the knee. "Florrie and I are going to bed, Mama."

She came awake, startled, and took off her glasses and asked what we'd been doing. Dink told her we'd been sitting on the porch.

"Be sure and drink a big glass of mineral water before you get in bed, son," she said. He made a face but headed for the kitchen. "Come here, Florrie," Aunt Mira said.

She had her bottle of holy water, and she crossed herself and sprinkled me. Dink came back from the kitchen and she sprinkled him, too. Aunt Mira walked around the living room turning off lamps, and then we climbed the stairs single file for bed. On the landing, Aunt Mira stopped and turned around to us. "We're all going to early Mass in the morning."

Dink shrugged his shoulders, and once again we started up the stairs. Mass was all right with me. I didn't mind. I would spread one of Aunt Mira's hankerchiefs over my hair, and when we went in the church I would dip my fingers in the pool of holy water and cross myself, even though I was not a Catholic. I, too, would kneel as we entered our pew, and I would kneel on the rail inside the pew and pray every time Dink and Aunt Mira did.

The Mass, said in Latin, was romantic. No matter to me that the words were mysterious, unknown. So, too, was God mysterious, unknown. The Catholic God appealed more to me than did Brother Gridley's God of wrath and thunder. The priest's robe was resplendent as was heaven, if there was one, and the choir, which sang high in the loft of the church, had the voices of angels.

Aunt Mira and I turned left at the head of the stairs, and Dink turned right. I told Aunt Mira I would get up early to bathe before Mass, and we said goodnight. I went into the guest room and closed the door. I would never want Aunt Mira to see me undressed.

After I put on my gown, I turned off the light, opened my door, and climbed into bed. Aunt Mira's light still burned in her room, and I knew she would lie awake late in the night reading the *Saturday Evening Post*. My feather mattress cradled me, gathering me in for sleep, and I closed my eyes.

I thought about Mama and felt guilty. I had not missed her, nor had I called her on the telephone. I would call her the first thing in the morning. With my conscience eased, I drifted down toward sleep.

I wished the days here with Dink never had to end, but now my coins of time were spent, my fortune flung among the fields and woods. Except tomorrow. There was still tomorrow, and with any luck at all the day would last forever.

ⵏⵏⵏⵏⵏ 8

Aunt Mira and Dorothy sat on the back porch peeling June apples. The yellow peelings curled in a downward spiral and dropped into the zinc tub that sat on the floor between them. A bushel basket of apples sat at Aunt Mira's feet. When Aunt Mira finished peeling an apple, she handed it to Dorothy, who sliced it over a bowl she held in her lap, throwing the core into the zinc tub.

Aunt Mira was making her yearly batch of apple butter. She brought the apples back from one of her tenant farms in Greenbriar when she went collecting rent on Monday. For supper tonight there would be hot biscuits dripping with butter and filled with the spicy, brown apple butter. My stomach cramped with pleasure when I thought of it.

"Florrie and I are going up on the road to Mrs. Wesson's to get a bottle of root beer, Mama," Dink said. Mrs. Wesson sold a bottle of homemade root beer for a nickel.

Aunt Mira looked up, the paring knife in one hand and a half-peeled apple in the other. She looked at us, suspicion turning down the corners of her mouth. Putting on my plainest face, I reached for an apple core in the zinc tub, nibbling it around the edges.

"That's the only place you're going?" she asked.

"There's not anyplace else to go," Dink answered. "We're just bored sitting around the house all the time."

"All right," Aunt Mira said. "You just be sure you're back here in a little while. I don't want to have to send Ralph Junior out looking for you."

Dorothy caught my eye, and she stopped slicing apples and smiled at me. I smiled back at her and she looked back down at the bowl, slicing apples again.

Aunt Mira pointed the paring knife at me. "Joel's bringing Julia home tomorrow, Florrie. Marcy's well, and when you get back this afternoon, gather up your clothes and make sure you've got them all. Be ready to go when Ralph Junior is, in the morning, you're so slow and you know how he hates to wait on people."

"That's all right Aunt Mira. Tell Ralph Junior not to bother taking me home, I'd rather walk, anyway."

She's past ready for me to go, I thought. The only reason she let me spend so much time with Dink was because it entertained him. But it was a burden for her, too, I knew, having to worry about what we were doing when we were out of sight.

Dink had never known what to do with himself when he was alone. If I was with him he'd swim or play croquet or anything I suggested.

"I don't like to be by myself," he told me once. "Everything's gray and I can't think of anything to do. When you come, Florrie, things come alive. It's like when they stop a reel at the movie with the picture still on the screen. When you come, the picture starts again." He smiled, embarrassed.

He was never a reader. One time he announced to me, proudly, I thought, "I've only read one whole book in my life, and I never intend to read another one. Worst experience of my whole life, reading that book."

78

When we were little, sometimes I got tired of games and went to sit under a tree and read. Dink would sit under another tree and sulk, glaring at me. Finally, I got tickled at the way his eyes bugged out when he got mad and played with him. He was so happy then that he danced around and hugged me, and we went to the porch to play doctor. Sometimes I lay on the glider screaming and hollering, having a baby, until Aunt Mira made us stop playing doctor altogether.

Dink and I walked up the lane, and I felt Aunt Mira's eyes following us. I kicked at a rock and then picked it up and threw it as far as I could. I was scared Aunt Mira would change her mind and call us back, and when we finally turned the curve out of sight of the house, I said, "Beat you to the top of the hill, Dink," and started running.

I couldn't run fast because I was barefoot and the rocks cut my feet and the hot dust oozed up between my toes. Dink passed me, running hard, and stood waiting at the top of the hill.

"If I'd had shoes on, you wouldn't have beat me," I panted as I ran the last few feet up the hill. "I thought you were supposed to be puny, drinking mineral water and all that stuff."

Dink smiled and then quit smiling. "Don't make me smile, Florrie, my soda will drop off."

His face was smeared with soda, and even when he didn't smile, it fell off him in powdery flakes. The soda was supposed to dry up his pimples. I stopped in the road and looked at him.

"Are you planning on not smiling all day long, Dink? Can't you forget your damn pimples for one day and have fun?"

We started walking along slowly and Dink looked at the ground, his hands stuck in his pockets.

"When you go back to school, Dink, you can dip your whole damn head in soda for all I care."

"No, I can't." He shook his head sadly. "Except at night,

and then it rubs off on the pillow. Father Sullivan won't let me wear soda to class."

"Dink, you can't expect a priest to understand about pimples. They just think about God and inner beauty, things like that."

The bottoms of my feet were burning, and I walked along the grass that grew on the edge of the lane, but too often it tapered away on the rim of a ditch, and then I had to walk on the sides of my feet.

Summer filled the lane. Everywhere you looked there was green. Meadowlarks sang from the fields and sweet William grew in the ditches and along the fences.

All at once I felt like I sprang whole from the earth, and I saw each grain of dust that lay in the lane. My sight blurred, and I melted and blended with the trees and grass and with the dirt in the field. "This is my world," I thought, and I watched Dink and me walking down the lane.

"Pimples are hell," Dink said.

"What?"

"Pimples, Florrie, they're hell."

"Oh. Well, they're not that bad, Dink. Everybody has them. I have them."

"Where?" he asked, stopping to look at my face.

"Here," I said, pointing to my chin.

"Ah, there's not but one. It's easy to make light of somebody else's pimples when you've only got one yourself."

"Goddamn, Dink. If anybody had told me yesterday that we'd spend our last whole day together talking about pimples, I'd have told them they were crazy. But here we stand, and all we've talked about so far is your pimples."

He started walking again, a hurt look on his face. He didn't say anything and I didn't say anything and we just walked along. I was sorry already for what I said, but I hated to always be the one that apologized. But I sensed, too, that in the future Aunt Mira was not going to let us spend so much time together. The day was ruined unless I apologized.

"I'm sorry, Dink," I said.

"That's okay." He was happy again. I had said I was sorry, so the day was saved. He smiled at me and whistled under his breath, and then we were at the woods. The bootlegger woods. We stopped walking, and Dink stared into the woods, squinting his eyes, trying to fathom its darkness from the safety of the lane. "What do you think, Florrie?"

I shrugged. "I don't know, Dink. Maybe we're wasting our time. We could go back and play croquet."

An ant bit my ankle, and I scratched and waited for Dink to make up his mind whether we would go in or not.

"Do you think I'm silly?"

"No," I said.

Finally, he took my hand. "Let's go," he said, and we stepped together into the gloom of the woods.

The change from sunlight to near dark was like flicking a light switch, and I shrank back toward the lane. But Dink squeezed my hand, pulling me forward.

I looked at Dink's white tennis shoes, coveting them in my heart. Pine needles stuck in the winter softness of my feet, and every stick I saw was a snake, ready to slither across my feet, its underbelly damp and smooth. I pushed close to Dink.

We crept along, bent over and breathing hard, but when nothing happened we straightened up, feeling braver. We walked farther, and I felt foolish, silly, like we were playing a part from the Campfire Girls or the Rover Boys. Dink and I were too old to be looking for bootleggers in the woods. The Rover Boys had looked for bank robbers.

The woods were quiet except for the twittering of sparrows. I had never been in woods such as these. My woods, behind our corn field, was a happy place with birds singing and squirrels clattering up and down trees. There were open places among the trees where sunlight flooded in and flowers grew thick and wild. There were forget-me-nots, honeysuckle, and grape hyacinths.

But not here. The trees were mostly pines, growing so dense they struggled upward, taller and taller, fighting for the sun. Their trunks were long and skinny, they had leaves only on the top branches. I saw no wildflowers.

I wanted to leave this gloomy place and go to swim in the woods or play croquet, and I would have, had it not been for Dink. This was one of his games, and if I wouldn't play, I knew, he would sulk as he always had when I got tired of playing. So I stayed, walking along beside him. We walked for so long that finally I got mad at him for wanting to come in here. It would be fun, though, to tell Daddy there were no bottleggers in here after all.

My stomach started growling. Breakfast was a long time ago according to the way my stomach felt, but I couldn't tell from the sun because I couldn't see it from in these woods.

Dink squeezed my fingers. "Hush," he whispered, even though I hadn't said anything.

"What's the matter?" I mouthed.

He tapped his ear for me to listen. I heard nothing at first, but then voices, not far away. My heart began a slow, fearful beat and I pulled Dink's arm and pointed toward the lane. He shook his head and pulled me along with him. We would be killed. Whoever was in there would come out and hack us to pieces and I would never see Mama again. And I wouldn't even have talked to her on the telephone because I forgot to call her this morning. When we came home from early Mass and I changed into my overalls and shirt, I felt guilty as I passed the phone on the stairs for not stopping and calling Mama. "I'll see her tomorrow," I had thought. "No need to call now." That was a mistake, because I wouldn't see Mama tomorrow or any other day, because I would be dead.

Whoever was behind the scrub pine bushes would have heard us coming if they had not been making so much noise. Dink and I were about twenty-five feet away, hidden in a thicket of pine saplings. And then I heard a woman's voice.

"Hand me that fresh bottle over there, sugar," she said and then the cork popped.

Dink dropped down on his hands and knees and crawled closer. Curiosity conquered fear, and I got on my hands and knees and crawled after Dink. When he got to the scrub pines, he stood up halfway and pushed the branches slightly apart. I stood up behind him, looking over his shoulder. The woman was facing me, and even in the half light I could tell who she was.

"My God," I breathed, "it's Maud Beggs."

Dink's elbow came back sharply in my ribs. It hurt, and I started to kick him, but decided I'd wait until we got to the lane. Mrs. Beggs sat on a campstool, her legs spread apart man-fashion, and her elbow propped on her knee. Her knotty fingers closed around the bottle of moonshine and she tilted back her head to drink. She held the bottle straight up, and her bright eyes shone from the wrinkled face, looking straight at me.

I thought she saw me, and my knees went weak, but then she finished drinking and passed the bottle to the man sitting next to her on a log, wearing bibbed overalls and a blue shirt.

There was a man sitting with his back to us, only his head and shoulders showing over the pine bush. He wore a white suit and a white Panama hat.

Mrs. Beggs was a widow with no income except her monthly

83

welfare check and whatever odd job she could find around Gray's Chapel. Sometimes she was a maid, sometimes a nurse for a new baby, and she had even chopped cotton. And she bootlegged. That was a job few people knew she had.

Dink stared enraptured as the bottle was passed around. The man in overalls passed the bottle to the man in the white suit. The man in the white suit pulled a handkerchief from his pocket and carefully wiped the mouth of the bottle.

"Well, now, ain't he nice," said Mrs. Beggs. "So proper he don't like our spit," and she slapped her knee and laughed close in his face.

"Get your stinking breath out of my face, old woman," he said.

It was Ralph Junior. There was no mistaking his voice. I looked at Dink. His jaw hung slack, and the look on his face was more interesting than the people gathered there in the woods to drink moonshine.

"Here's your money, old crow," Ralph Junior told Mrs. Beggs, and began counting bills onto her outstretched palm. He pulled the bills, one at a time, from his billfold, and when he stopped counting she said, "Okay, jack-leg rich boy. Don't try to cheat Maudie. Keep counting." Ralph Junior raised his hand to slap her, but she just laughed. "You don't scare me, rich boy," and her eyes glinted as she watched him.

He took another bill and slapped it on her hand. "You old whore," he said. "I ought to knock out the rest of those snag teeth."

She threw back her head and laughed, slapping her leg over and over. The man in overalls looked at Ralph Junior, grinning. Mrs. Beggs stopped laughing. "You keep your dirty mouth shut, Ralph Kirk." She leaned over and tapped him on the chest, her face no more than a few inches away. "If it wasn't for good old Mrs. Beggs and Sam, making your bootleg whiskey for you, how would you pay them whores those high prices you pay every Saturday night in Huxley?"

She sat back. "Sam," she said, "you reckon he's fixing to start asking his mama for money to go whoring?"

Sam said, "Yeah, he might just do that, Maudie. His mama would probably give him the money. I hear she's a mighty generous woman. She'd probably just hand it over and tell him to go straight from the whorehouse to the priest and tell him what he done."

They looked at each other and laughed, and looked away and then looked back at each other and started laughing again. They laughed so long that Mrs. Beggs started wheezing. Sam slapped her on the back.

Dink was smiling a happy, wide smile, his hands resting lightly in his pockets. Ralph Junior shouted for them to shut up, but they pretended not to notice him at all, so he quit hollering and covered his face with his hands.

Mrs. Beggs said, "Yeah, and after he got through telling the priest what he'd just done, the priest would probably get so excited he'd make Ralph show him where the place was so he could go get him some, too. Everybody knows how priests love tail, most especially nun's tail."

"Naw," Sam said, "you're wrong, Maudie. Priests don't like girls." Sam leaned close to her ear, talking confidentially, but looking at Ralph Junior. "You know the way those priests run around in skirts. They don't fool me none, with them crosses and the way they walk around with their heads bowed. They want you to think they're praying, but I know what they're really thinking about."

"What?" asked Mrs. Beggs.

"Boys. They're thinking about boys. Why, Maudie, them fellows are all pansies, didn't you know that?"

Ralph Junior jumped up and said, "All right, that's enough,

you scum. I'm paying for you to run that still, and if either one of you say another word, I'll break it up and you can find somebody else's whiskey to sell."

Ralph Junior opened his wallet and laid some bills in Sam's hand without counting them out. They didn't say anything else to Ralph Junior. I never in my life thought I'd be on his side about anything, but I was this time. Imagine, them having the nerve to talk like that about the priests and nuns. Common, that's what they were.

Mrs. Beggs grabbed hold of Sam's arm. "How much you got there, Sam?"

The man jerked his arm loose and glared at her. "Let me go, you old bag of worms."

Dink took my hand, and at his touch I turned away. He was still smiling. We crept along quietly, and when we could no longer hear their voices, we began to run. We ran until we were almost to the lane and could see the sunlight filtering through the trees. At last we stepped into the sunlight.

We stood there waiting for our hearts to slow down. The sun felt good after the damp woods, but the dust still burned my feet.

"How about letting me wear your shoes home, Dink? I don't think I can stand it any longer, my feet are blistering off."

Standing, he pulled his shoes off and handed them to me. I sat down and put them on, lacing them tight against their bigness. I looked at Dink's bare, white feet sticking out of his jeans and felt guilty. His feet were bony and too tender for the rough ground, but still, he ought to toughen up.

"Promise me, Florrie."

I stood up and looked at him, puzzled.

"Promise what?"

"Promise never to tell what you saw in the woods today. If it's ever told, I want to be the one to tell it."

"I won't tell anybody except Mama, and she won't tell."

"No. Don't even tell Aunt Julia. Promise me you won't, Florrie."

I really wanted to tell Mama, because I knew what a kick she'd get out of knowing something like that. But Dink looked serious and pleading, so I took his hand between my hands. "I promise, Dink. On this whatever the date is, day in June, I, Florence Lee Birdsong, do solemnly swear that I will never tell what or who I saw in the woods today, and that I will carry the secret with me to my grave."

Dink put his arm around my shoulder as we walked down the hill, but when we turned the last curve and came in sight of the house, he put both hands in his pockets.

He whistled as we walked along, stopping every now and then to turn and grin at me, his bare feet making big prints in the hot dust.

🌲🌲🌲🌲🌲🌲 9

The choir of female voices held the same high note. I lay prostrate before them, and until the sound ended, I could not move. I raised my head, trying to scream for them to stop, but no sound came. A singer with long blond hair, her eyes cast heavenward, reached out her hand to grip my shoulder.

I groaned and opened my eyes. Dink climbed into bed with me. "Go back to sleep, Florrie. You're just dreaming."

He wore long-sleeve pink pajamas, and his wavy hair stood straight up. The bedroom windows were crystal with early light as I cradled my head on Dink's shoulder. I went back to sleep.

The next time I woke up, a bell tinkled far away; Dink's head lay on my pillow, his breath moist on my cheek. I slept again.

I awoke the third time to the terrible sound of Aunt Mira's voice in my ear. She leaned across me, shaking Dink by the hair of his head. The breakfast bell she still held in her hand rang softly.

"I knew you all were up to something," she said, "I knew it all the time, I knew it . . ."

Dink jerked loose from her and jumped out of the bed, shrinking back against the wall. Outside, I heard Ralph Junior's car stop beneath the bedroom window, the sound of the motor dying as he turned off the key. Then the front door slammed.

I thought, "Lord, we've done it now. We've really done it now."

Aunt Mira turned on me. "What were you doing in bed with your cousin? What do you mean coming in my house and acting like a harlot?" She turned to Dink again. "Wait until I tell Father Sullivan about you. He'll get you straightened out in a hurry. Don't think he won't."

Dink sat down on the end of the bed. "Florrie was having a bad dream and I just came to . . ."

"To do what?" Aunt Mira smiled.

"To lie with her until she went back to sleep, but then I went to sleep, too."

"Don't try to put that kind of story over on me. I know how men are. I know what they want, what they're after."

"Mother, please, don't . . ." Dink said.

Downstairs, Ralph Junior and Dorothy were talking. Then the front door slammed again and I heard Ralph Junior start the car. The motor sputtered, caught, and the sound of the car faded away down the lane.

Aunt Mira stood in the bedroom door, holding the silver breakfast bell as if she were about to ring it. She was breathing hard, her chest curving out roundly to her waist. She had a short nose, but it was sharply pointed. "She looks like a mad pigeon," I thought.

"Dink, go to your room and get dressed. And get packed. I'm taking you back to school today."

I started out of bed.

"You, Florrie," she said, "You stay in bed until Dink leaves. It may not matter to you how you act, but it matters to me how you act in front of my son."

I got back under the cover and looked at the ceiling. Dink walked around the bed, and from the corner of my eye I saw him look at me, but I didn't look back. I despised him, with his pink pajamas and his pimples.

He left the room, and Aunt Mira came and looked down at me. "Did he do anything, Florrie?"

I got out of bed and went to stand at the windows, looking down into the driveway. "If I pushed the screen outward, I could jump before she could stop me," I thought, and for a moment I saw myself in my long white nightgown, lying face downward in the driveway. Tears stung my eyes and ran down my face. How pitiful Aunt Mira would be as she told Mama about my death, how pitiful as she begged her forgiveness.

"Florrie, I said 'did he do anything?' " Aunt Mira asked again.

"I don't understand what you mean," I said, turning around.

"Crying won't help anything now, Florrie. I mean you'd better tell me if you all did anything."

"You mean, did Dink and I have intercourse? No, Aunt Mira, we didn't."

She put her hand to her throat and walked out of the room. Outside the door, she looked back. "You are a sinful girl, Florrie. Pray for the Lord to forgive you. When I go to Mass on Sunday, I will ask Father to pray for you, too."

"And while you're there," I said, "ask him to pray for a dirty-minded old lady. You weren't happy until you ruined things for Dink and me. Don't think I haven't noticed how you've been watching us and set Dorothy to watching us, too. You've been hoping something would happen."

She closed her eyes, crossing herself. Then she left, but I stood there listening as she went down the stairs. She paused briefly on the telephone landing, and after a while I heard her push through the creaking swinging door to the kitchen.

Dink came to the door, still in his pajamas. He looked at me, and I turned away from him and began gathering my clothes. There weren't too many, just overalls and the dress I had worn to Mass. I folded them and got my brown paper bag from the closet. I looked at the door and Dink was gone.

Then I made my bed, even though I knew Dorothy would unmake it, later, to put on clean sheets. After I put on my shirt and overalls and there was nothing left to do, I walked around the room.

"Good-bye, Uncle Ralph," I said to the picture over the dresser. I never knew him; he died before I was born. But he looked sad. "Don't be sad, Uncle Ralph. You're not like other men. You even gave Aunt Mira a cemetery, and that's a lot more than other men can say they gave their wives."

I looked out the window toward the fields where Dink and I

gathered wildflowers the first day he was home. So long ago, it seemed. All at once, I wanted to see Mama. I got my brown paper sack off the bed and said, "Good-bye, room."

I left without looking back, and walked down the hall. As I passed Dink's room, I looked in. He was sitting on the side of his bed, already dressed except for his shoes.

" 'Bye, Dink."

"Wait, Florrie," he said, getting up and coming to the door. His hair was freshly combed and damp, the tight blond waves lying flat, still showing the teeth marks of the comb. He looked strange in his white starched uniform. His pants had a black stripe down the side. A black tie was knotted neatly at the collar of his white shirt. This was not the Dink who went into the bootlegger woods with me yesterday.

"You're not mad, are you?" he asked.

"Certainly not. Why should I be mad?"

He shrugged. "Just in case you are," he said, "I'm sorry for the way Mother acted."

"Your first apology, Dink," I smiled. "See you later," and I turned and ran down the stairs, taking them two at a time.

I looked up at the foot of the stairs. Dink was still standing there, watching me. I turned away from him and walked through the living room, the draperies pulled against the morning sunshine. Dorothy was talking to Aunt Mira in the kitchen.

I eased out the front door and headed up the lane toward home. I stretched my arms and breathed the morning air. Everybody knew when June came, there was no such thing as winter, that summer would go on forever.

When I came to the curve in the lane, I stopped and looked back. Another ending, I thought. Dink and I will play together no more, because we are too big now. I was surprised that I had admitted it. Sad but true. I am too big to play.

I had caught myself lately, since Goo-Goo died, thinking of

endings and the swiftness of things changing. And summer would end, I knew. Fall would strip the trees, and winter winds, following close behind, would freeze the fields.

I turned the curve and climbed the hill that led to the bootlegger woods. I was no longer afraid, walking past slowly, wondering if Ralph Junior was at the still. I thought, this time yesterday, Dink and I were at Mass, smiling at each other wisely, full of ourselves and our plans.

I came to the fields, and the house was in sight. I hoped that Mama was home. I started running and saw Daddy far across the field, plowing. I stopped and cupped my hands around my mouth, shouting, "Halooo!" From the tiny figure, a faint "Halooo" came back.

When I came to the iron gates, I tried not to look at the place where Dink and I had sat kissing. Terrible, terrible, I thought, and the memory came back, of how his cheek tasted of soda.

As I crossed the road, I saw Mama kneeling in the turnip green patch. "Mama," I called.

She was gathering turnip greens in a boiler. When I called, she looked up, lifted the boiler and waved it, turnip greens spilling all around her. "Hey, is your name Florrie, or Morrie?" she called.

I climbed over the gate, dropping my brown paper sack to the other side, and ran to the garden. I threw myself on her, hugging and kissing her until she fell over, sitting on the turnip greens.

"Mercy, have mercy, Florrie," she begged, laughing.

Then we knelt, side by side, in the garden, and I helped her pull the turnips, shaking off the black dirt before we dropped them into the boiler.

When we had picked all Mama said we needed, I sat with her on the back porch steps, while she cut up the turnips for supper. She told me about the day she rode the streetcar all over

Birmingham, looking at houses. "Marcy was feeling better, Florrie, or you know I wouldn't have left her."

Every now and then, she would stop cutting up the purple-bottomed turnips to clasp my arm. "It was wonderful, Florrie. You can go anywhere in Birmingham you want to go, just for a nickel. I didn't get back to Marcy's until after dark that day. I just walked the downtown streets, looking in windows. The lights were shining up and down the streets, it was like a fairy-land." She patted my hand. "Our day is coming, Florrie. Don't you ever forget it, one of these days when we get to town, we'll ride the streetcar and go to Nunnally's. You know what I did, Florrie? Before I went back to Marcy's that night, I went to Nunnally's and had an ice cream sundae. I wished you were with me."

I smiled at her and took the knife. I started cutting the turnips for her.

"What I really like the best, though," she said, "is buying groceries. Not having to dig your food or chop it or churn it. Just take it home in a sack and there it is. I wasn't brought up like this," she said, looking around her, "and I will never get used to it. Not if I lived here a hundred years."

We looked up as Aunt Mira drove through the iron gates, Dink in the front seat beside her. She stopped the car at the edge of the road, then turned and drove out of sight past the cemetery. Dink didn't wave or even look our way.

"Why, I didn't know Dink was here, Florrie. Why didn't you tell me?" I shrugged my shoulders. "There was nothing to tell," I said.

🌲🌲🌲🌲🌲🌲 **10**

"Mama," I said.

"What?"

"I'm going to buy a brassiere while we're in town today."

Mama turned from the mirror, the brush stopped in mid-stroke. She was still holding a swatch of hair. "I don't believe it," she said.

"Well, I am."

"Wonders never cease," she said. She started brushing again, twisting the swatch of hair into a bun on the back of her neck. I sat on her bed, watching her as she pinned her hair in place, hairpins sticking from her mouth. Her figure under the white slip looked young. But her feet were laced into the black oxfords that she said were good for them.

"Mama, while we're in town today, why don't you buy some white pumps?"

"Because I don't want any white pumps. And even if I did, where am I supposed to get the money to buy them?"

"From the five dollars." Daddy was digging a grave today, and Aunt Mira had given Mama the five dollars for it this morning.

"Florrie, that five dollars has been spent nine times over."

I lay back on the bed and watched her finish dressing. Poor Mama, I thought. She's getting old. She'll be forty-five in July. Imagine being forty-five! I looked at her, wondering how it felt to be so old, but she went on dressing, seemingly undisturbed about her age.

I stretched, pleased with myself for being young. It would be a long time before I got old. A lot of brassieres between the one I got today and the time I'd have to buy the special uplift kind like the ones Mama and Aunt Mira wore. Or a corset.

I swore never to wear a corset. They looked like medieval torture instruments. Mama wore no corset, and neither would I. Aunt Marcy wore a corset that was good for her back. When you put your arm around her, it was like hugging a board.

Mama leaned close to the mirror, dabbing on lipstick, her mouth puckered and round. "What changed you mind about wearing a brassiere, Florrie?" Mama said through the puckered mouth.

"Nothing changed my mind. I just decided, that's all, and I don't want to talk about it any more or I'm not going to buy one."

Mama stood up straight in front of the mirror, looking at herself. She patted her hair, smoothed her slip at the waist, and licked her tongue over her lips, moistening them. She looked pleased with her reflection, head cocked to one side.

I sat up on the side of the bed. "Vanity, thy name is woman," I said.

She laughed, and turned from the mirror. She went to her closet and took out her blue dress with the lace jabot. She pulled it carefully over her head, turning her lips in to keep from smearing her lipstick.

"Mama, why don't you get you a new dress? I swear to God, I'm tired of looking at that one."

Her voice, muffled, came from inside the dress.

"What?" I said.

Her head appeared through the opening of her dress, and she pulled it down over her hips, smoothing it and fastening the buttons. "I said, Florrie, I want you to quit cursing. It's not attractive at all. It makes you coarse and mannish."

I got off the bed and went to the dresser, picking up her "Pink Roses" lipstick. I turned to the mirror, smearing it hard on my mouth, going outside the outline of my lips. Then I turned to Mama. She stood by the open closet door, watching me.

"There," I said. "How do I look? Did that help my looks any? That makes me look goddamned sweet and feminine, don't you think?"

She didn't say anything. I turned to the mirror and looked at myself. The yellow pleated dress I wore was my best one, and I had loved it when I bought it last year. But now it was too tight across my chest, and too short.

I hated my shingled hair, with the sides long over my ears. I pushed at the bangs that hung just over my eyebrows, nudging them to one side. The pink lipstick was horrible with the bright color in my cheeks, and I rubbed at it with the back of my hand, smearing it over my face. "Mama, it's awful to be so ugly," I said.

She came and stood next to me, putting her arm around my shoulders. She looked at my reflection in the old dresser mirror, its silver peeling off in spots, and she smiled. "You're not ugly, Florrie. You're beautiful. Quit saying things like that about yourself. I don't allow anybody to talk to my girl like that."

I smiled sadly at her and turned my back on the mirror.

"Go wash your face," Mama said. "Then come back and put on a little lipstick. It looks nice on you when you do it right."

I went to the back porch and poured some water into the pan

from the bucket. I looked toward the cemetery and saw the grave Daddy was digging, close to our backyard fence. He was throwing up dirt with the long-handled shovel, but I couldn't see him.

"Hey, Daddy," I yelled.

He stood up, but only his head showed above the ground. He waved his arm, then disappeared into the grave again. I could see only the pick rising above the ground. He would keep digging the grave until it was six feet deep. Daddy could tell when he had dug six feet, because the top of the grave would be level with the top of his head. He was exactly six feet tall.

I lathered soap on my face and then rinsed it, but there was no towel, so I turned to face the wind that swept across the cornfield, bringing with it the smell of the maypops blooming along the road. They were almost ready to eat, with their sweet perfume taste. I flapped my hands and rubbed my face until they were dry, and then I went back to the bedroom.

Mama was through dressing, even to her purse hanging over her arm. She was wiping away the flecks of powder that had fallen on her dresser. Her room was neat and orderly, her comb and brush lying at an angle in the middle of her dresser. The bed was smooth where I had lain; no signs were here that she had lately undressed and then dressed again, except for the lingering odor of Lady Esther face powder and Campana Balm.

"Go out on the porch and see if the bus is in sight, Florrie. Come back in and tell me and then dab on a little lipstick. It's in the top drawer over there."

I went to the front porch and, standing on the top step, looked down the road. Heat waves shimmered in the air. July first. We were beginning the hottest month of the year. No bus appeared down that stretch of dusty road, and I went back inside.

"Bus isn't in sight, Mama."

"Hurry and get your lipstick on so we can get on down to the road. The bus ought to be here any minute. It's late already."

Mama opened the dresser drawer and took back out the gold tube of lipstick. I shook my head. "I'm blind from looking outside, and I guess I won't fool with it today," I told her.

She opened her purse and dropped in the lipstick. "If you change your mind, when we get to town, I have it in my purse."

I went to the front porch, and Mama walked through the house, checking. She would check the damper on the cooking range to make sure it wouldn't get too hot while we were gone, and she would make sure the lights were turned off. I heard her on the back porch, hollering to Daddy.

"Toli-*ver!*" she called.

"Yeah!" Daddy called back, a short burst of sound.

"Your lunch is on the back of the stove," she yelled, spacing each word far apart from the others. "We're going to town now, be back in a while."

Daddy didn't answer.

She came back through the house, stopping to lock the front door. She rattled the knob several times, to make sure it was really locked. "I've got things in there I don't want stolen," she said.

We walked down the front steps, Mama looking anxiously toward the road. "Wonder what's keeping it. I hope it hasn't had an accident. Frank drives like a wild man sometimes," but she smiled when she said it.

We walked through our yard and across the grass to the road. Mama talked happily, taking my hand in her soft, gloved one. We stood under a tree, facing in the direction the bus would come. At last a speck appeared, far down the road, and Mama said, "Well, it's coming." We walked to the edge of the road. She didn't say anything else until it pulled to a stop in front of us.

98

The big wheels of the bus threw up dust, and Mama held her handkerchief over her mouth and nose. When the doors opened, she pushed me ahead of her. Frank Sadler, dark and big, sat behind the steering wheel and smiled at me.

"Morning, Florrie."

"Morning, Mr. Sadler."

I handed him my nickel and moved back in the bus to let Mama on. When Mama started to climb the high steps, Frank jumped up and took her by the elbow. "How are you, Julia? It's been a long time since you've ridden my bus," he said.

Mama tried to give him her nickel, but he wouldn't take it. They walked back where I was sitting and Mama sat down next to me.

"You'll be the luckiest girl alive, Florrie, if you grow up to be as pretty as your Mama," Frank said.

"I know it," I said, sullenly, and looked out the window.

"Florrie's pretty now, Frank," Mama said, patting my hand. "She just needs a little more growing time."

I blushed and Frank laughed, and I wished she hadn't said that. Mama could really be embarrassing.

"Julia, you have the prettiest blue eyes I ever saw," Frank said, sitting down in the seat in front of us. He turned sideways to face us, pushing his bus-driver's cap to the back of his head. Mama laughed and patted her hair. "I swear," Frank said, "they get bluer every time I see you."

"I declare Frank, I believe I'm coming to town more often in the future," Mama said.

I looked at Mama. I didn't believe the way she was acting. We had come to town plenty of times and ridden the bus with Frank Sadler, but I had never before heard such talk.

"Mama, what are you doing?" I whispered.

Frank laughed, and walked back to the driver's seat. He started the motor and eased off the brake, and the bus began to roll. He honked the horn at Charlie Swinburne, walking down the middle of the road. Charlie jumped out of the way, laughing as we passed him.

I stared at Mama, puzzled. She had her head turned, looking out the windows across the aisle from us.

"Mama, you ought not to talk to Frank Sadler like that. What would Daddy think?"

She looked at me then, and the gaiety was gone from her voice. "It feels good to have a little fun once in a while." Then she looked straight ahead.

The bus was empty except for us, and we rode along in silence. A film of dust had settled on Mama's black purse, and she wiped it away with her handkerchief.

The bus pitched and bumped, and our arms stretched out to hold to the metal rail that ran along the top of the seat in front of us. We kept the window closed so our hair wouldn't blow, and I was so hot that my legs slipped in the warm sweat on the leather seat.

My dress stuck to my back and I leaned forward and shook it loose, then leaned back again.

"I'll be back tomorrow dragging in stove wood and wearing Ralph Junior's old shoes," Mama said. "Everybody's supposed to have a good time except me. Toliver drinking up at Charlie Swinburne's all the time, and you always gone so I never know where you are."

I wouldn't look at her and kept turned away, looking out the window.

She leaned around me, talking to the side of my face. I watched her reflection in the window. "I was myself before I married Toliver. Do you understand what I mean? I was myself. I haven't done anything for a long time that just concerned me, something that was mine. Except when I went to Marcy's and walked those city streets. That was mine. And I didn't miss you and I didn't miss Toliver."

That hurt, and I thought I would cry until I remembered that I didn't miss her either. I wondered if she'd felt guilty like I had.

"Getting married and having children, Florrie, doesn't mean you stop liking fun." She sat back in her seat again, looking straight ahead. "And I'll tell you something else, if you'd like to hear the truth. I enjoy talking to Frank. He likes the city like I do, and he says one day he's going there to live. And if I enjoy talking to Frank, why then, Miss, I'll keep on talking to Frank."

She didn't speak to me until we got to town. After we had walked along the streets for a while, and looked in the store windows, she was gay again. We went in Davis's, and she left me in the foundation department while she went to see about her job in the store office. I promised to meet her in the balcony tearoom in a half hour.

The salesgirl looked at me. "Hon, I can't tell just from looking what size bra you're going to wear. Let's go in the fitting room and let me measure you." I followed her through a curtained door and then into a smaller room. "Just unbutton your dress, hon, and slip it over your shoulders. What size bra do you usually wear?"

"I've never worn one before," I said, my face turning red.

"Probably you didn't need one before now," she said. She stood, hipshot, watching as I struggled to pull the dress over my shoulders. Finally I stood there in my petticoat, the top of my dress hanging around my hips.

She wrapped her measuring tape around my chest. She had heavy make-up spread thickly over her porous skin. Her black hair, piled high on top of her head and upswept in the back, had a strong oily odor. She wore purple lipstick and a purple silk blouse with a black skirt. Her feet were enclosed in black high-heel ankle-strap shoes.

"Hon, I can't get the right measurement over your slip. You're going to have to drop the straps down."

I closed my eyes and pulled down the straps, letting the petticoat top fall around my waist.

"My God," the girl breathed. "Whoever would have thought you'd have boobs like that!"

I turned my back on her, pulling the straps back over my shoulders.

"What are you doing, hon? Don't you want me to measure you? You got at least size thirty-six boobs there. Why have you been keeping them hid all this time anyway?"

"I've changed my mind," I said. "I don't need a brassiere."

"You need one all right, hon. What are you ashamed of? You could run the fellas all wild, you know that, don't you?"

I pulled my dress back over my shoulders and buttoned it, then turned around.

"It beats all I ever saw how you try to keep 'em hid like you do," and she shook her head. "Well, it's your business, but if you change your mind, you be sure and ask for Marie if you come back. Okay, kid?"

I nodded and followed her from the dressing room. She walked behind a counter and said to a red-headed salesgirl, "She's got beautiful boobs, beautiful," and they smiled at me as I left the foundation department.

I walked slowly through the store, people pushing against me and glaring when I bumped into them. Humiliation washed over me every time I thought about the way that girl stared at me. Anger welled up, and I thought I would go back and hit her. I could almost feel the smooth silk blouse under my hands

102

as I pushed her over. I stopped walking, the thought was so real.

"Young lady, you're blocking this aisle," a gray-haired woman said.

"Excuse me," I said, walking on. I got to the staircase that led upward to the tearoom and started climbing, looking at myself in the mirror that covered the wall.

It was a shock to see that I looked the same, that there was no outward sign that today I had been naked in front of a stranger. I looked down at the women on the floor below. The firm, round protuberances on their chests told me they wore brassieres. Did they all undress in front of common salesgirls?

I stood at the door of the tearoom and looked for Mama. She waved to me from a table next to the wall. I weaved through the noontime crowd and sat down in the chair across from her.

"What took you so long? Did you buy your brassiere?"

"Don't talk so loud, Mama. No, I didn't buy it."

"Why not? Why didn't you get it?" Mama asked.

"Because I didn't like the way the salesgirl looked at me, and I don't want to talk about it."

"I don't know what in the world you're talking about, Florrie, and I don't want to know. Because if I did, I still wouldn't understand it. It'll be a long time, maybe right before school starts, before we get to town again. If you want a brassiere, you had better buy it today."

I picked up a menu and read the list of desserts. Ice cream. Chocolate and vanilla. Apple pie. Chocolate pie. Lemon pie. Blackberry cobbler. Apricot pie. That's it, apricot pie. My spirits brightened when I thought about the rich yellow pie with the tall meringue.

"Mama, I'll have apricot pie and a glass of milk." Cold milk, milk that wasn't warm straight out of the cow's udder.

A waitress stood at our table, ready to write down our order. "Two apricot pies and one milk. And one coffee," Mama said. The girl wrote it down and Mama smiled at her. "You know, I'm going to work here this fall. I'll be working in the basement, selling shoes. I'll probably be eating up here, so maybe I'll get to know you."

"Is that right?" the girl said, and she didn't smile back at Mama. I looked down at the table and squeezed my hands together in my lap. Mama ought not to be so friendly with people like that. That girl didn't care about Mama.

The waitress left and Mama turned to me. "I've got another surprise for you, Florrie."

"What is it?" I asked, looking up.

"Mrs. Beggs is going to come and clean house and cook, when I go to work. For only two dollars a week."

"Are you telling the truth?"

"What's gotten into you, asking me if I'm telling the truth! One of these days I'm going to forget how big you've gotten and turn you over my checkered apron. I don't want you coming home from school and having to think about getting supper. So yesterday, when I saw Mrs. Beggs coming up the road, I stopped her and asked her. She said she'd be glad to, she needs the money this winter."

I wanted to tell her about seeing Mrs. Beggs in the woods with Ralph Junior and a man named Sam at the still, but I remembered my promise to Dink and I didn't tell.

The waitress came back, bringing our pie and milk and Mama's coffee. I slipped my shoes off under the table to feel the thick rose-colored carpet soft under my feet. Cool air blew on us from the grating on the wall.

When Mama started working here, she could eat apricot pie every day. I hated the waitress who didn't want to be her friend. After I ordered my second piece of pie, I would tell Mama not to ever speak to her again.

It was laying-by time. The planting was done, the crops cultivated. There was nothing for a farmer to do now except wait, and so Daddy sat most of the day on the porch, looking toward the fields.

"Lord, Florrie, it better rain soon, it better rain soon," he told me one night when we sat on the porch. It had not rained for two weeks, since the middle of July. We had walked together in the fields one day. "It will have to rain for a week to make up for a drouth like this," he said as we walked between the rows of corn. The stalks had quit growing, their roots caught in the grip of the hard, gray earth. He pulled loose an ear of corn, a nubbin, and stripped back the shuck. "Look at that corn, Florrie. It's no good except for the pigs." He rubbed his fingers along a corn frond. "Feel it Florrie, how brittle."

I felt a leaf and it was dry and crisp. "What are you going to do, Daddy?"

"There's nothing to do but wait and pray. If it rains soon,

we're all right. Just pray for rain, Florrie." He looked across his fields, across Aunt Mira's fields. "This is rich land, Florrie. If I farm it right, I can make it pay." He smiled at me. "I've decided next year I'm going to plant cotton. Cotton doesn't need so much rain. I've been scared of cotton since the boll weevil, but that's the way a farmer makes money. Maybe I can buy your mama a house and she'll be happy."

"She'll be happy when she moves to town," I said.

"I'd shrivel up and die in town. The land is where I want to be, Florrie. It's the only thing in this world that you can count on. It'll be here when I'm gone and you're gone, but somebody will be farming it, and then their children. The land goes on. One of these days I'm going to own a piece of it, too, and when I die it'll be yours."

We walked together out of the field, but he turned and walked up the road to Charlie Swinburne's. I watched him out of sight and then I went home. He woke me up when he came home late that night, fumbling at his bedroom door and bumping against the wall. There was always moonshine to be had at Charlie's. Mama and I had eaten supper alone. "Well, I guess Mr. Birdsong's off somewhere getting drunk," Mama said while we were eating.

Mama's birthday had come on the nineteenth of July. I didn't have any money to go to Huxley and buy her a present, so I wrote her a poem. I worked on it for a week before her birthday, and then at supper on the nineteenth I gave it to her. I had copied it in ink on notebook paper, and I put it in an envelope on which I'd written, "Happy Birthday, Mama." I called my poem "Remembrance," and she sat at her place at the table and read it.

Remembrance

My loneliness is sharp today.
Autumn is here and summer was
Sacrificed in her bright fires
To Winter's God.

Like the summer
You are gone, and oh, the
Years we had together were too few.
I haven't many summers to remember
That belonged to you and me.

My sorrow is keen today, and
In every falling leaf and last lonely
Winging bird I feel your loss.
I look for you in the brown earth,
In the brown trees.

I look for you in the brown of my
Soul, but you are not there,
In those drab shades.
I see no color now.

But in a while Spring will come and I will walk in
The green grass, the warm wind will blow.
You will take my hand and
Sadness will vanish with Winter,
When Spring is here.

Mama looked up and there were tears in her eyes. "Florrie, that's beautiful. I didn't know you could write poems like that." She wiped her eyes and put the poem back in the envelope.

I smiled at her and was proud that she liked my poem.

*　　*　　*

The humid heat of July turned into the humid heat of August. It would be at least two or three more weeks before Daddy could harvest any of his crops.

Dog days came with August. Dogs had fits, running in circles until they fell exhausted on the ground. Sores wouldn't heal, and if you got sick you stayed sick longer. Nights were almost as hot as the days, and Mama and I sat on the front porch steps trying to catch a breeze.

Daddy sat with his feet propped on the bannister, smoking Bugler cigarettes. Mama sighed and shifted her legs. "I don't see how you can stand to smoke, Toliver, hot as it is."

"If you've got the habit, you smoke whether it's hot or cold. I remember you had the habit when we were living over in Georgia."

"I didn't have the habit," Mama said. "I just smoked to keep Fannie company. She's the one had the habit."

"I don't believe Fannie smoked at all," Daddy said.

"Pshaw, Mr. Birdsong, that's all you know about it. Fannie could roll a cigarette good as a man any day."

Mama still smoked. I hadn't known it until a few days ago when I came back to the house to get a book. I'd just left and Mama didn't expect me to turn around and come right back. She was sitting by the fireplace in the living room blowing the smoke up the chimney. I watched her take a few puffs before I let her know I was there.

"Mama, what in the world are you doing?"

She jumped up and threw the cigarette in the fireplace. "Florrie, I wish you wouldn't slip up on me like that. One of these days I'm just going to keel over dead. So now you know. I've been smoking off and on ever since you were born. You just better not tell Toliver, that's all. If he knows I'm smoking tailormades, I'll have to divide with him or go back to rolling my own, and I cannot stand Buglar tobacco. Promise, Florrie, you won't tell."

"I won't tell, Mama," I said, and followed her into the kitchen. She went to the pantry and poured some coffee into her hand and chewed the grounds. Then she went to the back porch and spit them over the bannister and came back to the kitchen and sat down at the table.

"I learned that from Mr. Birdsong's brother. It's good to get liquor off your breath, too."

"Mama, you don't drink, too, do you?"

"Of course not, Florrie. But Ernest did. Ernest loved a joke, and drank, and used to get me to smoke with him. That's the way I thought Toliver was when I married him. Molly—you know, Ernest's wife—was jealous of me one time in Atlanta. She thought Ernest had a crush on me, and he did, only I denied it to her and tried not to get with Ernest by myself."

We sat on the porch steps almost every night until it was time to go to bed and try to sleep. Mama slept naked on the floor with nothing but a sheet to lie on and a pillow for her head.

I often went to the sleeping porch and sat in my window for a while, sometimes until the moon had set. I thought about Billy Paul, dreaming that he loved me, and about Dink, wondering if he was lonesome. I started to write to him once, but decided not to, because it was over with us and I wanted it to stay over. We could never go back to where we were before Aunt Mira found us in bed together.

This morning at breakfast, Mama asked me if I would like to go to Huxley with her and help her bring back a few things we needed at the store. We sat there, Mama and Daddy and I, drinking our coffee. It was hot and I was irritable and all I could think of was getting to the woods and lying in the shade with my book. The bookmobile was coming by, and I wanted to swap the books I'd read. The bookmobile wouldn't be by again for two weeks. I was already dressed, waiting for it.

"Can you wait to walk to Huxley until I swap my books?"

"No. I want to go before it gets too hot. It's a long walk. You go ahead, I can make it all right by myself."

"Hell, I'll go with you."

"If you curse me again, I'll slap your face, Florrie Birdsong. This is your mother you're talking to. What's the matter, did you get up on the wrong side of the bed?"

"No, I didn't, I felt fine until you hopped on me the first thing with things to do."

"What do you do to help around here anyway?"

"When I get married and have children, my children aren't going to have to bring in stove wood and walk four miles for groceries."

"Unless you start wearing a brassiere, nobody's ever going to marry you, because people are going to start thinking you're like Lucinda. I wouldn't want a son of mine to go with a girl that didn't wear a brassiere."

I was so furious, I stood up and threw my cup of coffee against the fireplace. It bounced once on the hearth and when it hit again, it broke, coffee splashed on the floor.

Daddy stared down at the table and didn't look up. Mama turned in her chair, looking out the kitchen window.

"See what you make me do," I said and the tears started. "See how mad you make me?"

I went out the back door and sat on the steps. I leaned my face against the house, the rough pine boards, which Daddy had stained green last fall, pricking my cheek.

Lucinda, Mama said. Poor Lucinda, because that's what people in Gray's Chapel called her. Poor Lucinda, they said, she's not quite bright. Lucinda was the daughter of Mr. and

Mrs. Simpson. When Lucinda was little, she was precious with her long black curls and brown eyes. She played in her front yard, and when someone passed by she would run to meet them, pulling at a trouser leg or the hem of a dress. "Play with me," she begged, "please, play with me."

When she was six years old she went to school, but the teacher sent her home after a few weeks with a note. The note said that Lucinda was not ready for school yet. Better to wait until next year. She went again the next year and was sent home again. Mr. and Mrs. Simpson sent her one more time, and when she was sent home the third time, they didn't send her to school anymore.

Dr. Fairfax said she'd outgrow it, but she didn't. She grew bigger and bigger and still played in the front yard to watch for people passing by. Only people didn't think she was cute anymore when she ran out to pull at their clothes.

"Go on now Lucinda," they said, shaking loose. "Your Mama ought to make you play in the back yard."

One day I passed her house and she was sitting on her front steps, holding her doll. She stood up and yelled to me, the rag doll bouncing down the steps. "Play with me, play with me," she called in her baby voice. She was standing barefoot on the steps. She wore a red cotton print dress, too small for her. It was high above her knees, stretching tight across her breasts. Her black hair was cut short, and it curled around her face. One side fell over her eye, and when she lifted her hand to push it back, for a second I saw a pretty young girl with a soft curving body, her arm raised in a womanly gesture to her hair.

But then she bounded down the steps, running after me, and yelling: "Play with me, please play with me."

I looked at her as she ran toward me. I turned and ran, and when I looked back she was chasing me, her breasts bouncing up and down. The next time I looked back, she was sitting on the side of the road, her legs pulled up with her head resting on her knees. She was crying.

"Lucinda," I called, "I'll play with you some other day." She didn't look up, so I went on home.

Mama stepped around me as she went down the steps to the store. I watched her walk across the yard and go out the gate, not looking back.

I thought, what if I never see her alive again and we were mad at each other. I stood up and ran toward the gate.

"Mama," I called.

She turned and waited until I caught up with her. I put my arm around her neck, pulling her head down to kiss her goodbye.

"Florrie," she said, kissing my cheek, "what am I going to do with you?"

"I'm going to clean up the house and wash the dishes. Everything will be clean when you get back."

Mama left me and crossed the grass. She turned right on the road heading toward Huxley, and then I saw the bookmobile coming. I ran to the house and got my books, running back to the road to flag it down. I swapped my books for a Grace Livingston Hill that I hadn't read called *Crimson Roses*. There was a book about Beethoven's life, and I took that one and one by Faith Baldwin. I could have only three.

The lady that rode in the back with the books sat at a desk and stamped my card and asked if I was ready for school to start, and I told her I certainly was not. I got off and waited for the bookmobile to pull away; then I crossed the road, cutting through the cornfield to the woods.

✝✝✝✝✝✝ 12

The sun was low in the sky; it sank beneath the branches of the hickory tree where I was lying, turning my shade into late afternoon glow. It lit the pages of my book so brightly that the type jumped out and hung shimmering above the fuzzy texture of the paper.

I lay flat on my back, my legs pulled up, and rested my book on my stomach. Sunlight washed over me, warm and liquid. I stared at the round red sun balanced on the edge of the horizon, then closed my eyes and watched its burned-in image flickering on the retinas of my eyes.

I had been in my woods all day. When I got here this morning, the two smallest Beeton boys, Ronald and Jerry, were playing here. People seldom came in here because the woods ended on a dried-up creek bottom and were a short cut to nobody's house.

I knew there could be no reading with their whooping and hollering going on. But neither could I order them out. The woods belonged to no one that I knew of, and besides, they'd probably go home and tell. It wouldn't do to get their old daddy mad at you. He was mean and trashy.

People called Mr. Beeton "Peachtree," because when he came home drunk he broke off a long peach-tree limb and whipped Mrs. Beeton and the children. Mr. Beeton said there wasn't any switch as good as a peach-tree limb. People who lived close to them said the whole family, seven of them in all, would run around and around the house, Peachtree waving the switch at them, his blue tick hound nipping at his heels. "Here, now, Blue," Mr. Beeton said, shaking his foot, but he never hit the dog.

The children screamed and cried, and sometimes one of them broke the circle and ran in the house and the others followed him, like a game of follow-the-leader. Then shouting came from the house for a while until one of them ran outside again. Then the chase started all over again, until Peachtree caught someone. Then they all stopped and Peachtree walked up and down the line, whipping them.

A neighbor went to Huxley once and brought back the sheriff, but when he got there he just stood and grinned, watching them. After a while he got in the car and left. "A whipping every now and then is good for kids and wives," he said.

This morning I called to Ronald and Jerry, and they came and stood in front of me.

"What you want," Ronald said.

"I just want to warn you about the bootleggers."

"What bootleggers?" he asked.

"Well, I heard my Pa say this morning," I said, "that when he was in the cornfield yesterday, he heard some bootleggers in here talking."

"He did?" Jerry asked.

I nodded. "My Pa said he heard one of them with a *mean* voice say if he ever caught him a little boy in here, he was going to kill him and use him to help ferment the mash."

114

They thought about it for a minute and then Ronald said, "Come on Jerry, we better get out of here," and they left.

I waited a few minutes to make sure they weren't coming back, and then I lay down under the oak tree.

I didn't go home to lunch because I couldn't quit reading *Crimson Roses*. I finished it and lay there thinking about it for a while, and then started the story of Ludwig Beethoven. I read the rest of the afternoon, and when I came to the end of the story it was hard to shake free of the spell of that magnificent man.

I believed that I understood his pain at going deaf, to never again hear an orchestra play his music. Mama and I listened to the symphony on our radio on Sunday afternoons. It was an old table radio that Aunt Mira had given us when she bought her new one, and it squawked and sputtered, the sound fading away and coming back. But still I felt the beauty of the music, and thought, how awful to be deaf.

I stopped up my ears and watched the pantomime in the woods: birds with no voices, trees moving without the sound of the wind. To be deaf would be to see musicians ready to play, their instruments poised. The conductor raises his arms for the music to begin and the violinists move their bows across the strings, the flutists' fingers rise and fall delicately over the air holes, horns are raised to pursed lips, the big fiddles are plucked. But there is no sound.

I looked again at the picture of the orchestra in the book. The book said that Beethoven could hear the music in his mind. When I stopped up my ears, I could not hear the birds' song.

It was almost dark. The rosy mouth of the horizon had swallowed all but a half-moon sliver of the sun, and as I watched, it too slid down the gullet of night. Frogs croaked from the creek bottom and a mockingbird, who later tonight would turn into a nightingale, sang practice notes from the limb above me. Too soon the day ended, and it was time to go home.

I stood up and brushed off my clothes. I itched in a dozen different places, and knew I had red bug bites from lying in the dry grass. I gathered up my books and ran for home. I was scared of snakes in the dark, so I hardly let my bare feet touch the ground, running on tiptoe. Mama was going to be mad at me for staying out so late and for not cleaning up the house after I said I would.

I ran from the darkness of the woods into the twilight of the cornfield. I stopped, sucking air for a minute before I started to run again. Over the top of the corn I could see a light in our kitchen window. I was starving from having had no lunch, and I thought that from here I could smell the sour milk corn bread cooking in the stove.

I pushed my books up under my arm and ran again, pushing through the corn, straining toward home. The hot sun had burned the ground between the rows of corn from black to gray until finally it was bleached so chalky white it seemed now to have light of its own and glowed in a wavy path stretching to the road.

Something grabbed my foot and sent me crashing headlong into the corn. I threw my arms out to catch myself, books flying around me. I lay there on the ground, trying to get back the breath that had been knocked out of me. After awhile I sat up and pulled my left foot up so I could examine it.

My big toe was numb, and I could see where the toenail had been torn back. Blood, black in the fading light, dripped onto the ground. I reached out and pulled at the root that tripped me, but the more I pulled, the longer it got, going deeper into the ground. Tomorrow I would come with the hoe and chop it in two.

I crawled on my hands and knees, picking up my books. I

reached for the last book leaning against a stalk of corn, bracing myself with my right hand on the ground. Then I heard a sound like a baby shaking its rattle. I looked around. A rattlesnake crawled from under a broken corn stalk, its mouth open, its tongue flicking in and out. It had a big head. I cried out, I wanted to run, but if I did it would surely strike. And I knew that people who got rattlesnake-bit died almost every time, that it was a miracle when they lived.

My right arm began to shake from the weight of leaning on it, and my left hand still reached for the book. If I stay still, he won't hurt me, I thought, and silently I prayed: Oh, my God I am heartily sorry for having offended Thee and I detest all my sins because of Thy just punishment, but most of all because they offend Thee, O God, Who art all good and deserving of all my love. I firmly resolve with the help of Thy grave to sin no more and to avoid the near occasions of sin. Amen.

Someone walked through the cornfield not far away from me and I prayed again, Hail, Mary, full of Grace, the Lord is with thee, blessed art thou among women and the fruit of thy womb, Jesus. Amen.

A crow flew over, dipped low, cawed, and flew off over the woods. I closed my eyes and thought that I would faint, but then something cool touched my hand. The coolness crept up and over my hand, flowing like a stream of spring water. All my strength flowed into the ground and my lips moved silently. It seemed a long time before the horny rattles passed over. Then there was nothing, but still I knelt, a statue in the field.

I opened my eyes to darkness. I closed my hand around the book I had reached for and stood up. My right arm hung lifeless at my side; the muscles jerked with spasms when I lifted it.

I walked slowly from the field and crossed the road to our house. It was strange, but I didn't hate the snake. He hadn't

117

hurt me because I hadn't scared him. I felt strong, and thought, I must have a soothing power over the wild animals. Like Snow White, the way the birds would come and sit on her finger.

I went in the yard and stopped inside the gate, leaning against the post. I was so tired I thought I could not take another step. It was black dark, the moon shining full over the trees. Far across the cemetery, the stained glass window of the church winked purple and green in the moonlight, like some gaudy jewel of God.

I started toward the back door of the house and heard a long, mournful cry, so hopeless and lonely that gooseflesh rose on my arms. I started running. "Mama, Mama, what's the matter," I screamed, and jumped all three steps to the back porch. I burst into the kitchen. Mama was sitting at the kitchen table, her head on her arms. She looked up at me. She was crying.

"Where have you been, Florrie, I thought you were dead! You've been gone all day, and when you didn't come home for supper, I called and called. Toliver's out looking for you now. Where have you been?" Anger was in her voice.

I sat down in the chair next to her, touched that she was so worried about me, and put my arm around her. "I forgot what time it was, Mama. The bookmobile came. I got new books and went to the woods, and before I knew it, it was almost dark. I was in the woods behind the cornfield reading."

"No, you weren't, Florrie. Don't lie. I sent Ronald Beeton in there to look for you. He came up the road when I was calling, and he said he saw you in there early this morning. I sent him to get you, and when he came back he said you were gone. Even Toliver is worried about you."

"I was in the cornfield, Mama, and I saw Ronald Beeton, only I didn't know who it was then. I've been standing out in the yard looking at the moon. I saw a snake in the corn field."

Mama sat up and took the handkerchief out of her pocket

and blew her nose. "Florrie, can't you stay home and read sometimes? Do you always have to be off somewhere? One of these days something really will happen to you, and there won't be anybody that knows where you are so we could help you."

Daddy came in the back door and when he saw me, he smiled. "Well, here you are, Florrie. I knew you were all right. I kept trying to tell your mother you were all right, but you know how excited she gets."

"You were worried, too, Mr. Birdsong, quit trying to fool somebody. You'd better start taking as much interest in your daughter as you do your corn, or the Lord only knows what's going to happen to her."

Daddy looked at me behind Mama's back and shook his head not to say anything. He went on the front porch and Mama got up to get my supper. She had made a pot of soup, and there was corn bread.

"Did you make the corn bread with sour milk, Mama?"

"I sure did."

"I knew it," I said. "I knew it when I came out of the woods. I could smell it cooking all the way across the corn field."

🌲🌲🌲🌲🌲 **13**

I woke up at dawn, so hot I couldn't sleep, so I got up and went to the cemetery. There seemed always to be a cool wind blowing through there, and I walked among the graves enjoying the quiet.

"Good morning, Mrs. Hobson," I said. "We're going to have another hot day."

The twin boys of Sarah Culpepper lay under a blackjack oak. The two tiny graves were outlined with a white iron fence. Poor little things, I thought, they didn't even live to be a month old. I read their tombstone. It said in slanted script, *"Do not weep, for God has called them home to be his angels. Born April 1, 1935—Died April 27, 1935. Twin sons of Sarah and Robert Culpepper."*

I remembered their funeral, the two little coffins lying side by side over their graves. Sarah was still too weak to be at the funeral, and the neighbors picked flowers off the wreaths and took them to her.

"Good morning, little Culpeppers," I said. "I hope you are God's angels and that it's lots of fun."

120

I walked along in the half light, sleepy from not having had my morning coffee. An early morning wind rose, bending down the tall grass next to the fence; a bird balanced on a branch, then flew away, flapping its wings hard against the wind.

Dawn gave way to morning, and the joy of the new day caught at me. I started dancing, my nightgown whirling around my ankles; I leaped across graves, then back again, so that bad luck would stay away. I ran the length of the cemetery and fell exhausted in the grass under a tree.

I lay on my back and looked up through the leaves to the sky. No one to see, no one to care that I danced among the graves. No one to look at me and frown and say, Don't do that, people don't act that way.

I thought that some day I would go and live in the woods like Thoreau, to be by myself and do the things I wanted that hurt no one. Do what things, I asked. I don't know for sure, I answered. Run with joy when I feel like it, or shout, or throw my arms around someone I love. Just be myself, I suppose.

Mama called from the back porch. I lay there and listened to her call a few more times before I stood up and walked to the fence. "I'm coming," I shouted.

"Come home," she called.

I walked toward the yard and when I came to the cemetery gate, I climbed over. Gray smoke, trickling upward from the chimney, lay crossways in the air. The morning breeze was gone, and there was no sign at all that rain would come today to save the crops.

Daddy stayed gone most of the time now, and yesterday I saw him ride past with Charlie Swinburne in Charlie's old Ford. When he came home for supper Mama wouldn't speak to him, and when he spoke to her it made her mad.

"I don't have a thing to say to you, Mr. Birdsong."

"You're glad the crops are burning up, Mrs. Birdsong," Daddy said. "You're glad because then you can say 'I told you so.'"

"I've been saying 'I told you so' for almost twenty years, and it hasn't made an impression on you. I doubt that this year would be any different."

I started up the steps of the back porch and Biddy, Mama's pet chicken, ran out, thinking it was to be fed. I stepped on its rough foot and it ran squawking under the house. Biddy was the last of our chickens. Daddy had raised chickens for a while, but Mama kept making pets out of them or giving them away.

"Hell, a chicken is just something to eat," Daddy said. "I'm not wasting any more time raising them for pets."

Last summer we had a black hen that Mama was crazy about. She made a long rope out of strips of old sheets knotted together and tied one end to the hen's leg and the other to a bush or tree, leaving enough rope for her to walk around. Mama was afraid she would leave the yard and go to the road and get run over by a car.

Every day we had to keep moving the old black hen to the shade as the sun went across the yard. One day Mama and I went to town, leaving her tied in the shade. Neither of us thought about it getting sunny while we were gone, and Daddy didn't come home for lunch that day because we were gone. He took his lunch with him and worked in the far field.

When Mama and I got home in the middle of the afternoon, the black hen was lying in the broiling sun, her wings fluttering feebly in the dust. She had pulled the rope tight, straining toward the shade of the trees, but it was just beyond her reach.

Mama and I took her in the kitchen and poured cold water on her. Mama even took the little bottle of whiskey out of her sewing-machine drawer and put some in a teaspoon, pouring it down the hen's throat. But she died a few minutes after we brought her in.

Mama sat down at the kitchen table and cried, her face cupped in her hands, her elbows resting on the table. "Florrie, why didn't I think to move her before we left," she said.

Daddy came in from the field and I told him what happened to Mama's chicken. "I don't think that chicken is hurt a bit," he said. "There's no sense in wasting it, Florrie. Fry it for supper."

"You're just a durn fool," Mama said, and we took the old black hen in the woods behind the cemetery and buried her with the rope still tied to her leg. It was right after that that Daddy quit raising chickens.

I went in the kitchen, and the first thing Mama did was jump on me.

"If you had to do the washing around here, Florrie, you wouldn't wear those long gowns around and lie in the dirt in them. Just look all over the back of your gown, it's filthy. The least you can do is dress when you get up in the morning. I have never in my life run around in my nightgown during the day. Nor failed to comb my hair."

"Well, you're just good," I whispered under my breath. If Mama had hair like mine, she wouldn't comb it either, because it looked the same combed or uncombed. I went to my room to get dressed.

I changed clothes and went back to the kitchen and sat down to eat. Daddy was already at the table. His eyes were red, and I thought, too much moonshine. Mama put the biscuits and syrup on the table. And butter. Mama had churned yesterday, and there was a fresh cake of butter, milk still seeping from around the edges.

"Is this all we're having?" Daddy asked.

"Mr. Birdsong, if you know of something else I can put on the table, I'll put it. You're lucky to have syrup for the biscuits," Mama said. "I took the last of the two dollars Joel gave me last week and got the syrup."

"I like meat with my biscuits," Daddy said.

"Well, if you know where some meat is, go and get it." Mama sat down and began to eat, pouring the syrup onto her plate. It spread in a thick, golden pool, and she stirred the fresh butter into it. Then she spread it with a knife onto the biscuits.

"If I knew where my hog was, I'd go and get some meat. I'd like to get my hands on the son of a bitch that took my hog. I believe that rotten sheriff was in on it, because he sure didn't look for it very hard."

I looked at Mama, and she was as calm as I'd ever seen her. She spread syrup daintily on her biscuit, taking care that it didn't get on her fingers. "You might as well forget about that hog," she said. "It's gone. You better start thinking about what we're going to do this winter if the rain doesn't come soon."

"The rain will come in time," Daddy said. "The land will take care of us."

"I start to work tomorrow," Mama said. She stood up from the table and began gathering the dishes, dropping them into the dishpan of hot water on the stove.

"I thought you weren't going to work until after school starts, Mama." I didn't want her to be gone during summer vacation, and I dreaded having Mrs. Beggs come here. Disappointment stabbed my stomach, and I pushed back from the table, no longer hungry.

"Mira Gray came by the house early this morning and said they called from Davis's yesterday. They told her to tell me to come in tomorrow so they could start teaching me the stock.

They want me there for the school trade. Is that all you're going to eat, Florrie?" Mama asked as she took my plate.

"I'm not hungry," I said.

Daddy stood up and walked to the back door screen, pushing it partly open. "I don't think a mother ought to work. It's her duty to take care of the house and children."

"I don't own a house to take care of, and my girl is almost grown up. Besides, in two weeks she'll be in school all day. My duty is to myself as well as to you, Mr. Birdsong. Times have changed. Women don't have to stay home anymore if they don't want to. I'm still a young woman with a lot of years ahead of me, and I don't expect I'll spend them sitting on this farm."

"There's no reasoning with a fool," he said, and went out the door. Mama didn't say anything until he passed the kitchen window. He had on his straw work hat, and I wondered what he would find to do in the fields.

"Florrie, I want you to walk up the road to Mrs. Beggs and tell her to come on here tomorrow. If she can't, ask her what's the first day she can come."

"All right," I said, standing up.

"While I'm thinking about it, Florrie, I want to remind you to help Mrs. Beggs out when she comes, and try to keep Toliver out of her way. You know how he talks, and she won't get a thing done if he sits around talking to her all day."

"All right," I said and left the kitchen, heading for the front porch. Mama followed me to the front screen door, and when I went down the steps she said, "Remember, if she can't come tomorrow, be sure and ask her which day she'll come. If she can't come tomorrow, you'll have to spend the day with Mira Gray."

I walked down the road past Mrs. Goggins's house. All seventeen dogs ran to the gate barking at me. If those dogs ever got loose and got hold of somebody, there wouldn't be anything left to pick up. I hurried by.

I went about a quarter of a mile and passed the Simpsons', glad Lucinda wasn't out front. I climbed the hill, then cut across old man Higgins' pasture. The cows mooed and looked at me, but didn't start toward me. I would have run. I was scared of cows, though Daddy said that was foolishness. I climbed through the fence on the other side of the pasture and was in the narrow dirt road that led to Mrs. Beggs's.

I walked down the road for about a quarter of a mile and there, in a grassy clearing, was Mrs. Beggs's house. It had only two rooms and a porch. Her privy sat nestled among some trees in the back and was the same colorless gray as the house. The wood had gone so long unpainted that it had petrified.

An old Model T Ford with no wheels sat in the front yard, and on the porch was a rusted wringer washing machine. Mrs. Beggs sat in a straight chair next to the washer.

"Morning, Mrs. Beggs."

"Morning. You Mrs. Birdsong's girl, ain'tcha?"

"Yes, Ma'am," I said. "She told me to come and ask you if you could start work tomorrow instead of two weeks. She said if you can't start tomorrow to please tell me what day you can start. They called Mama yesterday to come to work tomorrow."

She untied her blue print sunbonnet, took it off, and fanned herself. "I reckon I can come tomorrow, all right. But I can't come the next day. That's Friday, and I got business to attend to."

"Yes, Ma'am, thank you Mrs. Beggs. I'll tell Mama what you said. Good-bye."

She nodded, and I turned and walked from her yard. I went back down the road and wondered if it were true that she had a tall, black-headed son, like some people said she did. They said he loved his mother and told her that when he made some money he was coming back to get her. Mama said she didn't believe it, that Mrs. Beggs had lived here for ten years and there never had been any sign of him.

I started running to tell Mama what Mrs. Beggs said.

✝✝✝✝✝✝ 14

I got up early so I could have a cup of coffee with Mama before she left for work. She was already dressed except for powdering her face. She wore her blue eyelet dress, which she had washed and pressed yesterday, and her good black shoes. Daddy was still in bed, because he came home drunk last night, and while I was still half asleep I heard him fussing with Mama in the kitchen. I had put the pillow over my head and gone back to sleep.

"Florrie, you remember what I told you," Mama said. "Stay close around the house, and if Toliver looks like he's keeping Mrs. Beggs from getting her work done, tell him to go on down to Charlie Swinburne's and leave her alone. It'll be a waste of the two dollars I'm paying her every week if I have to come home and go over what she's done."

"I will, Mama. I remember everything you told me. Quit telling me again every five minutes."

"Besides, he's supposed to finish digging the grave that they're going to bury that old soldier in," Mama said.

"Will it be a military funeral?"

"I don't know, Florrie, I guess it will. I'm nervous and don't feel like worrying about funerals right now. You remind Toliver when he gets up that he's supposed to finish that grave or Mira Gray will get somebody else to do it." Mama took a last sip of coffee and stood up. She fluffed up the lace jabot. A horn blew out on the road.

"It's Frank, already. Run and tell him, Florrie, that I'll be there in a minute. Don't just sit there, run and tell him. It looks like it's all you can manage, to do the least little thing I ask you."

"Well, hell, I'm going as fast as I can. He's not going to just pull off and leave you," and I went out the kitchen door and down the back steps to the yard. Frank Sadler was standing outside the bus smoking a cigarette.

"Hey, Mr. Sadler," I yelled, waving my arms.

He looked toward the yard and waved back.

"Mama says she'll be there in a minute."

He waved his arm and went to stand under a tree.

I squinted my eyes as I watched him, and when my eyelids began to tremble, he danced up and down on the dappled grass like a puppet suddenly gone crazy.

I heard the screen door open, and then Mama came down the back steps into the yard. She looked funny dressed up so early in the morning.

"Florrie, I'm going to count on you today. It'll be about six o'clock when I get home. Be a sweet girl, and I'll see you tonight. I love you."

She kissed me, but wouldn't let me kiss her back because she was afraid I'd smear her powder or mess up her hair. She turned away from me, swinging her purse as she walked. I watched her as she opened the gate and walked across the grass to the road. I felt like crying because she was going to town without me.

She walked up to Frank, who was standing under the tree, and he took her arm and helped her onto the bus. The doors closed and then the big blue and white bus pulled off. I watched it until it went past the church and disappeared around the curve.

I climbed the steps to the back porch and saw Daddy sitting at the table. I shaded my eyes with my hands and looked through the screen door at him. He had a cup of coffee. He sat with his back to me.

"Good morning, Daddy."

He twisted around to look at me. "You're up mighty early, sugar pie."

"I got up so I could see Mama before she left for work."

"Has she gone?"

"Yes," I said. "Just a minute ago."

He turned back to his coffee and said, without turning around, "Come on in and have a cup of coffee with me."

"I've already had two cups. Mama said for me not to drink any more than that."

He didn't answer.

"It looks like there's a good chance it might rain today, Daddy. The clouds are really boiling up back in the southwest."

"Is that right? Rain will help, but it won't save the crops. Not now. All I'm hoping for is that I make enough for the winter."

"Do you want me to cook you some breakfast, or do you want to wait until old lady Beggs gets here?"

"Old lady Beggs is *here*," a voice said from the yard.

I nearly jumped out of my skin, and she laughed. I watched her as she climbed the steps, and I was embarrassed that she heard me call her old lady Beggs.

She wore a black long-sleeve blouse, hanging over a gray skirt. Her wrinkled face smiled at me from the same blue print sunbonnet she had worn yesterday. A large red straw bag hung over her arm.

"Old lady Beggs, eh? So that's what you call me behind my back," she said, when she got to the screen door where I was standing.

"I'm sorry, Mrs. Beggs, I was only teasing, I didn't mean anything . . ."

She laughed as she went in the kitchen. "Good morning, Mr. Birdsong," she said. "The first thing I'm going to do is cook you some breakfast," and she pulled the iron skillet to the front of the stove. Then she took off her sunbonnet and put the straw basket down on the floor in the corner. She smoothed her thin brown hair, which was curled tightly in permanent-wave curls all over her head.

"Come in here, Florrie, and show me where things are. I can't cook in somebody else's kitchen unless I learn where things are."

I went in the kitchen and opened the pantry door. "All the food's in here, and things like flour and sugar and baking powder. The dishes are in here, and on that bottom shelf the pots and the skillet. Mama keeps the butter and the milk, too, when there's any milk, in a bucket down the well, where it's cool. We don't have an ice box." I was ashamed to tell her that.

"I don't have an ice box either, Florrie, so don't let it bother you. It's a wonder the things people can do without."

"When you need milk and there's not any in the bucket,

Daddy will milk it for you. I've never learned to milk because I'm scared to death of cows."

"That's funny," Mrs. Beggs said. "I'm scared of cows, too, that's why I stopped drinking milk," and she winked at Daddy.

Daddy laughed, his face turning red. "Milk's for sissies, isn't that right, Maude?"

Mrs. Beggs laughed and started slicing salt meat and dropping it into the skillet. I was surprised at Daddy calling her Maude. Mama would be mad if she knew about that, and I decided it would be best not to tell her.

"How about some breakfast, Florrie?" Daddy said.

"I had something to eat with Mama and I'm not hungry. Mrs. Beggs, unless you need me to help you, I'm going across the road to the woods and read."

"No, I don't need you, Florrie. You go ahead and do what you'd do if I wasn't here."

I started to leave, and then I thought I ought to remind Daddy about digging the grave like Mama told me to.

"Daddy, Aunt Mira wants that grave finished today."

"I know it. I'll see to it after breakfast, Florrie."

"The funeral's tomorrow afternoon."

"I know it, sugar pie."

"It's a military funeral, I'm pretty sure."

"I know it is, Florrie," Daddy said, impatience in his voice.

"Well, I'd better go get dressed now. I'll be back in a little while to see how you're doing, Mrs. Beggs." I used the same tone of voice I'd heard Aunt Mira use with Dorothy.

"Yes, Ma'am, Miss Florrie," Mrs. Beggs said.

She leaned over her straw bag in the corner and pulled out a fan. She went back to the stove, fanning with a Bremar's Funeral Home fan in one hand and turning the meat with the other.

It was too bad if she didn't like what I said, but if Mama

131

came home and found she hadn't done anything and Daddy hadn't finished digging the grave, I'd be the one in trouble. After all, Mama said she was counting on me.

I went to my room and changed to jeans and a shirt. The only time I had worn a dress this summer was when I went to church. I buttoned the white shirt and let it hang outside. Then I went back to the kitchen.

I wished it was Mama setting the plates on the table. It was unpleasant to see Mrs. Beggs handling Mama's dishes and cooking breakfast in our kitchen. I wished that the crops had been so good this year that Mama needn't have gone to work and that Daddy really could buy us a house.

"Mrs. Beggs, I'd like some biscuits and white meat to take to the woods with me, if you have plenty. I probably won't be home in time for lunch."

She fixed me three biscuits with meat. I looked at the back of Daddy's head while she wrapped the biscuits in a piece of newspaper. His hair grew down the back of his neck, gray mixed with black. If Mama was forty-five, I realized, Daddy must be almost fifty, because he was over four years older than her.

It had been too long since he'd been to Huxley for a haircut, but he said he hated to spent the twenty-five cents. His fingers curved around his knife and fork as he cut his meat, and the knuckles were big from years of grasping plow handles. Grandpa Birdsong had set him to plowing when he was eight years old.

"You didn't get many years of playing when I was growing up," he said. "Some days I wanted to play so bad I didn't know what to do and Papa would tie that harness around my waist and tell me to take the mule and go on out to the field and get to work." He sounded mad when he told about it. "It wasn't

132

Papa's fault, though. It was all he could do to keep the place running, having three children to provide for. And Mama, too."

Those weren't the kind of farm stories he told Mama.

Mrs. Beggs gave me my lunch and I left. I went through the living room and picked up my book. I would read *Crimson Roses* again. The clock on the mantel said nine-thirty. I hollered good-bye to Daddy and went out on the front porch and down the steps, headed for the woods.

The day stretched ahead endlessly, and the two weeks before school started was forever.

🌲🌲🌲🌲🌲 15

      I came home at dusk. Heavy white clouds had been building all day, higher and higher, stretching upward like a mountain. They were dark on the bottom at first, but as they spread and moved across the sky, they turned dark all over. The wind came in gusts and brought with it the smell of rain that was already falling over the hill.

When I went through the gate to the back yard, the first drops were falling, spattering and darkening in the dust. As I walked toward the house, I held back my head, sticking my tongue out as far as I could to catch a raindrop. When I neared the kitchen window, I stopped and listened.

Mama was yelling. Words like "slut" and "whore" came through the open window. Daddy must be drunk again. I shivered and rubbed at the rain on my arms. I wondered if they would fuss until we went to bed, as they sometimes did.

All at once, the sky lit with an eerie yellow glow, and as I watched, the sun set behind the dark clouds far in the west. The rain was over, the ground pockmarked with rain drops. Still no rain for Daddy's crops. And I was sorry that there would be no storm, because then we could leave and go to Aunt Mira's, and that would put an end to their fussing.

As I started up the back steps, Mrs. Beggs came bursting out of the kitchen, pushing the screen door so far back that its spring stretched and popped in the middle, the broken ends dancing and slapping against the wood. I jumped back flat against the wall as she ran past me. She jumped down the steps to the ground, not bothering to take them one at a time.

Mama's dishpan flew through the open screen door, landed on its side, and rolled across the porch before it spun like a top and settled upside down.

Next, our iron cooking pot flew through the door and fell on the porch, spilling turnip greens. Their juice ran in streams down the wood floor.

Terrified, I ran through the kitchen door and saw Mama take her arm and sweep the kitchen table clean of everything on it. Plates crashed and broke, the sugar dish emptied in a white mound on the floor, and the salt and pepper shakers rolled under the table.

"Mama—what's the matter?" I cried.

She was still dressed as she was when she left for work this morning, and she whirled and looked at me. She clenched her fists and screamed: "Where have you been all day? Why didn't you do what I told you to?"

"I did what you told me to, Mama," I said. "What's the matter with Mrs. Beggs," and I began to cry. I held out my arms and went toward her.

"You stay away from me," she said, backing away, "Don't come near me."

Her eyes watched me like the shiny eyes of trapped rabbits watched Daddy as he held them by their ears and cut the big vein in their necks. Then he unloosed them, and peeled back the bloody fur from the raw, red skin.

Mama put both hands to her head and started to pull her hair, crying. I ran to her, pulling at her arms. "Mama, tell me what's the matter. I love you, please tell me."

"Lord, Lord," she said, sitting down at the table. "Lord have mercy, Lord have mercy. Toliver's disgraced us again. He disgraced us over in Georgia, everybody laughing at him behind his back the way he drank with the colored people. He tries to make you think he doesn't like colored people, but he does. He loves them."

I sat down in the chair next to her. "Don't talk about Daddy like that, Mama. He's good, and I don't care if you don't love him, I do. What about you and Frank Sadler? Everybody in Gray's Chapel talks about that, too."

Her arm came up from the table, and she slapped me across my face with the flat of her hand. I dropped my head to the table and sobbed.

"I told you to stay around the house today. I knew if you were here, he wouldn't fool around with old lady Beggs. But you couldn't do that, you had to go off in the woods, reading. You're living make-believe, Florrie. *Crimson Roses*. That's really funny. I sat down and thumbed through that book after you went to bed the other night. A handsome man that leaves his sweetheart one red rose on her seat at the theater. That's not real. What's real is we don't ever have enough money, and we live out in the sticks, and we live in my sister Mira's tenant house."

I raised my head; my tears lay in a puddle on the walnut table.

"If you'd stayed home today, all this wouldn't have happened. I can't go back to work anymore now because I can't let old lady Beggs back in this house. And I can't leave you and Toliver every day by yourselves."

I stood up from the table and got the dishrag off the back of the stove. I wiped away the tears from the table and rubbed it across my face. It smelled like dishwater.

I sat down and Mama looked at me, sadly. "Was the book so good?" she asked.

I shook my head and took a deep breath to hold back the tears. "I wish I'd stayed home, Mama. I'm sorry it turned out like this. If you'll go on back to work, I'll go stay at Aunt Mira's every day."

"No," she shook her head, "You can't. Mira wouldn't want you there every day."

"What happened with Daddy and Mrs. Beggs, Mama?"

Mama rested her head in her hand, her elbow braced on the table. "When I got home, they were both drunk. I didn't even know old lady Beggs was still here, because she was in my room, asleep on top of my cover." Her voice was flat. "Old man Birdsong was sitting at the table. Just sitting there, not doing anything. When I came in the kitchen door, he didn't even look up, he just sat there staring down at the table. The only sign of supper was a pot of turnip greens put on the stove to cook. But there wasn't even any fire in the stove. The one I built this morning had gone completely out. I said to Toliver, 'Toliver, what's the matter with you, where's Florrie?' He stood up then, but nearly fell off the chair. He headed out the back door, but he like to never got out, because he kept hitting the side of the door." She quit talking, and took a deep breath.

"Finish telling me, Mama."

"I went through the house, calling you, and when I saw you weren't in the house, I went to my room to undress. There she was, lying on her back, her arms and legs stretched out. My room smelled like a still, and her mouth was hanging open and she was snoring."

"That's just terrible, Mama. That's the worst thing I've ever heard of."

"I started screaming for her to get off my bed and to get out of my house. I will say one thing, I like to have scared her to death, anyway."

"You should have seen her jump down the back steps," I said.

Mama shook her head. "What in the world's going to become of us, Florrie?" She put her hands over her face, pressing at her eyes with her fingers. "Florrie," she said, "I don't feel good."

I stood up and put my arms around her. "Come on and lie down for awhile, Mama. You'll feel better."

"I wouldn't lie on the cover that woman's been on."

The kitchen was almost dark, I pulled the chain of the overhead light, and in the sudden brightness we looked at the broken plates and the spilled sugar.

"I'll clean it up, Mama, and you can lie on my bed. I'll change the cover on your bed for you."

She stood up and grabbed at the table as she swayed, her face and lips pale in the electric light of the kitchen. "Florrie, help me," she said as she fell. I screamed and grabbed her, but

I couldn't hold her up, and she fell to the floor. I knelt beside her. Her stockings were rolled with round garters, and I pulled the blue eyelet dress down over her knees.

"Mama, what's the matter?" I cried, and kissed her all over her face. She only lay there, with her eyes closed. She looked dead, with her hair so red next to her white skin. I ran out the back door to the fence and screamed and screamed for Mrs. Goggins. The dogs barked and jumped on the fence.

The lights were out in her house, and I ran to the woods at the back of the yard, calling Daddy, but he never answered.

I ran back in the house and looked at Mama, lying on the floor among the broken dishes. I went out the back door and down the porch steps, heading for the road. I would get Aunt Mira to come. I crossed the road and ran down the lane, my hands pressed against my mouth.

I whispered, "Mama's going to die, Mama's going to die."

The lane stretched ahead, bright in the moonlight, and the dust was cool on my feet. I ran and ran, and for a moment came outside myself and watched myself running through the night. I ran between the fields, the ghostly corn waving and nodding to me as I passed.

A bell tinkled, and Beautiful Eyes mooed at me over the fence. Daddy hadn't brought her back to the barn. Her udder would be almost bursting with milk by morning.

I passed the bootlegger woods and turned the curve at the top of the hill, stopping for the first time since I had left home. Through the trees I saw a light at Aunt Mira's house. A breeze began to blow as I ran down the hill.

I ran past the flower beds, and when I came to the croquet court, I heard the wooden crack of my mallet as I knocked Dink's ball almost to the spring house. And there came the sound of my happy laugh, from a thousand years ago.

I took the steps two at a time to Aunt Mira's front porch, and

138

flung open the front door. The radio was playing, and Aunt Mira and Ralph Junior were sitting in the brocade chairs. They jumped up when they saw me.

"You all come quick, Aunt Mira, something's the matter with Mama."

✝✝✝✝✝✝ 16

I sat in the back seat of Ralph Junior's Plymouth. Aunt Mira sat beside him in the front seat. "It's Mr. Birdsong's fault," she said. "If Julia dies, it's his fault. He could find a job in town if he wanted to. He is a mess. He's always been a mess."

I trembled, my teeth chattering.

"You're a lazy girl, Florrie. You could help your mother if you wanted to. You're a big strapping girl who could have worked this summer but wouldn't. I am a widow with two sons to support. I cannot support Julia's family, too."

Aunt Mira got me a job at Kress's in Birmingham, and Mama, furious, wouldn't let me take it. I had been glad. "No girl of mine will work behind a counter," Mama said. "You just keep quiet, Florrie, and I'll tell her." But Aunt Mira kept blaming me for not taking the job.

The car passed between the stone pillars of the gate.

"Ralph Junior, you ride on to Huxley and bring back Dr. Fairfax. Tell him not to worry. I'll take care of his bill."

Aunt Mira and I got out and Ralph Junior turned his car down the road, his red taillights disappearing around the curve.

I ran across the road and to the back of the house, my legs shaking so that I could hardly climb the steps. The screen door was still wide open, and bugs swarmed in the light that spilled from the kitchen. I ran through the open door. Mama was gone.

"Mama," I called, and went in the living room. Daddy sat in the dark on the wicker love seat.

"Where's Mama?" I said.

"Your mother is on her bed." His words were thick and slurred.

Is she dead?"

"No, she is not dead," he said.

The front porch door opened, and Aunt Mira walked into the living room. "Where's Julia?" she demanded.

"None of your goddamn business where she is," Daddy said from the darkness.

"Look here, who do you think you are, to talk to me like that?" Aunt Mira said.

Daddy stood up, and walked unsteadily to stand in front of her. He wore his khaki field clothes.

"I think that I am T. J. Birdsong. Toliver John Birdsong is what my mother named me. You may call me *Mister* Birdsong." He bowed low in front of her and almost fell. "Oops," he said. "I almost fell on her ladyshit."

"You are disgusting," Aunt Mira said, and went into Mama's room.

"Florrie, if you will take my arm and help me to my room."

"Daddy, did you take Mama to her room?" I asked, as we walked arm in arm to the back porch.

"I came in and found Mrs. Birdsong lying on the floor," he said. "I picked her up and carried her to her room and lay her on the bed. I think she's sick." He leaned on the bannister and looked up at the star-filled sky. "Well, it's over," he said. "The crops are gone, Florrie. What are we going to do now?"

"Nothing to do now, but go to bed," I said.

"That's the right answer, go to bed. And tomorrow, when I wake up, it will be raining, and the corn so tall you can climb it into heaven."

I walked him to his door and watched as he fell across the bed.

"Good night, Daddy." But he didn't answer.

I went back to the living room and looked through the door to Mama's room. Aunt Mira had helped her on with a gown, and she lay under the covers.

"Mama, how do you feel?" I asked.

"I'm all right, don't worry, Florrie."

Aunt Mira sat in the rocking chair by her bed, holding her bottle of holy water. "Julia, I'm going to say a prayer for you," she said.

I walked to the end of the bed. Mama looked better, the color back in her face, her lips pink again. "All right, Mira Gray," Mama said.

Aunt Mira whispered, then crossed herself and sprinkled Mama with holy water.

I walked around the bed and kissed Mama on the cheek, then went and sat in the dark of the living room. After a while, I heard Dr. Fairfax and Ralph Junior on the porch.

I went to the door and let them in, then turned on the lamp.

Dr. Fairfax nodded to me, taking off his hat. His bald head and rimless glasses glowed in the lamplight. He set his black bag on the end table next to the love seat. "Where can I wash my hands, Florrie?" he asked.

I took him to the back porch, and poured water for him and handed him the soap. "I'm sorry you have to wash in the dark," I told him. "We don't have a sink in the house."

"Don't apologize to me, Florrie. You're living in a castle, compared to some people I've seen. I've just been to see a sick child before Ralph came to get me." I handed him the towel that hung on the wall, over the wash pan. He shook his head, and dried his hands by waving them around in the air. "The mother and two little boys live together. There's no father. They're living under the foundation of an old house that burned down. The children play around the woods during the day and the mother goes to beg. When she comes home at night, they eat whatever she's begged, and then they crawl under the floor and sleep. I took the sick boy home with me. I don't know if he'll make it or not."

I shook my head at the sad story. Then I followed Dr. Fairfax into the kitchen. "My grandfather was a doctor, you know," I told him. "He was a horse-and-buggy doctor in St. Helen's County."

"I know that," Dr. Fairfax said. "From what I've heard, he was a good one, too."

"I might decide to be a doctor," I told him. "I've thought about it," I said, and was surprised. That was the first time I'd ever had the idea.

"That's a fine ambition. The medical profession needs more women, Florrie. It needs their kindness and gentle touch," and he smiled at me and turned away, his shoulders round and humped under the crossed suspenders.

I stood in the kitchen door and watched him go into Mama's room and close the door. Ralph Junior was gone. I went to sit on the front porch. The wind was rising, clouds scudding across the sky. I felt the agony of hopeless wishing for rain to fall in time to save the parched corn and string beans and potatoes.

142

"Florrie," a voice said in the darkness. I jumped, turning toward the sound. It was Ralph Junior. He sat in a rocking chair at the end of the porch closest to the cemetery, his legs crossed at the ankles and propped up on the bannister. He wore his white Panama hat pushed back on his head. "How's Julia?"

I sat down on the top step and looked toward the road. A car went by, its headlights illuminating for a moment the tall grass that grew in the ditch. Then it was gone, the road dark again. Two cars, Ralph Junior's and Dr. Fairfax's, sat in the darkness in front of the house.

"I don't expect I want to talk to you about my mother," I told him. "You don't even respect her enough to call her aunt, like you do Aunt Marcy." I leaned back against the post.

"Julia's not much older than I am," Ralph Junior said, after a while. "I remember when she ran away from Stillwater and came to Birmingham to live with Aunt Marcy. I was just a kid, but I still remember the first time I saw her. She was working in Papa's store, and I went to buy new shoes."

I rolled and unrolled the hem of my shirt between my fingers. I looked beyond Ralph Junior toward the cemetery; the tombstones were dotted like white mushrooms that had sprung up in the night.

A square of light lay on the end of the porch, shining through the living room window.

"I hadn't seen Julia for years," Ralph Junior went on with his story. "She came to help me pick out shoes, and she had on a white dress and white shoes. I was fifteen years old, and I couldn't believe that anyone so beautiful was kin to me. Her hair was redder than it is now. Papa said she could have had her pick of any man that worked in the store."

I didn't believe that Mama had worn white shoes, and neither did I like Ralph Junior knowing things about my own mother that I didn't know. I stood up to go inside.

143

"I like Julia," Ralph Junior said, standing too. "I hope she's all right. Tell Mother I've gone on home, Florrie."

He passed in front of me and walked down the steps, then stopped and looked up at me. "I used to watch you and Dink together. You all had so much fun," he said. "I don't remember playing myself. Seems like I've been grown all my life."

He walked down the path to the front gate and got in his Plymouth and drove away. I watched his car cross the road and move down the lane. I tried to feel sorry for him, but I just couldn't manage it. He was mean to Daddy, and whatever he felt for Mama didn't make me feel any kinder toward him. It was strange, the way he'd been talking, though. In all these years, he never had said more to me than was absolutely necessary. Nor I to him. He was just somebody that I was glad was gone, especially when I was with Dink.

The door to Mama's room opened, and I went back inside the house. Dr. Fairfax closed the door softly behind him, then looked at me, his pale blue eyes magnified behind his glasses. He took me by the arm and walked me to the settee, and we sat down, side by side.

"Florrie, you're a big girl," he said. "I understand from people that know you, that you're a smart girl, too. Like school, do you?"

"No," I told him. "I despise school. They take the most exciting things in the world and make them dull."

"You mean the teachers do that?"

"Yes," I said.

"What, for example, have they made dull for you?"

"The American Revolution, for one thing. I checked a book from the library and found out for the first time how wonderful it was. The colonies struggling for freedom, I mean. I know how they felt, because I feel that way too."

"How do you feel?" Dr. Fairfax asked, smiling at me.

"That to be free is the most important thing in the world. More important than love, or sex, or money. Free to be myself, whatever it turns out to be."

"That's deep thinking for a girl of what . . . fourteen, is it now?"

"I'm fifteen. I'll be sixteen next February."

"It doesn't seem like almost sixteen years ago that you were born. You were born right there in that room," he said, nodding toward Mama's room. "I sat in there all night, with Julia asking first me and then the good Lord to help her." He laughed and shook his head, remembering.

"I ought not to laugh, because Julia wasn't built to have babies. You were born at dawn, kicking, feet first. I told Julia not to have any more children because the next one might kill her. I'm glad she hasn't."

"What's the matter with her now, Dr. Faixfax? When I left to get Aunt Mira a while ago, I thought she was dead."

"She fainted, that's all," he said. "You know what happened here tonight, Florrie, I don't. And I don't want to know, except as how it concerns her health. Julia's not a strong woman. Never has been. And she didn't eat lunch today. Said she forgot about it, learning stock at that store."

Mama didn't go to the tearoom and get apricot pie. That was astounding news, that she would forget that, because when we went to town, we never forgot Davis's tearoom.

"Daddy got drunk on moonshine with old lady Beggs. Mama said she can't ever go back to work in that store again. She was madder than I've ever seen her in my whole life."

"She fainted from not enough food today, and too much emotion," Dr. Fairfax said. "She might have suffered a slight heart attack, along with it."

"Oh," I cried, and he shook his head. "No. No. No. Florrie, control yourself," he said. "Nothing serious, just an irregular heart beat from too much excitement. I've given her a pill and she'll sleep all night. I want you to go to bed, too."

"No, I won't go to bed. I'm going to stay with Mama. You tell Aunt Mira it's all right for her to go on home. She just takes over, Dr. Fairfax, and bosses you around, until you can't stand it. That wouldn't be good for Mama, it would make her nervous."

Dr. Fairfax stood up and picked his bag off the table. "It's because I trust you to take care of your mother, Florrie, that I'll tell Mira Gray to go on home. I don't think Julia will wake up before morning, but if she does, you give her one of those blue tablets I've left in an envelope on the table by her bed."

He went back in Mama's room, and when he came out Aunt Mira was with him. She argued about staying, standing first on one foot and then on the other, but finally Dr. Fairfax convinced her she should go. She went back to Mama's room and came out with her purse and her holy water.

"Ralph Junior said to tell you that he's gone on home, Aunt Mira. He thought you were staying the night . . ."

"My car's out here, Mira Gray, I'll take you," Dr. Fairfax told her, nodding at me behind her back. "Florrie knows what to do, she'll take care of Julia tonight." He urged Aunt Mira out the door by her elbow. "Florrie, I'll be back sometime tomorrow to see about Julia. You get some rest if you can."

I stood in the front door and watched them down the steps. He helped Aunt Mira into his car, their voices floating back, but I couldn't hear what they said. Then Dr. Fairfax climbed in beside her. His bright headlamps cut through the night, and a cat's eyes gleamed for a moment in the yard, then disappeared.

I pushed the door to and locked it, although we never closed our doors in the summer. I walked to the mantel and looked at the clock. Nine o'clock, but it felt much later.

I walked through the house, lonely and half scared, closing

windows and pushing at their rusty unused locks. They wouldn't budge, and I turned away and went to the kitchen.

The broken screen door was wide open, and I pulled it to. Moths swarmed around the kitchen light bulb, and I heard the thin whine of mosquitoes. I looked through the screen to the back yard, but all I could see was the bulky outline of our barn. Tomorrow there would be sunlight, but I ached for it now, for fear would run from the sun as the clouds had run before the wind.

I latched the screen and closed the door, then went back to the living room. I would leave the light burning tonight, and not let Mama know that I did. The house was quiet and strange, and I was afraid to let in the darkness that pushed against the windows and the doors. I was afraid that the darkness would flood in like black ocean waves and Mama would be carried away on its dark tide.

I kept on my clothes because I felt safer that way. I got my book of Beethoven off the end of the mantel. I would sit in the rocking chair and read in Mama's room until morning. Then I would send Daddy to Huxley to call Aunt Marcy to come. It was terrible, to be scared by yourself.

I tiptoed into Mama's room. The light from the living room shone across her bed, and I stood looking down at her. She lay on her back, breathing softly, a worried frown between her eyes. I leaned over and kissed her on the forehead, and her breath had a sweet, medicinal smell. She sighed and moved restlessly, then was still again.

I pulled the rocking chair to the living room door and sat down, pushing the door so Mama's bed was in darkness but the light shone at an angle across my book. I propped my feet on the iron rail of Mama's bed and leaned my head on the high back of the chair.

I prayed, the words forming in my mind. Dear Lord, if you

147

will let Mama be all right, if you will let her live, I promise to help her with the work and never to talk back to her again. I promise that I will never miss church on Sunday, morning or night. Amen.

I hoped that the Lord and I had struck a bargain.

✟✟✟✟✟✟ 17

The rifles cracked. One—two—three—four—five—six. I counted the shots. A bugle blew taps, the notes wavering, hanging mournful in the mid-afternoon heat. I stood at the living room window, looking at the crowd gathered in the middle of the cemetery.

"Who's shooting?" Mama called from her bed.

"It's the military funeral for that old soldier. You remember."

"I can't sleep with all that noise," Mama complained. "It's hot enough by itself without having to listen to all that shooting."

"Don't try to sleep, Mama, just rest."

Then she was quiet.

It was too far away to recognize anybody at the funeral, but I watched the four soldiers. They stood in twos, facing each other while folding the American flag; then they handed it to somebody, but I couldn't see who it was. The funeral was almost over, and I was sorry to have missed it. Military funerals were far between.

"Florrie," Mama called, "come and sit with me."

I went and sat down in the rocking chair. She held out her hand and I took it, and soon she was sleeping again. I pulled my hand loose gently and leaned back, rocking.

I had sat here all night last night, dozing. When dawn came I stayed awake until the sun rose high enough to come in Mama's window. It shone across her bed, turning her patchwork quilt as bright as Joseph's coat of many colors. Then I went to the kitchen and looked around, not knowing what to do.

Daddy had come to the back door and knocked, and I unlocked it and let him in. His shoes were caked with wet mud, his blue work shirt drenched with sweat. He had been up since dawn to finish digging the old soldier's grave. He built a fire in the stove and we had coffee together, but no breakfast. Then I came back to Mama.

When Frank Sadler stopped the bus and blew the horn for Mama early in the morning, she sent me to tell him not to stop anymore. "Don't tell him what happened last night, Florrie," she said. "He'll hear about it soon enough, anyway. Just tell him I'm sick, but don't go into details. Tell him I'll let him know later if I want him to stop any more."

I ran to the road and told him what Mama said. He nodded his head all the time I was telling him. "I feel bad about that," he said. "She was so excited yesterday, she talked all the way to town about that job. I'll drop by and see her when she's feeling better."

"You better not do that, Mr. Sadler. I don't think Mama would want you to do that."

He got on his bus and drove away.

"Florrie," Mama said.

"Yes'm? I thought you were asleep."

She pushed herself to sit up and I got up to help her. "Sit back down, Florrie. I don't need any help. Don't treat me like an invalid."

She reached both arms behind her and pushed the pillow into a brace for her back. She leaned her head against the iron headboard, her hair falling about her shoulders.

"Mama," I laughed. "You look like Rapunzel in the fairy story. Only your hair's red instead of blond."

She smiled and held her arms out. "Come here, Florrie," she said.

I sat on the side of the bed, and she pulled me to her and held me tight against her chest. I heard her heart beat. It was steady.

"I'm sorry I hit you. I won't ever forgive myself for doing that. I'll regret it the rest of my life."

"It's all right, Mama, don't talk about it." I went to sit back down in the rocking chair, and I thought, this time yesterday I was in the woods. I wish I were in the woods today. I felt guilty as soon as I thought it.

"It seems like it doesn't matter how hard you try, you can't change things," Mama said. "The pattern's set, like the preacher used to say back in Stillwater. We just get up each morning and play the part that's already been chosen for us."

"If that's true, then I'd rather be dead," I said. "Besides, I don't believe it. Once I get grown, I'm in charge of what happens to me. Nobody tells me what to do."

"That's a fine plan if you can carry it out, Florrie. I hope for your sake that it's true, because if it isn't, you've got some hard knocks coming."

"I'm just going to make sure I don't make a mess out of things like you and Daddy have," and then I was sorry to be so cruel.

Mama closed her eyes. "It's something you think will never happen to you," she said.

"Think what will happen?"

"That the tiny baby you held in your arms and nursed and looked after and loved more than you ever thought you could love anything, would grow up and sit in judgment on you." She opened her eyes and looked at me. "But it turns out fair in the end, because one day your children will judge you, too, and you'll be found wanting just like you've found me wanting. It always happens that way."

"Mama, I didn't mean that the way it sounded. I mean that I don't want to be at somebody's mercy like you and Daddy are at Aunt Mira's. And I don't want to be told what to do and have to do it."

"I'm coming around to that way of thinking myself, Florrie. For twenty years I thought I didn't have any choice except to move from one farm to another when Toliver told me to. It's just the past year that I realize what a fool I've been."

I looked out Mama's window toward the road. Cars drove past one by one, headed home now that the funeral was over. Women walked arm in arm down the side of the road, waving to the people in the cars as they passed. Later on this afternoon, I would go to the cemetery and look for shell casings from the firing of the rifles.

"I can look back now and see that Toliver and I ought to have stayed in Georgia. I regret coming here to live in Mira Gray's house; but I was sticking out to here with you—" she rounded her hand in a wide arc over her stomach—"and I was scared to stay over there in those woods with you coming. I wanted to be close to a hospital. Still, I didn't go to a hospital because we didn't have the money." Mama frowned. "It's terrible, the pain it takes to have a baby."

She formed her middle finger and thumb of her left hand into a circle; making a fist of her right hand, she pushed it against the circle. "It's just like that, having a baby. Just like trying to push your hand through that little hole."

"Oh, Mama," I said, "you're exaggerating. Trudy Hunt didn't say it was like that to have a baby when she had hers. She said it was easy as anything."

"That's because she's common," Mama said. "Common people have babies like a cat having kittens." She pressed her lips together and shook her head with disapproval as she thought about it. "Beside, Florrie, how come you're talking about having babies with that common girl, anyway?"

"I'm old enough to talk about having babies, Mama. It was at church one Sunday while we were waiting for the sermon to start."

"That's really a good subject to talk about in church. Besides, you're the one that makes me forget how old you are. You're the one that won't wear a brassiere. I don't understand yet why you didn't buy one that day in town."

"Mama, if you knew how sick I am of that subject, you would never bring it up again."

She didn't say anything, and I rocked and listened to the afternoon sounds. A rooster crowed and there was the sound far away of someone hammering. A breeze came through the window next to the porch, and the white, ruffled curtains ballooned out; then the breeze died and the curtains collapsed and were sucked back against the screen. The heat of late summer swam around me, and I wanted to sleep. I lay my cheek against the warm, smooth wood of the chair and closed my eyes.

"Are you asleep, Florrie?" Mama asked.

"No, Ma'am," I said, but kept my eyes closed.

"Why don't you go stretch out on your bed?"

"It's too hot to get on the bed. I'd rather sit here with you," and I opened my eyes and smiled at her.

Sunlight, shining through the tan windowshade, filled the room with shimmering half-light, like the glow in a movie theater.

Mama swung her legs over the side of the bed, and I jumped up, alarmed.

"Lie back down, Mama," I said, pushing at her.

"No, I'm tired of lying down. I'm going to sit up for a while and rest my back." She pushed her hair off her shoulders, letting it hang down her back.

I sat back down.

"Where's Toliver?" Mama asked.

"He just got back from Huxley. He called Aunt Marcy to come and help out. Now he's walking around in the field, watching the corn dry up, he says."

"I wish you all had asked me before you got Marcy to come. I'm not sick enough to need her, Florrie. But what's done is done, and I'll try to get her to go home as quick as I can without hurting her feelings. No sign at all of rain?"

"No."

"Toliver's no farmer, rain or no rain. Every year he talks about how good next year's going to be, and here we are, twenty years later, with not even a roof over our heads to call our own. Me, a forty-five-year-old woman, still struggling for a place to call her own."

"I think Daddy's a good farmer, Mama. Farmers have good years and bad years."

"Well, I'm ready for some of the good ones, believe me. I've had plenty of the bad. Toliver's father was no farmer either, though Toliver tries hard to make you believe he was. Before we were married, he wrote letters to me in Stillwater, telling me about his father's plantation. Toliver told me in his letters that sons of the old slaves still lived on the place and were loyal to the family. He said there was a white picket fence that went around acres of land that the house sat on. There was a long drive that led to the house, he said, lined with weeping willow trees, and we would live in a white bungalow that was on his father's land. In the letters he called it our little white 'B.' " She clasped her hands on her stomach, and twirled her thumbs around each other as she talked. "I really loved Toliver then. When he talked about the old home place, he could make me see those fields of cotton and the white house. He was handsome, and wore his hat with the brim turned up all around. I thought he was the jolliest man I'd ever met."

This was the first time she'd ever talked so much about the days in Georgia, and I held my breath, afraid that she would stop talking. In the dim light of her bedroom her face was young again; she gazed over the top of my head, her eyes blurred with remembering.

"I told Toliver I'd marry him, and I broke my engagement to Mr. Gentry. Mr. Gentry was at least fifteen years older than I was, and he'd given me lots of presents. I was wearing a diamond wrist watch he gave me, and when I told him I couldn't marry him, he took the watch off my arm right then. He was really mad. Mira Gray was mad, too, that I broke my engagement. She was mad because I let all that money get away. Mira Gray liked for a lot of money to be in the family. I got on the train and rode to Birmingham to meet Toliver. We were married at the Baptist church, and Mira Gray wouldn't come even though she was living right there in Birmingham. Marcy and Joel came. They were the only ones who were at my wedding."

She lay back down on the bed, stretching out on top of the

154

cover. She didn't say anything for a long time and I thought she'd gone to sleep, but then she started talking again.

"After we were married, we went to Tolbertville, to the old home place. When we got there I just about fainted from shock. It was a nice farm, all right, but it was a long cry from a plantation. And there wasn't any driveway or weeping willows or bungalow. And there wasn't any picket fence that went around acres of land, and there weren't any darkies singing in the field. It was in the middle of nowhere. The closest neighbor was a colored family about two miles away. Your Grandmother Birdsong was dead, but your grandfather was living. He was a fine old man, and I think the world of his memory. I didn't say anything to Toliver about the lies he'd told me, and to tell you the truth, Florrie, I don't think he thought of them as lies. He was as proud as he could be of that farm, and took me and showed me the fields where the cotton was planted, but I started right then planning. I started planning how to get him off the farm and into town."

Mama sat up and got off the bed and went to stand at the window. She let the shade all the way up, and late afternoon light flooded into the room. The sun was behind the trees, but it would be after dark before the room started to cool off. She looked toward the fields.

"This is the last farm I'll ever live on," she said. "I've lived in the woods in Chaffee, Tolbertville, Chattanooga, and Gray's Chapel. I have gone the second mile with Toliver, and the third and fourth mile on my own. Toliver's talking now about moving up to Pine Mountain in Tennessee. President Roosevelt's giving away land to get people to come and farm it." She turned away from the window. "I'm not going to Pine Mountain or any other mountain. I'm going where the bright lights shine, and if I have to live the rest of my life without seeing another tree, it would suit me fine. All I want is pavement and street lights and neighbors so close we can reach out the window and touch each other."

"Mama, you wouldn't just walk off and leave Daddy, would you?"

She turned to look back out the window. Her hair hung almost to her waist. The last time it was cut was when I was born.

"That's the first time the question's been put to me. I haven't even put it to myself." She sat down on the side of the bed. "Florrie, I've lived in so many woods that if I don't get out of them, I'll go stark, staring crazy. It's all I think about any more. When we lived in Chattanooga, Toliver got a job working at the bakery in town all night long. I didn't sleep a wink until he came home about dawn. I had an old pistol that I carried in my apron pocket, but if it'd come to it and I'd had to shoot, I'd have shot myself, because it backfired. I just felt better knowing it was in my pocket. There were bootleggers all around there, and one night they ran right through our yard, the sheriff after them. That was during Prohibition, and while we were living in Chattanooga the police broke bottles of bootleg whiskey and poured it in the Tennessee River. People were down on their hands and knees, lapping it off the ground.

"When the sun went down, you couldn't see anything but black everywhere. I didn't go to bed, but went from room to room checking locks and taking the pistol out of my pocket when I heard a sound. Every morning when Toliver came home, I lit into him. I told him how scared I was down in those woods after dark, but he didn't care. He just said I was overly excitable, and then he'd go to bed and sleep a while and then get up and go out to the fields."

She took my hands; hers were cool and damp in the heat of the room. "Yes, I will leave him, Florrie, if that's what it takes. I won't stay here any longer than it takes for me to get away."

I pulled my hands loose from hers and stood up. I would try to keep from crying, try to keep from upsetting her. I believed now, as I hadn't believed before when Mama talked about leaving, that what she said was true, that our time left here was short. One day, and not too far away, we would leave Gray's Chapel.

"You don't have to go with me, Florrie. You're old enough to have a choice. I didn't know I had a choice for twenty years."

I nodded my head, but couldn't speak because tears were too close.

"Don't ever think that life is easy, Florrie. Especially for a woman, because so much of what happens to you depends on the man you marry. Except it doesn't for me anymore. I'm a free woman as far as that goes, and it feels good not to have to worry any longer about what Mr. Birdsong does. Look at your mother, Florrie, and learn a lesson from her. Make something out of yourself so you won't have to depend on anybody, especially for money. That's the most degrading thing that can happen to you."

"I don't know what I'll do, Mama. I just want us to stay together, you and me and Daddy."

Just then, the evening paper bumped on the front porch, and I left the room before she could answer. I went to the porch and picked up the paper and sat down in the rocking chair to read.

"Florrie," Mama called. "Bring me my glasses off the mantel, and the front page of the paper."

I turned the pages of the paper until I found the funnies, pulling them loose from the rest of the paper. Then I went in the living room and got Mama her glasses and the paper.

I sat down in her rocker and read my favorites first, Brick Bradford and the Phantom, then skipped to Skeezix and Tillie the Toiler.

"Well, I declare," Mama said.

"What?"

"This contest they're advertising in the paper today."

I leaned over to see.

"This Old Gold contest. All you have to do is work these puzzles and send them in with an Old Gold wrapper. This is the first puzzle and there'll be one every week for twenty-four weeks. The first prize is ten thousand dollars," she said, "and there are five one-thousand-dollar prizes and ten one-hundred-dollar prizes. What do you think about that, Florrie?" She was excited.

"That's wonderful," I said.

"I'll stop buying Lucky Strikes and buy Old Golds," she said, without looking up.

I left her sitting in the middle of the bed, the paper spread on the bed in front of her. I went to the cemetery.

The old soldier's grave was covered over with flowers. There was a flag at each corner of his grave, two American and two Confederate, fluttering in the late afternoon breeze.

I walked through the cemetery, pushing at the grass with my toes, looking for shell casings. But I could find only two. The children at the funeral had taken the rest.

🌲🌲🌲🌲🌲 18

Aunt Marcy and I sat on the front porch. I was on the steps, and she rocked in the rocker. Yesterday, she and Dr. Fairfax had come at dusk, Uncle Joel's black Packard and Dr. Fairfax's black Ford pulling up in front of the house at the same time.

Uncle Joel didn't come in. He sat in the car and I spoke to him through the car window. He smiled, the nervous tic in his jaw twitching, then he kissed Aunt Marcy good-bye and drove away.

Dr. Fairfax came out of Mama's room, smiling. "Julia's doing fine, just fine, she'll be up in no time. You two nurses make her rest for at least a week. No work, you understand?"

Aunt Marcy laughed and said that was just what she was here for. Dr. Fairfax left, saying he'd be back in a day or two.

Aunt Marcy sat rocking, fanning with a folding fan she carried in her purse. On it was a picture of pink and white old-fashioned ladies with daintily pointed shoes peeping from beneath ruffled skirts. They were hiding their faces behind fans just like this one. Gentlemen, dressed in blue satin knee britches and shirts with lace jabots, bowed low over their outstretched hands, forever about to kiss the pink-tipped fingers.

Aunt Marcy let me hold her fan, and I sat on the steps, opening and closing it, freeing the timid ladies and the gallant men, then closing them again into their accordion prison.

She had been here for a week, and I was ready for her to go home. Now that I knew Mama was not going to die, I wished Aunt Marcy would leave. She was pleasant and sweet, but every night I had to roll up her hair for her, and pluck the wild hairs from her eyebrows.

Besides, I was tired of fried chicken. Mama loved chickens as pets, but Aunt Marcy loved them fried. Aunt Mira had sent Ralph Junior to our house with a crate of fryers the day after Aunt Marcy came. One of Aunt Mira's tenant farmers had brought them to her as rent the day before, in his pickup truck.

Aunt Marcy had a system for catching chickens. She stood in the yard until she spotted the one wanted. Then she walked slowly toward it, clucking and calling softly, "Here . . . chick, chick, chick." She held up her apron in one hand, pretending there was corn in it, and with her other hand threw make-believe corn on the ground. When the chickens got interested, she stopped walking and stood there, waiting for the chicken to come to her.

Soon the chicken started toward her, stiff-legged, its head cocked, one eye watching her all the time. When it got close enough, she grabbed it and wrung its neck, all in one motion, the chicken swinging round and round.

Daddy thought it better to chop off their heads, letting them bleed to improve the flavor of the chicken. He held them down with his foot, laying the head on the chopping block and bringing down the ax. The bright blood spurted as the head left the body, and another chicken would run with the head, dropping it to peck at the eyes.

Daddy admired Aunt Marcy. He said she had a good attitude for a city woman. If Mama were more like Aunt Marcy, he said, he'd go to chicken farming again.

One night after Aunt Marcy had cooked fried chicken, I took my plate and ate with Mama in her room. Mama leaned over from the side of the bed and whispered, "If Marcy cooks chicken one more time, I'm going to cackle or lay an egg, one or the other."

I laughed so hard, Aunt Marcy came to the room and said it wasn't good for Mama's digestion, all this noise.

"I'm going to miss you, you litle old monkey, when I go home," she said. "I'm going to miss having you to roll up my hair at night." She patted her brown, wispy hair.

"You ought to stay longer," I lied.

"I'll have to go on back. You know how a man is," she laughed. "I've been away from your Uncle Joel too long now."

She rocked and fanned, an almost pretty woman, with her large brown eyes. She was slim, except for her big legs, as big at the ankles as at the calves. She thought of herself as sickly, often saying she was the delicate one in the family.

She wore ruffled voile dresses and big leghorn hats in the summertime. She went to the big Baptist church in Birmingham, and had never told any of her friends that Aunt Mira was a Catholic.

"I know it's a sin for me to be like that, Florrie," she said, "but I'm still ashamed that Mira Gray married a Catholic. Ralph was a good man, though, and he didn't take the Catholic religion as serious as Mira. She makes me sick, running around the way she does with holy water. If I were Julia, I'd make her stop that sprinkling with the holy water all the time."

Tomorrow would be Saturday, and Uncle Joel was coming to pick her up. Yesterday we had washed her dresses. I showed her how to use the flat irons, heating them on the stove, but her face turned red and she said she felt faint. So I ironed the dresses for her, folded them, and put them in her suitcase.

She started to cry as she watched me iron. "I wish you and Julia could get away from here. I'm almost glad Mama's not living, because it would kill her to see how Julia has to live. I've told Julia, over and over again, that if she ever leaves Mr. Birdsong, I want you and her to come live with me."

"Mama's not ever going to leave Daddy, Aunt Marcy. We love him, and lots of times we all have a lot of fun. It's not bad all the time, you know."

Aunt Marcy and I slept together in my bed. She was afraid of the night sounds the first night, but when I told her what they were—Mrs. Goggins's dogs howling and Beautiful Eyes mooing—she fell asleep before I did.

I stretched and looked toward the fields and watched Daddy hoeing the watermelons. They would be a good crop in spite of the dry spell. I went with him to the field one day, and we burst open several watermelons, standing there eating until we were bloated.

"Florrie," Daddy told me, standing there in the field. "I don't know how much longer I can stand those tea-party meals your Aunt Marcy is putting on the table. The fried chicken is good, but we need some big crumb biscuits and chicken gravy to go with it. I'm about to perish to death."

I stood there in the vines with him and thought about biscuits and gravy; then I helped him load the watermelons onto the wagon. I climbed on Dixie's back and Daddy led her, pulling the wagon, to the house. We stopped in the road near the front porch and called Mama to look.

She came and stood in her nightgown at the top of the stairs. "Well, I declare," she said, and went back inside.

Daddy put a sign on the highway that said: "WATERMELONS

FOR SALE," but two weeks went by and nobody stopped. He took the sign down and fed the watermelons to the pigs.

Aunt Marcy stood up from the rocker and smoothed her dress. "I better go in and start cooking our last supper, Florrie."

"That sounds mighty religious," I said.

She frowned. "What do you mean?"

"You know, last supper, Jesus' last supper. It was just a joke."

"Oh, I see," she laughed. "That's pretty funny," and she turned to leave the porch.

"Can I help you do anything?" I asked.

"No," she said, "and I don't want you or Julia either one to come in the kitchen. I have a little surprise."

She opened the screen door and went in, her small feet at the end of her big legs pointed slightly outward.

I walked down the steps to the front gate, my hands shoved deep in my overall pockets. Next Monday was Labor Day. What a terrible holiday, I thought, to come on the day before school starts. The only thing exciting to look forward to at all was the Harvest Ball in October.

It was a high school dance, held every year at harvest time. I went last year with Nell Barfield. Nell was asked to dance right away, but I had stood with a bunch of girls, unpopular girls that no one would ask to dance. This year I would go to the dance, but I would not stand with them. If I had to be unpopular, I would be unpopular by myself.

I hoped that this year Billy Paul would dance with me, that he would put his arm around my waist and we would whirl away, looking into each other's eyes. I leaned on the gate, my heart beating against the warm metal, and closed my eyes, dreaming.

"Hi there, Florrie," a boy's voice said.

I squealed, and looked into Billy Paul's eyes. All my strength ran out through the soles of my feet.

Billy Paul laughed, sitting back on the bicycle seat.

My face turned red. I could feel it turning red. "I didn't hear you coming," I said. "I was thinking about school starting next week."

"School . . . ugh!" he said.

"That's what I think, too," I said.

"I didn't know you felt that way about school," Billy Paul said. "Every time I see you, you're reading a book."

"Just for fun," I said, "Not school books. As a matter of fact, I plan to skip classes more this year than I did last year." I decided that only at the moment I said it.

"Yeah?" he said, looking at me with interest. "I didn't know girls did things like that."

I shrugged. "I don't know about what *girls* do. I just know about what I do."

"I better be going," he said, pushing the pedal up with the top of his foot.

I nodded and he reached out his hand and touched me lightly on the cheek. I started for the house, the afternoon light a blur all around me.

"Hey," he called.

"What?" I said, turning around.

"You forgot your paper."

"Throw it to me."

He pitched it underhand, and it fell right at my feet. He waved his hand and rode away, gaining speed as he coasted across the grass toward the road. I watched him, loving his back, until he was out of sight.

I picked up the paper and went in the house to Mama's room. She was sitting in the rocking chair by the window, and I handed her the paper. She opened it and began to look through, page by page, for the contest.

"Florrie, when I get well, are you going to help me with the puzzles?"

"I sure am," I said.

Aunt Marcy came to the door. "Florrie, your face is red," said Aunt Marcy. "You better stay out of the sun."

I linked my arm through hers. "Come on, Aunt Marcy, and show me the surprise you've got for supper."

We walked, arm in arm, to the kitchen. A platter sat on the table, covered with a drying cloth. She pulled it back to show me a pyramid of fried chicken, watching to see my pleasure.

"It was the last three chickens," she said. "I knew Julia wouldn't want to fool with them after I go home."

I stared at the heap of delicately browned drum sticks and breasts and wings. "That's wonderful, Aunt Marcy, just wonderful," I said, heading for Mama's room. I would tell her the news, chicken again for supper.

✝✝✝✝✝ 19

Aunt Marcy went home, and I was glad to have things back the way they were. Uncle Joel came to pick her up and came up on the porch to speak to Mama. Mama had gotten up early in the morning and put on her red-striped house dress and wound her hair into a bun on the back of her neck.

She sat in the rocking chair, looking as she always had, except she was still pale. Uncle Joel blushed and asked her how she was feeling, then reached in his pocket and gave her a hand full of change.

"There's no need for that, Joel," Mama said, but reached out and took it.

I walked Aunt Marcy and Uncle Joel to the car, carrying Aunt Marcy's suitcase for her. I leaned in the car window when she was settled and kissed her good-bye and thanked her for coming. As they drove away, I hollered after them, "Don't you all take any wooden nickels now," and Aunt Marcy waved.

The car turned and passed out of sight behind the fence of the cemetery.

I helped Mama for a few days, happy that she was up. I looked at her neatly made bed, and it was hard to remember her lying there so sick. Dr. Fairfax said Mama ought to take life easy for a long time, and I swore that never again would I forget to bring in the stove wood for her. But Mama told me to forget it, she'd rather bring it in herself than stand around waiting for someone to do it for her.

The last few days before school slid by, one like the other except for the changing color of the sky. It turned from the pale, bleached blue of deep summer to the dark blue of the coming autumn, and already hazy, dreamlike days were on us.

I strained backward to summer, unwilling to admit that it was almost over. I walked on the road and told myself, see there's still a bloom on the maypop bush and the heat on your back is the hot sun of summer.

But it was September, and the halcyon days of Indian summer were here, and I was bewitched. I left the house early in the morning, making the most of the time left before school started; soon I stopped being scared that Mama would get sick again.

Labor Day came, and I went to the picnic at the church. Everybody packed a box lunch and brought it with them, leaving it in a stack next to the spring. After the games were played —three-legged race, catch the greased pig, walking race— everybody picked out a lunch from the pile, making sure it wasn't his own. I didn't go because of the games. I went to eat somebody else's food.

It was strange, but the same food we had at home, when it was cooked by other people, tasted different. And it looked different. It was like when Mama and I ate in town; it was regular food, but it tasted funny.

I begged Mama to go to the picnic with me, but she wouldn't. Mama had never been to church with me except once, when I was ten years old. I didn't understand why she went then, unless it was to show the people of Gray's Chapel that she was talented.

The Methodist church had a new organ, and Mrs. Johnson was looking for someone to sing a solo for the morning church service to dedicate the organ. Nobody wanted to sing, and when the Missionary Society met at our house, Mama spoke up and said that she would sing. The only singing I had heard Mama do was sitting on the front steps at night.

"Come on, Florrie," she'd say. "Harmonize with me on 'In the Evening by the Moonlight.' "

I sang alto to her soprano. It was passable singing for a summer evening, but I never dreamed that Mama thought she could sing well enough for a church solo.

The Sunday for her singing came, and Mama stood up from the chair where she was sitting on the pulpit behind Brother

Gridley. She stepped forward a few feet and waited while Mrs. Johnson played the first introductory bars of "In the Garden."

I slid down on the bench and squeezed my eyes shut, embarrassed for her. Mama cleared her throat and began to sing. It was the wrong place and Mrs. Johnson started over, again playing a few bars of music. Mama started at the right time and sang all the verses, her voice wavering at times, but pure and on key.

I opened my eyes when she was through, and as she walked down the aisle to sit by me for the sermon, people reached out and touched her, smiling and nodding their heads. She took a deep breath as she sat down, but she looked proud, and I smiled at her, happy that she was my mother.

Mama was fixing my lunch for the picnic. She was spreading peanut butter on big crumb biscuits and I looked at them, horrified.

"Who do you think you're fixing *those* for?" I asked.

She stopped spreading the peanut butter and looked heavenward. "Dear God, I prayed that just this one time she wouldn't say anything, but I guess that was asking You for too much." She looked at me. "I'm making your lunch for the picnic. I may give you the pleasure of making it for yourself, if you fool with me even a little bit."

"I'm not going to take biscuits to the picnic. My God, Mama, even the Beetons don't take biscuits!"

"Florrie, I'm fixing all there is to fix. If you don't like the food we've got, go out and fuss at Mr. Birdsong. I'm going with Mira to Pitilla's for groceries in a little while, but it won't be in time for your picnic. Do you want me to fix this lunch or not?"

"Go ahead," I said, and she started spreading the peanut butter again.

"Mama, you don't understand. Sometimes I think you try not to understand. I told you, the lunch isn't for me. Everybody puts their lunch in a pile and you pick out somebody else's, so you don't eat your own lunch."

"That's unsanitary," she said. "You don't know if whoever fixed the lunch even washed their hands or not. You eat your own lunch, you understand?"

"I'd rather lie down and die than let anybody see me eating biscuit sandwiches. Everybody else's sandwiches will be made out of light bread."

Mama got mad. "Do you think that eating light bread sandwiches makes you refined? I wouldn't be ashamed to eat anything I brought in front of those country people."

"Well, I am, and whoever gets my lunch sure better have lots to drink to wash it down. Have you ever had peanut butter and biscuits stick in your throat?"

"I'm not going to the picnic, you are. If I were going, I'd eat them and be proud of it. Even Toliver says nobody can make biscuits like I can."

Mama put her arm around me, but I stood rigid and unfriendly. She turned back to finish my lunch, and I left the kitchen and went to get dressed.

Cars had already parked along the road, and people were passing the house on their way to the church. Women wore their best lace, and ruffled sunbonnets and starched dresses. Men wore shirts with turned-back collars, and work pants with a crease that stood out razor sharp. Children ran ahead of their parents in their freshly ironed clothes.

"Stay clean," their mothers called to them.

I put on my blue chambray Sunday dress with the white collar and cuffs and my black shoes with the strap across the top. I brushed my bangs across my forehead, spitting on them and separating them to make me look older.

I went to Mama's room and tilted the mirror on her dresser until I could see myself all the way to the floor. The dress

169

pulled tight across my chest, and I rounded my shoulders enough to make the bulges disappear. I made a face at the girl in the mirror and turned away.

I went back to the kitchen. Mama was sitting at the table, the Old Gold contest spread in front of her. I put my arm around her shoulders. "Come with me to the picnic, Mama, please."

"No. I'm going to stay here and work on my contest. When you get back, maybe you could help me some. You're pretty good at working these puzzles, Florrie. If I win, I'm going to give you, let's see, a thousand dollars," and she laughed. "If I ever do get my hands on some money, I'm going yonder."

"You'll have some money one of these days," I said. "I better get going, hardly anybody's passing the house now."

She handed me my lunch, wrapped in newspapers, and I bit back the words that I wanted to say to her about wrapping it in newspapers. "How do I look?" I said.

"You look fine, except you need a brassiere. Humping your shoulders over like that doesn't hide them."

I flounced out of the kitchen, slamming the screen door behind me. I jumped down the steps and started up the path that led to the cemetery. I looked back over my shoulder; Mama was standing in front of the kitchen window. I stopped and looked at her, and ran back to the kitchen.

I hugged her around the neck and kissed her, and I don't know why, but I felt like crying. I left again and went up the path, only this time I didn't look back but went straight through the cemetery to the church.

It was about eleven o'clock when I got there, and people were standing around in groups talking, the children hollering and running around. People had put their lunches down underneath the oak tree by the spring. Some were in white bakery boxes, some were in light bread wrappers, and some were in grocery sacks. There were a few in newspapers, like mine.

170

The lunches wrapped in newspapers would be the last chosen, the ones in bakery boxes, the first. Light bread wrappers and grocery sacks were in the middle, equal in desirability. I sidled over with my lunch, looking around to see if anyone was watching. I wanted no one to see which was mine. I put it at the edge of the heap and turned to see Billy Paul watching me. He was leaning against a tree and wore white pants and a blue shirt. He was holding a stiff straw hat in his hands.

I was weak with happiness that he was here. I walked to the tree where he was standing. "Hello, Billy Paul. I didn't see you standing there."

"This is where I'm supposed to meet Elaine. If she doesn't come on pretty soon, I'm liable to go on off with some other pretty girl." He smiled at me.

My face flamed red, and I walked around him, going to sit on the steps of the church and watch the children play. There were girls my age there, but I knew them only to speak to. They walked past, their arms linked together, laughing and flirting with the boys. Billy Paul and Elaine passed, and I watched them as they walked down the grassy slope at the side of the church. People were gathering on the picnic ground for the games. I wished that Nell were here. The picnic would be a lot more fun if she were here to walk with and laugh at the games with.

I went back to the spring, thinking I could hide my lunch better than I had, but Mrs. Johnson was standing there, to keep the dogs away, she said. I offered to take her place.

"Gracious, Florrie," she said. "You're not supposed to stand and guard the lunches. You run on and have a good time with the young people."

I left and went to stand under a tree at the top of the slope, looking down at the people. Fans moved slowly back and forth, and men had spread their handkerchiefs on the ground and were sitting on the white squares. Children stood on the stone picnic tables, ready to watch the race for the greased pig.

Inside a towsack, lying on the ground, the pig was greased and ready to go. A dozen men stood in a line across the picnic ground. Brother Gridley untied the towsack, and the pig squealed and ran across the grass, heading for the woods. When Brother Gridley yelled "Go," the men ran after it, stumbling and falling over each other.

"Sooey, sooey, sooey," they yelled, and in a few seconds the pig and men all had disappeared into the woods. Shouts of "There he goes" and "Got him" and "No you don't" drifted back from among the trees. The people were cheering and yelling, the boys stamping their feet, and even the women were standing on the tables to see who came out first.

After a while, Grady Beeton ran from the woods, the pig squealing and wriggling in his arms. "I won, I won, I got him!" he cried.

The crowd moved out to meet him, and as they came together, they gathered around him and Grady was gone from sight. I was disgusted. Might have known it would be a Beeton.

I went back to the church. There was no use watching any of the other games. They were silly; people didn't care what kind of fools they made of themselves. I went inside the church, the bright sun still flashing and jumping behind my eyelids.

I sat down and rested my head on the back of the seat, listening to the shouts from the picnic grounds. There was a picture of Jesus hanging in the back of the pulpit. He was kneeling to pray, rays of light streaming through the clouds onto His face.

Someone was walking up the aisle. I turned around and saw Billy Paul walking toward me out of the gloom. He sat down in the seat in front of me and turned to face me.

"What are you doing in here all by yourself?"

"I just don't care much for games," I said.

172

"Me either," Billy Paul said, and then we sat, not talking.

I was uncomfortable in the silence, and I tried to think of something to say. But there was nothing.

"I guess you're ready to go back to school tomorrow."

"No, I'm not, I'm not ready to go back to school," I said, unwilling for him to think that I liked school.

He laughed and stood up. "See you later, Florrie," he said, and I watched him leave, unable to think of a way to keep him there.

I was alone again, and I looked at my hands folded in my lap. I hated myself for being so dull that Billy Paul would not stay to talk, and I hated Mama for telling me that I was pretty when she knew I was not.

I sat there until I heard the people laughing and talking as they came up the slope and around the side of the church, heading for the spring. I went back outside.

People were milling around the pile of lunches, picking out the bakery boxes first. I hurried and reached around Belton Beeton and got the bakery box he was reaching for. He let out a squawk and looked around to see who had stolen his treasure, but I disappeared into the crowd.

I walked down the slope and sat at a table by myself. I tried to open the box, my fingers fumbling with the string. I could hardly wait to see what I had gotten. Potato salad and chocolate cake, maybe, or was it barbecued pork chop. The knots were too hard to untie, so I ripped the box from around the string.

Fried chicken. A whole box of fried chicken with two biscuits. I stood halfway up, thinking I would take it back to swap, but the box was torn, so I could not. I sat back down and picked up a drumstick, and looked at it. There was nothing to do but eat it. I raised it in silent tribute to Aunt Marcy.

People sat down at the table with me, and I looked anxiously

at each lunch as it was unwrapped. Mine was not there. Thank
God I would not have to watch them choke on my peanut butter
sandwiches. The tables filled all around, and I slipped a spotted
white dog one of my drumsticks.

When I looked up, I saw Elaine sitting at the table in front of
mine, and next to her was Billy Paul. I stared with fascination
at his fingers curling around Mama's big crumb biscuit. With a
small gesture, he raised the sandwich and smiled at me. Humiliation washed over me, and I looked down at the table and
didn't look back up again until I had finished eating.

When I finally looked up, Billy Paul was gone. I didn't see
him anymore that day, because I went on home.

🌲🌲🌲🌲🌲 **20**

School started on time. The building did
not burn down or get blown away by one of Mama's cyclones,
as I'd hoped. I went to the road and waited for the school bus
that first morning, and looked across the cornfield to the
woods. "See you in a little while, woods," I whispered.

After a while the bus came, and when I got to school I stood
outside the building waiting for the bell to ring. The wind blew

through the halls and out the front door; the air smelled musty from the building being closed all summer. It smelled of wax, too, for the floor inside the door was polished and gleaming.

Teachers that I hadn't seen since last year went up the whitewashed front steps, smiling at the greetings of the girls and boys.

Mr. Saxon, the bachelor English teacher, stepped from his slate-blue Ford roadster, blushing as the girls gathered around him, flirting with him. He was plump, his flesh spilling over the starched collar of his shirt; his eyes were blue, the lashes the pale color of his hair.

This year I had him for English. Audrey Patton told me that I'd be sure to cry when he read us *Sonnets from the Portuguese*. I had read them already, and they made me happy, not sad.

I went to the school library that first day and checked out *Jane Eyre*. I cried at the same places every time I read it, cried for the heartbreak and agony of Mr. Rochester's love for Jane.

What a wonderful man he was, to stay loyal to a crazy wife chained in the tower! I sat at the kitchen table and cried as I read, while Mama worked her contest. Mama looked up from her puzzles and saw the tears streaming down my face. I told her why I was crying.

"Florrie, quit reading such sad books. It's not good for you to have your mind on crazy people. It'll make you nervous."

But I read it anyway, and then I read *Wuthering Heights*, only I didn't let Mama see me cry when I read that one.

Mornings were so cool now that you needed a sweater, even though it got hot later in the day. Daddy came in the kitchen one morning, his hands and face scrubbed for breakfast. "There's going to be cold weather early this year. I feel it in the air. It won't be long until hog-killing time," he said. Then he told Mama and me his yearly hog-killing story, called "The Year the Meat Went Bad."

When he was a boy at home in Tolbertville, he said, the weather turned cold in October one year. His daddy killed all the hogs that were big enough and dressed the meat, hanging the hams and bacon in the smoke house. The next week the weather turned warm as summer. "We never did have any cold weather that year," Daddy said, "and all the meat spoiled and turned putrid. We had to take it down in the woods and bury it."

After Daddy told the story, he said he believed he'd wait until Christmas to kill hogs this year, but I knew he wouldn't. The first cold snap, we'd hear the pigs squealing as he drove the knife into their hearts. Charlie Swinburne would come to help dress the meat, taking home a ham or some sausage for his pay.

A washtub of chitlins would sit on the back porch, smelling like something dead way off in the woods, until Dorothy came up from Aunt Mira's and took as many as she could carry home with her in a big bucket. Dorothy would get on Frank Sadler's bus and ride with him to Huxley. He would make her raise all the windows and sit with the chitlins in the back of the bus.

Whatever chitlins were left would be thrown away because, as Mama said, "We're not the kind of people who eat chitlins."

I went with Mama to the woods behind the cemetery to help her gather the wild plums that grew there. We took along a tablecloth and spread it under the tree; then I climbed up and shook the branches. Mama laughed and rubbed her head when the plums hit her as she knelt on the ground to draw the tablecloth into a sack; then she stood and slung it over her shoulder like a beggar's pack.

I helped her wash and cut up the plums, and then she put

them in water and sugar in an enamel dishpan. After a while the fruit began to boil, froth rising on top like foam on ocean surf. Mama stood over the dishpan, skimming off the froth and putting it in a bowl. When I started to stick my finger in to taste it, she told me not to, that the froth was the impurities cooking out of the plums.

Later, after it had cooked for a long time, she poured the hot red syrup into a saucer and let it set for awhile to see if it would jell. When it cooled, we got a spoon and ate it, the tart jelly making the saliva pour from under my tongue.

Mama said she wouldn't cheat and use pectin like Mrs. Goggins did, that knowing just how long to cook it was all the fun of making it. Sometimes Mama's jelly didn't jell and was like syrup, and we could pour it from the jar onto our biscuits.

We still sat on the porch at night, even though it was cool after the sun went down. Daddy chain-smoked, flipping the butts over the bannister. Mama went out every morning with a trash sack and picked them up, saying the tobacco was killing all the grass up around the porch.

"That just shows all you know about how grass grows," Daddy said.

The end of September brought the rain. It was the first we'd had that was enough to wet the ground. It rained steady for a week. The house was damp from so much moisture in the air, and when you climbed in bed at night, the sheets were cold and clammy.

At night, Mama and I sat at the table in the kitchen listening to the dull drumming of the rain on the roof. Mama worked her puzzles and I read my books and did homework. It was the fifth night of the rain when Daddy came through the kitchen on his way to bed. He stopped and watched Mama working on the puzzles. He looked tired and spent, like an old man. He rubbed his hand over his mouth. "The only way you get money is to work for it, Mrs. Birdsong. And even then you might not get any."

Mama didn't say anything and she didn't move. Daddy looked up at the ceiling. "Listen to the rain fall. It falls on the just and the unjust and it falls on the fields and washes away the topsoil. And it falls on the corn and potatoes. But it's like pouring medicine down a dead man's throat. It's too late to do any good."

He left and Mama's pencil started to move again, unscrambling the letters of the puzzle.

"Mama, I feel sorry for Daddy," I said. "He worked so hard this year, and the crops started off so good. All that work for nothing."

Mama got up from the table and went and opened the drawer of the worktable. She reached behind some bread wrappers and pulled out her pack of Old Golds. She shook a cigarette from the pack and sat back down at the table. She scraped a long kitchen match across the floor, lit her cigarette, and took a deep puff.

"I don't feel sorry for him. I used to, but not any more. Some people get sense after awhile, learn better than to think you can make a living scratching around in the dirt, but not him. Not Toliver Birdsong. He's trying to live those stories his daddy told him. Toliver is a great believer in the stories of how it used to be."

She leaned over and flipped ashes in the open eye of the stove, took one last puff, and dropped the half-smoked cigarette into the red coals. "Come help me, Florrie," she said.

I pulled my chair around next to hers, and together we figured that the picture of the tulips meant "two lips." We finished the puzzles about ten o'clock, and she put them in an envelope addressed to New York. I took the envelope and rubbed my fingers across the words.

New York was a big city. I knew that. And it had a lot of people. I knew that, too. But beyond that, I did not know and could not imagine. And I was glad that it was the letter and not me that was going so far away.

Mama took the letter out of my hand. "One of these days we'll go there, Florrie. I'd saved a hundred dollars to go to Washington and see the Capitol when I married Toliver, and didn't get to go. But if I win some money in this contest, we'll get on the train and go to New York. That'll be better than Washington."

She went to the work table and got another cigarette, lighting it from the coals in the stove. When she straightened up, she said, "I love a train. I lie in bed at night and listen to them whistle when they climb the hill in Coal Town. It's the lonesomest sound in the world and I feel like crying when I hear it, but I don't want it to stop. I used to flag the evening train at the depot in Stillwater and give the engineer the mail sack. About every two or three runs, he'd give me a box of candy or a box of crystallized fruit. The first time I took a box of candy home, Wilbur took it and threw it away. He said it was low women that took presents from men they didn't know, so I got so I'd slip it in the house and hide it. At night when I went to bed, I'd turn off the lights and eat candy in the dark." She smiled and shook her head. "Sometimes I think it's a wonder I grew up halfway normal, having to live with Wilbur so long. It finally killed Ruby. She got sick and went to bed. The doctor came, but he said he couldn't find anything wrong with her. Finally, she just died, I think to get out of her misery. Wilbur never was good to her. He went out of town and left her for weeks at a time to take care of that store of his. She never did get to do anything just because it was fun. At least I had the sense to know I had to get away from him."

She sat down at the table and smoked her second cigarette

and told me some of the stories I had heard before. But always it seemed like the first time, and, like the first time I ever heard them, I hated Uncle Wilbur for being so mean to my mother.

✝✝✝✝✝✝ 21

Mama made me a new dress for the Harvest Ball. She went to town while I was at school one day and bought lavender taffeta cloth that turned silver when you moved in the light. She bought it with the money Uncle Joel had given her when she was sick.

She pulled off her shoes and sewed barefoot, pumping the treadle so fast that the needle blurred and disappeared. Aunt Marcy had given Mama the sewing machine when she bought her new electric one, and Mama cherished it. It sat next to her bed, under the window. I begged Mama to let me use the machine, but she wouldn't. She promised to teach me when I got older.

About a year ago, when I was home by myself, I decided to sew on the machine anyway. I got a piece of cloth out of Mama's rag bag and began to sew. I thought it wasn't nearly as hard as Mama made out. But soon the thread tangled and knotted, and I couldn't get the bobbin out of its holder.

I was scared to death when I told her what happened, expecting her to be furious when she saw the mass of knotted and twisted thread. But she sat down calmly and untangled the thread. "Be sure your sins will find you out, Florrie, be sure your sins will find you out."

She made my dress from one of the patterns she kept in a shoe box on her closet shelf. It came almost to my ankles, and had tight puff sleeves. The sleeves had tiny outside seams all around the band that fit around my arm; Mama had made the tiny stitches by hand.

I watched Mama's hands as she pulled the needle through the cloth. She thought her hands were ugly because they were square, her fingers short and stubby. She was ashamed of her thumbs most of all. They were short and wide at the tips, the nails wider than they were long. She was self-conscious about them, and had gotten into the habit of tucking them into her palms, her fingers closed around them.

She thought my hands were pretty, with my long fingers and tapering fingernails. Sometimes she would take my hands and hold them in hers, looking at them, and she would tell me that I had an artist's hands. "Take care of them, Florrie, and keep them looking nice. One of these days, you're going to play the piano. Quit cracking your knuckles, or you'll make them big."

I told Mama I thought her hands were pretty too, but secretly I did think mine were prettier. But when I looked at her hands, I felt sorry for her, not because the fingers were short and blunt, but because you could see how hard she'd worked from the stubby nails and calluses. And they looked like she was easily hurt, like the back of Daddy's neck looked vulnerable.

I started writing a poem about Mama's hands. I haven't finished it yet, but the first two lines say:

My mother's hands have never graced a banquet table,
Nor casually arranged a Russian sable.

When I finish it, I'm going to give it to her.

The Harvest Ball was next week, on Halloween, and every night I creamed my face with Mama's cold cream, and brushed my hair a hundred strokes. And I sat in the window and prayed. I prayed that Billy Paul would dance with me, and that I would know all the right things to say.

I sat in my window one night and looked up at the stars, and I said, "Help me, stars." But they only sent back their cold light, and I knew that all the help I got with Billy Paul would have to come from me.

🌲🌲🌲🌲🌲🌲 22

Halloween was cold and clear. We had our first frost the night before, and it settled on the last of the wildflowers. They drooped over, weary already with the weight of winter, their petals burned brown and crisp.

In the afternoon Mama put the finishing touches on my dress, and I stood in front of her mirror and tried it on. It had a sweetheart neckline that came to a point between my breasts.

I stood barefoot while Mama knelt on the floor in front of me, turning up the hem. Pins stuck from her mouth like metal cat whiskers, and she fussed as well as she was able, not being able to move her lips, when I twisted from side to side to feel the cool, slick cloth move on my legs.

Daddy said it was beautiful when I modeled it for him, but he said it to me, not to Mama. The only compliment I ever heard him give Mama was that she made good crumb biscuits, almost as good as his mother's.

I took the dress off and Mama sat at the machine and began to whip in the hem. "At the risk of making you mad, Florrie," she said, "I bought you a brassiere when I bought the cloth for this dress." She held up her hand when I started to speak. "No, don't say anything. I've decided that you either wear the brassiere or you stay home from the party."

I looked at her, not speaking, but she didn't look at me, just kept her head bent over the dress.

"All right," I said, angry, "give me the goddamn thing. One of these days, I won't have to do what you say. I'll be my own boss and I'll run around naked and not wear underpants or brassieres, and I'll do anything I decide I want to do."

"You don't know, Florrie, how glad I'll be for you to be your own boss. You think you know it all. I hope I'm around the day you find out you don't know it all, because you'll be the most surprised person in the world. Don't you care that people laugh at you and think there's something wrong with your breasts flopping around like they do?"

"I said, give—me—the—goddamn—brassiere! I don't care about your advice. I'll do what you say because I have to. So give it here."

Mama went to her dresser and opened the top drawer. She took out a small Davis's sack and handed it to me. I took it to my room and lay it on the bed, but I didn't try the brassiere on.

I lay down on the bed and went to sleep, and when I woke up, Mama was shaking me by the shoulder.

"It's six o'clock, Florrie. Come and get some supper, because the Pattons will be here at seven o'clock to pick you up. Come on now, and eat something so you won't get to feeling bad."

I sat up, my stomach curling with excitement. The time had finally come. "I'm not hungry, Mama, I can't eat a thing."

"Come on, now, and eat a bowl of soup. That's not heavy, but it'll keep you from getting weak."

I followed her to the kitchen and sat at the table with them. Daddy complained about the supper being so meager, and I could eat only a few spoonfuls of soup because I felt sick with excitement. I went to my room to dress.

I had bathed earlier in the day, sitting in the zinc tub full of water in the kitchen, so all I had to do was put on my clothes. Mama had rolled the sides of my hair in curlers, and I was thrilled when I thought of my hair with waves in it. I began to unwind the wire curlers. My hair hung around my face in cork-screw curls that I would brush out when I put on my dress.

Mama came and stood in the door, watching me.

"Mama, don't stand there looking at me. It makes me nervous. I'll call you when I'm ready."

She turned and left, closing the door behind her. I had hurt her feelings, but I could not stand to let her watch me put on the brassiere. I took it out of the sack, looking at it for the first time. It was pink cotton, and had a pink and blue rosette in the center. I held it up by the straps and thought, God, how ugly!

Then I put it on and fastened it in the back. It was too tight, and I felt my heart beating under the tight band. Still it would have to do, or I couldn't go to the dance.

I pulled my petticoat over my head, and then my dress. I would need Mama to button it up the back for me.

I went to the door. Mama was sitting at the kitchen table,

already working on her puzzles. "Mama, will you come help me get my dress buttoned?"

She looked up at me. "You mean you can't do it by yourself? I don't know whether I'll help you or not. If my mother was living, I wouldn't talk to her like you talk to me."

"I'm sorry, Mama," I told her. "Please button my dress for me."

She stood up and I went back in my room. I stood by the bed and turned my back while she fastened the buttons. "Turn around and let me see how you look," she said.

I turned to face her. She smiled. "I didn't do a bad job on the dress, if I do say so myself. It looks nice on you, Florrie. You just act as nice as you look, and you'll be the prettiest girl at the dance."

I threw my arms around her, and hugged her and kissed her cheek. Her breath still smelled of supper coffee.

"Go in my room and use my brush to brush your hair. Just be sure you leave it on the dresser when you finish."

I went to Mama's room and stood in front of her mirror. I brushed my hair with her wide tortoise-shell brush, and my hair waved softly around my face. The dress turned silver when I moved in the electric light, my breasts thrusting outward. I had never seen myself with breasts that showed under my clothes, and I turned sideways to see myself in profile.

I was pleased. I pushed my chest outward, making my breasts even larger and I felt a sense of power, felt that for the first time I had a weapon in my battle to make Billy Paul notice me.

I took my fingers and pulled the dress lower between my breasts until I could see where my breasts curved downward into the brassiere.

It was almost time for the Pattons to pick me up. Their two daughters, Audrey and Harriet, would be with them. They would have on pretty store-bought dresses, I knew, because they had more money than most people had in Gray's Chapel. Mr. Patton worked at the powder plant in Coal Town, not farming at all. But Audrey had graduated from high school last year and still had not married. Mama said Mrs. Patton was getting awful nervous about Audrey finding a husband.

Lots of girls quit high school to get married, and Mrs. Patton was disappointed that Audrey hadn't. I think it will be a lucky thing for Audrey or Harriet ever to get married, because they look like the ugly stepsisters in Cinderella.

Audrey's big white teeth looked like Dixie's, and Harriet's blond hair was thick and straggly. But Mrs. Patton dressed them in pretty clothes and that helped some, though not much. Harriet was in my room at school, but we had never been friends. I didn't want to be friends with her, because all she talked about was boys. And not only that, but she thought Grady Beeton was cute.

A horn honked outside, and I took one last look in the mirror, then ran to my room to put on my shoes. Then I went to the living room. Daddy was reading the paper. When I came in, he lowered it from in front of his face and said I looked nice.

I went to tell Mama good-bye and found her in the kitchen. She was sitting at the table again, working on her contest. "How do I look, Mama?"

"You look beautiful. Be sure and tell everybody I made your dress."

"I'm not going to tell them it's homemade, Mama. Everybody else will have dresses from the store, and that's where I'm going to say mine came from. You don't care, do you?"

"No, I don't care," she said. She stood up from the table and went to her room. I followed her as far as the living room; then the horn blew again. She came out and handed me her coat. It

186

was rust-colored, and had a huge fox collar that Mama had sewn on it years ago.

I would wear it in the car, but I would pull it off as soon as I got into the building, because I was ashamed to let people see me wearing it. I was sure they would laugh.

Mama walked with me to the front porch, telling me to be sure to stay in the gym, to stay where it was light, because such terrible things were happening these days. "I don't want you in a car with anybody but the Pattons," Mama said. "Don't you go joy-riding with any of these country boys, you hear me?"

"I'll be careful, Mama," I said, and went down the steps. The late October air was cold, and I pulled the coat close around me. The fur collar felt soft as down against my face. I looked up at the sky as I walked toward the car, and found the Big Dipper without hunting for it. It hung with its bowl tilted over the woods across the road, the North Star bright at the end of its curved handle.

I reached the car, and Harriet hung her head out of the window. "What took you so long, Florrie? You're the slowest girl I know, no wonder you're the last one in the room every morning."

I didn't answer, but opened the front door of the car and squeezed in next to Mrs. Patton. Mr. Patton grunted and moved over, and I slammed the door closed. Mr. Patton said, "Helen, don't get your leg in the way of the gear shift. I might just shift your leg instead of the gear."

Harriet and Audrey and Mrs. Patton laughed at the unfunny joke. I guess they were scared not to laugh, because Mr. Patton had a quick temper and ruled all of them with an iron hand. Audrey and Harriet always asked him permission to go places; they never asked Mrs. Patton. That seemed funny, because I always asked Mama.

Mr. Patton was a big, heavy-set man, bald with big jowls. He smoked cigars and bought Mrs. Patton an electric iron for her birthday, and they always had a late-model Ford.

They even had a telephone. But the telephone belonged to Mr. Patton. Nobody could use it without asking him, and then he stood over them, listening to their conversation, telling them when it was time to hang up. When he wasn't home, he kept the telephone locked in the hall closet.

Mrs. Patton had lots of pretty dresses, but he picked them out for her, going to town and buying them and bringing them home to her. The only place she could go without asking his permission was to church.

We rode through the night, not talking, and I hugged Mama's coat close around me, because Mr. Patton rode with his window down, and the car was cold and drafty.

Mr. Patton slowed and turned onto the side road that went over Hog Pen Branch and wound around to the school. Harriet leaned over the back seat and asked me who I wanted to dance with, but I didn't bother to answer her, and she didn't ask me again.

We came to a car parked on the side of the road, our headlights outlining a boy and girl straining awkwardly in a kiss. We passed on, leaving them to the darkness, like startled woods animals surprised in the night.

The road dropped suddenly down a long hill, ending in a low place over the Branch. There was a wooden bridge, but there had been so much rain that the water lapped over its edges and ran onto the road. Mr. Patton eased down the hill, putting on his brakes and taking them off again so that we rolled a few feet and then stopped. Finally we crossed the bridge and made the sharp right turn that let you on the road that led to the school.

I heard the music first. It came faintly through the woods,

188

and Audrey and Harriet began to giggle and chatter, making me more nervous than I already was. I wished they would be quiet. I pushed closer to the door, looking straight ahead. Then Mr. Patton stopped in front of the school steps, and I opened the door and stood in the gravel. Harriet and Audrey got out too, and Mrs. Patton, and then there was a car behind us, honking for us to move on.

People walked toward the building, their long shadows melting as they met in the brightness of the lights that streamed from the school windows. The music was louder now, and I began to tremble, wishing I had stayed at home with Mama to help her work her puzzles. Mrs. Patton pushed at me gently as she got from the car, and took me by the arm, urging me forward. Harriet and Audrey linked arms, hurrying toward the front door.

I walked with Mrs. Patton, and we became a part of the flowing tide of people. Mr. Patton would pick us up at eleven o'clock. When we started in the front door, I slipped my coat off and hung it over my arm. I looked with envy at Harriet and Audrey. They had rabbit-fur capes.

A rush of warm air blew in our faces as we stepped into the front hall, and I stopped shivering, but suddenly felt drowsy. I pushed through the crowded hall, almost not recognizing old classmates with their curly hair and rouged faces.

Once, I caught a whiff of singed hair, and I knew that someone had let the curling iron get too hot.

Teachers lined the hall, looking strange in their long dresses and their smiles. Most of them never smiled in class. Mr. Saxon stood blushing in his black suit and bow tie, speaking to parents as they stopped to talk.

Gradually, I dropped behind the Pattons, slipping unnoticed to the edge of the crowd. I walked close to the wall, moving out only when I came to a radiator. I saw Harriet looking over her shoulder, but she didn't see me, and I was glad.

I turned with the crowd at the end of the hall, and headed for the gym. The music floated down the hall, and orange and black balloons hung from the ceiling. An orange pasteboard moon hung from a string, and printed on both sides in black letters was "HARVEST MOON DANCE."

Black paper cats with arched backs hissed silently from behind orange pumpkins on the bulletin boards. The senior class had spent all week decorating. I passed familiar class rooms that looked strange with the lights on and the day's lessons still on the board.

Teachers sat behind their desks, their smiles pasted on, available to be spoken to if anybody wished to.

At the gym, I stood just inside the door. People flowed around me, moving toward the punch table, and toward the chairs that lined the wall. I would not sit in those chairs tonight.

In the middle of the gym, people were dancing, mostly young people, but some mothers and fathers. I could not imagine Mama and Daddy dancing together. The Victrola was turned up loud, and Mr. Saxon wound it up and put on the records. Bing Crosby was singing "Deep Purple."

The senior class had turned the gym into a barn. All around the door frame were dried ears of corn, with the shucks pulled back and held on with adhesive tape. At the far end of the gym were two stalls, complete with hay and a manger. Along the wall where I stood were pumpkins and bales of hay, a pitchfork sticking from the hay.

Mrs. Patton stood guardian of the punch table, ladling out the green liquid sparingly. I walked over to her. "I'd like a cup of punch if you please, Mrs. Patton," I said.

190

"There you are, Florrie," she said, dipping up the punch. "I wondered where you'd gotten off to."

"We just got separated in the crowd, I guess. Where're Harriet and Audrey?"

She nodded toward the dance floor, smiling. "They were asked to dance right away. Someone will ask you soon, don't you worry, dear."

I searched among the dancers until I found Harriet. She was dancing with George Bentley. "Oh, I see Harriet," I said, walking away. "She's dancing with fat George Bentley."

I was thirsty, and gulped down the cup of punch. It tasted of pineapple and limes and sparkling water, and it was sweet and cold. I wanted another cup, but I would be embarrassed to go back and ask for more so soon.

A group of girls stood like a clot in a bowl of tapioca pudding near the Victrola. They were laughing and pushing at each other, showing everybody what a good time they were having. They danced with each other, but fell quiet when a boy passed by, hoping he would notice them. But the boys would not ask them to dance, and the girls knew it.

I knew, because last year I had been with them, sitting on one of the chairs, shrinking down at the way they acted. Nell and I came together last year, and Nell sat with me because she didn't want to leave me.

Boys came and asked Nell to dance, reaching through the other girls to tap her on the arm, and she refused them time after time. Finally I told her I was going home if she didn't dance.

She walked to the dance floor with the next boy who asked her, her face bright, her black hair tumbling around her shoulders. Her red dress was cut low in front, and when they put their arms around each other and jitterbugged, her breasts bounced and pushed upward from the front of her dress. The boys lined up, and she only danced a step or two with one of them before she changed partners.

I sat drinking punch and watching her until she disappeared with a boy out of the side door of the gym. I wondered how it felt to be so popular.

This year I would stay by myself. If I was unpopular, I would be unpopular by myself.

I took the punch cup and set it on the table. I stood talking with Mrs. Patton, longing to dance. Glenn Miller's orchestra played "Moonlight Serenade," and I saw Elaine with her head cradled on the shoulder of some boy I didn't know. He looked like a senior. My eyes slid over to the stag line, and I saw Billy Paul. Our eyes caught, and he left the stag line and circled the dance floor, heading toward me.

I was so scared, I turned abruptly and left Mrs. Patton talking to herself. I started for the gym door. I would hide in the girl's rest room until I stopped shaking. There was a touch on my arm, and I turned to see Billy Paul smiling at me.

"What do you want?" I asked.

"Don't get mad," he said. "I just wanted to ask you if you'd like to dance. Would you?"

Bing Crosby moaned once again that deep purple had fallen over sleepy garden walls.

"Yes," I told him, "I would like to dance," and I followed him to the dance floor.

Mrs. Patton stared and I smiled at her as we passed, but she didn't smile back. I was so excited that I thought my heart might stop beating. I turned my head away from the group of unpopular girls when we passed them, much as I turned my head away when I passed a dead animal on the road.

Billy Paul put his arm around my waist, and I put my arm

192

around his shoulder, and it was just like I had imagined it. We stood still for a moment to catch the beat.

Dancers slid by, bending and swaying, girls smiling over their partners' shoulders to speak to Billy Paul, their faces blank when they looked at me. That was all right, I was dancing with Billy Paul, not them, and I was sorry for them.

The music stopped almost as soon as we started to dance, and I was heartbroken that I hadn't even gotten to dance a whole record.

But Billy Paul held onto my hand, waiting for Mr. Saxon to change the record, and I knew that we would dance again. Sweat was moist in my palm and I wished that I could wipe my hands on the handkerchief I had pinned to my waist. But I couldn't, and we stood waiting for the music to start again.

Mr. Saxon wound up the Victrola and Bing Crosby began to sing "Temptation."

"Mr. Saxon sure is a Bing Crosby fan," I said.

"Don't you like Bing Crosby?" Billy Paul asked, and I was sorry I had mentioned it.

"Oh, I'm crazy about him. Mr. Saxon seems to be, too," I said.

We danced, Billy Paul holding my right arm down low at my side. He smelled of hair tonic, and I could see the dark pores on the side of his face where his beard grew out. I had never thought of him with a beard, and all at once I didn't like being so close to him. Our cheeks, where they touched, were slick with sweat.

"I can't dance to this beat, Billy Paul. I'm sorry," I said, turning away from him. I left him standing among the dancers and went back to the chair where I had left my coat.

I walked out the side door of the gym. It was cold, and I draped the coat around my shoulders and walked through the little children's playground, past the swings hanging like ghosts in the dark.

I went down the long flight of concrete steps that led to the baseball field, then walked across the wet grass. I sat down on the wooden bench that the baseball players sat on, waiting to come up to bat, and I looked up at the stars. Now the Big Dipper was straight over the pitcher's mound.

It's all over, I thought, and disappointment was sour in my mouth. Why are things never the way you imagine them to be?

I saw something move from the corner of my eye, and when I looked at the steps, there was a dark figure. I jumped up, terrified.

"Who's there?"

The figure started running toward me; I ran, trying to climb the bank, toward the school, but slid on the wet grass, falling down on my hands and knees.

I could hear the footsteps now and I stood up, running toward the woods. It was like nightmares I'd had, my legs heavy and hard to lift.

Soon I'll wake up, I thought, but the dark was real, and the heavy breathing of somebody behind me was real, too.

A hand closed around my arm, and I moaned. I turned to see Billy Paul's teeth shining white as he smiled at me. We stood there, gasping for breath, and I jerked my arm loose.

"What in the hell do you mean, chasing me like that, scaring me like that, Billy Paul? You ought to be ashamed." I pushed past him and walked toward the school.

His hand closed on my arm again. "Not so fast there, Florrie. You know you like being alone with me." He pulled me toward him, and pressed his lips against mine. He put his hand inside the low-cut front of my dress. His hand closed around my breast. I struggled with all my might, kicking him as hard

194

as I could. He turned me loose and I ran, but he caught me again and we fell on the grass, rolling around.

I raked my fingernails down the side of his face and brought up my knee, smashing into the softness of his stomach. He turned and groaned, writhing on the ground. I thought, I may have killed him. I crawled over to him. "Are you all right, Billy Paul?" and I sat back and cried.

Finally he sat up, still hugging himself across his stomach. He rested his head on his knees, and I went back to sit on the baseball players' bench. After a while, he came and sat next to me.

"How come you did that, Florrie, how come you hit me in the stomach like that?"

"Because you came chasing me, putting your hands all over me. Just who do you think you are?"

I leaned back against the tree that grew behind the bench and pulled my coat close around me. Billy Paul laughed.

"Go ahead and laugh, Billy Paul. I don't see anything funny."

"I wasn't laughing at you. I was laughing because you beat me up."

I didn't answer, and knew that he never could love me now. How could he love a girl that wrestled him to the ground and beat him up?

He reached for my hand and held it, and I didn't take it away.

"How come you came out here?" I asked. "How come you aren't inside, dancing with Elaine?"

"Because we had it made up between us."

"Had what made up between you?"

"That I'd try to get you alone and scare you. We thought we'd get a good laugh out of it, talking about it later. Elaine said you were stuck on me."

I pulled my hand loose from his, and stood up. "I was stuck on you," I told him, "but not any more. How can you be stuck on a boy you can beat up?"

I walked away from him, and he called to me in the darkness. "You looked pretty tonight, Florrie. You ought to wear dresses more often."

I crossed the baseball field and climbed the steps to the playground. I sat in one of the children's swings and pushed high into the night, the cold wind rushing around me.

My breath steamed and hung on the air, and I thought, it's cold enough now for Daddy to start his fall plowing.

✟✟✟✟✟✟ 23

Fall blazed in the woods for weeks before it was quenched in the hoarfrost of winter. The trees flamed red and gold in the fall sun, trembling with life, but it was a trick, for death touched them beautifully only for a while before they burned brown and fell to earth.

The cemetery was deep with fallen leaves. They lay in gentle mounds over the graves, and settled in drifts against the tombstones. Barren corn stalks left standing in the fields had turned their roots loose from the ground; you could pull them up without straining.

Everywhere you looked was gray, except for the green of the pines and cedars, dotted among the bare hardwood trees.

The birds were gone, except for the jorees, who would stay all winter. Flocks of birds flew over the house, and sometimes it looked like a hundred or more would leave the flock and drop like stones to the ground, pecking at the rimy dirt.

Mama and I put out pans of water and sunflower seeds for them, then stood on the back porch to watch.

Mama leaned over the bannister, following their flight south over the cornfield.

"I wonder where they're going," she said.

"They're going to South America, because it's hot this time of year."

She laughed. "They're not going because it's hot, Florrie, they're going to the city because they're tired of the country, like I am."

"For all you know, they're flying to the country, Mama."

She watched the birds until they disappeared over the trees. "Sometimes I dream I can fly." She spread her arms wide, moving them slowly up and down. "In my dreams, I move my arms like this, and I rise up slowly off the ground until I'm higher than the church steeple. Toliver stops plowing and watches me, and you're running after me, Florrie, holding up your arms. Then I begin to fall. I fall faster and faster until I almost hit the ground, but then I jump, and wake myself up." She smiled. "Wonder what that means?" she said.

We went to Aunt Marcy's for Thanksgiving. Uncle Joel picked us up early on Thanksgiving morning, and Mama sat in the front with him. Daddy and I sat in the back seat. People stared at us from their wagons and along the side of the road as the big black Packard drove through Huxley.

I sat back on the seat, trying to act like I rode in a Packard every day.

Later, Daddy said that for once in his life, he didn't get up half starved from Aunt Marcy's table. She had a baked turkey, but Mama made the dressing, and had stayed up late the night before making three skillets of cornbread. She put it in a bowl and took it with us.

When we got to Aunt Marcy's, Mama finished making the dressing, pouring the stock out of the pan that the turkey was baked in. Aunt Marcy stood at her elbow, making suggestions. Finally Mama stopped stirring. "Marcy, if you want to make the dressing, just say so. But my dressing tastes better than yours, so why don't you just go on and do something else?"

Aunt Marcy clapped her hands together and told me, "Come on, Florrie, let's you and me go play the piano."

They had a Pease upright that Uncle Joel had given her when they were married in 1900. Aunt Marcy told me that it was going to be mine when we moved to town. She sat down at the piano and played "Nola" and "Kitten on the Keys" and "Humoresque," telling me when to turn the pages.

She called Mama to come and play. Mama played by ear, mostly marches, her short fingers belting out the music in ragtime. Mama came and sat down at the piano, pushing the stool far back, so that her arms were stretched almost straight out. She played loud, nodding her head from side to side in time to the music. Uncle Joel even patted his foot when Mama played the "Stars and Stripes Forever."

When she finished, she twirled on the stool to face us, her face bright with happiness.

"That's a mighty good piano you all have," Daddy told Uncle Joel. Mama shook her head, and went back to the kitchen to finish the dressing.

Aunt Marcy and Uncle Joel had a big house in the fashionable part of town. They had no more children after little Janie died, but they had stayed in the house, which had five bed-rooms.

After we ate, Uncle Joel took Daddy home, but Mama and I spent the night on Thanksgiving, and Mama let me pick out the bedroom we would sleep in. I picked out the pink one, with white twin beds.

Before I went to bed, I soaked in a tub of warm water, using some of Aunt Marcy's violet-scented bath oil. Then I stretched out between the smooth sheets that smelled like soap and starch, and watched Mama kneel by her bed to pray. Then she climbed into her bed.

"At home, I kneel down in the kitchen, Florrie, and pray for the Lord to take care of you. I tell him to let me go in rags, but to take care of my girl."

I closed my eyes, waiting for sleep, but it wouldn't come. The light from the corner street lamp shone through the window and I got up to pull down the shade. There were lights in the house next door and I could see people moving around in the rooms.

After supper, Mama and I had taken a walk, strolling along the smooth sidewalks, looking at the houses with the small patches of lawn. Most of them were two stories high and close together, and there was light everywhere. When you looked up, you could barely see the stars.

"Mama, look how pale the stars are," and she looked up but didn't say anything.

"I like the dark around me at night, Mama. I can't stand all this light."

"Not me," she said. "I like the light. Sometimes I feel like I can't ever get enough light." She turned her face up to the electric bulb of the street lamp. "I'm like a flower turning its face to the sun. I thrive in electric light," and she laughed.

199

I pulled the shade and climbed back in bed. This time I slept, and the next morning Uncle Joel took us home.

December came, and it got dark at five o'clock. When I got off the school bus at four-thirty, the lights were already on in our house. The days were cold and it rained almost every day, a light rain that soaked through my coat and even seeped through the Cat's Paw half soles Daddy put on my shoes. He was through the fall plowing, and sat every night in front of the fire, pasting the black rubber over the holes in my school shoes or weaving baskets out of white oak strips. The baskets were to hold the cotton that he would grow next summer.

I sat afternoons in my room, and studied and read and added to the poems in my composition book. I wrote them first on scrap paper, then copied them in ink into my notebook. I wrote one poem on the death of love, which was about Billy Paul and me.

I saw Billy Paul at school the day after the Harvest Ball and he looked awful, with the long, red scratches down his face. But he grinned at me, and I was sad that I didn't love him anymore. I looked for some other boy to love, but there was no one. I tried to like a big, blond boy named Fred, but when he smiled you could see his gums. So that was the end of that.

I read and stared out the window at winter, and read *Jane Eyre* for the fourth time. I wondered if there would ever be a Mr. Rochester for me, and if there would ever be an end to winter.

✝✝✝✝✝✝ 24

Christmas, 1938. I lay in bed looking at the unfamiliar sun that streamed through my window and over my bed. "Hello, sun, it's good to see you," I said, and stretched gingerly, so as not to move too far from my warm place.

Two weeks away from school, two weeks Christmas vacation. I felt like shouting for joy, because the best part of vacation was being away from Miss Crenshaw, the history teacher. For two weeks I would not have to listen to her voice droning in a monotone as she read the textbook to the class. I nearly went crazy in Miss Crenshaw's history class, until I saved my sanity by making up poems in my head or counting my pulse, timing it by the second hand on the clock. It was usually seventy-two beats per minute.

When school started, everyone had raced to get seats in the back of the room because Miss Crenshaw smelled so bad under her arms. She was small and soft, but she smelled of stale sweat that must have been in her crepe dresses for years. She had three dresses, blue, red, and brown, and with them she wore clean, freshly starched white linen and lace detachable collars.

She called me to her desk once to explain a mistake in a test paper, and it was all I could do to stand there, my eyes watering from her strong smell. I looked at the boys in the back of the room as she marked corrections on my paper, and they were holding their noses, making silent gagging motions. I got tickled and laughed, and Miss Crenshaw asked me if I thought mistakes were funny. She marked my paper with a big red F and told me to bring it back signed the next day.

I stretched again and shivered when my leg touched a cold part of the sheet, and listened to Mama as she moved around the kitchen. I knew she had gotten up early, as she did every Christmas, to make her Japanese fruitcake. It had rainbow layers, pink and white and yellow, the top one chocolate and smeared with white icing and coconut.

Last week Mama and I had walked down the lane to Aunt Mira's, both of us shivering in the fine, misty rain. Mama wanted to ride to Huxley with Ralph Junior when he went, to buy the coconut and the food coloring for her cake.

We walked up the driveway and when we were almost to the front porch, Aunt Mira opened the upstairs bedroom window. "Julia, I'm working on my books for the cemetery," she hollered down, "I don't have time to visit with you today."

"I want to ride to Huxley with Ralph Junior, Mira Gray, to get the coconut for my Japanese fruitcake," Mama called back.

"I don't have money for you to spend on coconut, Julia," Aunt Mira said, lowering the window.

"We don't need your money," I yelled to the closed window, and under my breath added, "you old bitch."

"Hush, Florrie," Mama said. "You stop talking like that, Mira's my sister. You quit cursing like that."

"Why don't you curse her out then, Mama? You ought to be ashamed, letting her talk to you that way."

"Hush," she said again, squeezing my hand.

We walked home through the lane, and Mama took her hand out of her pocket and showed me a dollar bill.

"I had the money for the coconut. I took a dollar out of the candy box. After all, Christmas is next week, and you can't let it go by without doing anything."

By the time we reached the iron gates, I was so cold I couldn't feel my feet, but picked up numb lumps and set them down again. My hands were cold, too, even though I had them in my coat pockets. I was hurrying to reach the house, and could almost feel the heat of the fire as I turned myself in front of it, thawing out. Mama stopped in the road.

"You ain't game if you don't walk with me to Huxley to buy the coconut."

"You're kidding," I said, horrified.

"No, I'm not. If we hurry, we'll get back before dark."

"Mama, it's four miles there and four back. That's eight miles we'll have to walk. Let Daddy go for you."

"When I get my mind set on something, I usually do it. You go on home and get warm by the fire. I'll be back before dark."

She started down the road, walking in the ruts that the cars had made. I watched her until she got past the cemetery, and then I ran after her, because I knew she wouldn't change her mind and come back. After she got past the Fowlers' house, a half-mile on the other side of the church, there were no more houses until she got almost to Huxley. I was scared for her to go alone.

I caught up to her and linked my arm through hers. "If you're game, I'm game, Mama."

We walked and walked, and after we'd gone about two miles it seemed that I'd been walking all of my life. I thought of the stories I'd read about the cold north, and for the first time understood about freezing to death. Tomorrow they would find

Mama's and my frozen bodies on the side of the road, and no one would ever know that we had died for a coconut.

The wind swept down through the woods, and I hunched down further into my coat. I looked at Mama, and her nose and face were blood-red. She had tied her blue wool scarf around her head, and she plodded along, her hands shoved deep in her pockets. Straight in front of us, the red sun broke through the clouds and began to set; I knew that we wouldn't make it home before dark.

We saw the first house on the outskirts of Huxley. Smoke came from two chimneys and I wondered who the lucky people were who got to be inside by the fire. There was a curse on Mama and me; we were doomed to walk the rest of our lives.

"Come on, Florrie, run," Mama said, and we ran, holding hands and weaving like we were drunk.

We ran down the hill and there was the café, the truck stop called "Greenwood's." "Let's go in and get a cup of coffee," Mama said.

We pushed through the door, and the heat almost stifled us. We sat down on stools at the counter and drank hot coffee. Soon needles started pricking and stinging in my feet, and I could wiggle my toes.

Mama laughed and joked with the waitress who worked behind the counter, and asked for a pack of Old Golds. The waitress brought them to her, and Mama opened them and shook out a cigarette.

"Mama," I whispered, "you're not going to smoke that here, are you?" I looked around to see if anybody was watching her.

"I certainly am," she said. "I don't do anything at home I'm ashamed to do in public. See all those men? They're smoking aren't they?"

"Yes, but women don't smoke in public."

I looked down at the counter while she smoked. And she talked about me cursing! This was much worse, I thought.

Mama finished her cigarette and we left. We went to Pitilla's grocery store and bought the coconut and food coloring. When we left the store, Mama reached down in the sack and handed me a cellophane wrapper of peppermint sticks. "Merry Christmas," she said. I took out a peppermint stick and pretended to smoke it as we walked along.

It was twilight, and before we were halfway home, I was frozen again.

"When you're married and have children, Florrie, you can tell them about the time we walked eight miles in the freezing snow."

"It's not snowing, Mama."

"I know it, but it'll make a better story that way." She laughed.

In another few minutes it would be full dark. I wanted so to be home that I pulled Mama by the hand, and we started to run. We ran and ran. When we came around a curve in the road a man stepped from the woods into the road a short way in front of us.

We stopped, and Mama pushed me behind her. The man stood there not moving, watching us. He carried a long stick, taller than he was, and wore an old overcoat with no hat. His pants were baggy at the knees.

"Evening," Mama said.

The man didn't answer.

"You live around here?" Mama asked.

Still no answer.

"My husband's coming along behind us. He'll be here in a minute."

The man smiled and started toward us.

"What's in that sack, lady?" he said.

Mama stepped backward. "Run, Florrie," she said, but just then headlights shone around the curve in the road and Frank's bus came toward us out of the night. Mama ran down the middle of the road, waving her arms.

"Stop, Frank, stop Frank!" she shouted, and I ran behind her, looking back to see if the man was chasing us.

Frank stopped his bus on the side of the road; the man raised his stick threatening us, and stepped back into the black of the woods.

Mama and I climbed on the bus. "You got here just in time, Frank. The Lord must have sent you, because if you hadn't come when you did, Florrie and I would have been knocked in the head."

We rode the rest of the way home with him, talking all the time about what had happened.

"It must have been the Lord looking after you all, Julia, because usually I'm not this late on the run home from town. I had a flat outside Huxley, and it took me nearly an hour to get it fixed."

He let us off at our mailbox, and when we got to the front steps, Mama said for me not to tell Toliver, he'd be mad we went off like that by ourselves.

Mama's cough was worse the next day, but other than that, you couldn't tell we'd walked almost eight miles in the freezing cold and on top of that nearly got knocked in the head, too.

I decided it was time to get up and wish Mama a Merry Christmas. I threw back the cover and ran for the door, the floor cold on my bare feet. When I opened the kitchen door, the air was warm with the smell of cake baking. Mama was kneeling by the oven door.

"Walk easy, Florrie, so the cake won't fall. I've got the last two layers in now."

On the work table by the window, four golden-brown layers were cooling. I walked to the table and started to pinch one at the edge.

"Stop that, Florrie," Mama said. "Sit down at the table and eat your breakfast. I don't want a cake that's ragged around the edges."

I sat down at the table, and Mama put biscuits and apple butter in front of me. Butter had seeped through the biscuits, all the way through the crisp bottom crust. Mama saved the lemon peel for me, and I fished it out of the jar and held back my head, dropping it into my mouth. I ground the tart peel between my teeth. Mama sat down at the table with me.

"Christmas gift," she said.

"Mama, you said we weren't giving presents this year," but I was glad she had one for me.

"I couldn't let Christmas go by and not remember you, Florrie. This time next year we might not all be together, so we ought to have the best Christmas we can."

"Did you get Daddy something?"

"No, I didn't get Daddy something. Why should I? Do you think *he* ever remembers me on Christmas or on my birthday, or on our anniversary, or anytime, for that matter?"

I shook my head that he didn't. She left the room, and I thought about last Christmas. Daddy got drunk on Christmas Eve with Charlie Swinburne and didn't come home until Christmas morning. He was happy when he got home and walked over to Mama, who was cooking breakfast. She was standing at the stove, frying bacon, and he put his arm around her. Mama pushed him away.

"Leave me alone, Mr. Birdsong," she said.

"Merry Christmas and go to hell, Mrs. Birdsong," he said.

Mama came back to the kitchen and handed me a small, thick square of tissue paper. I unfolded it, resting the paper on the table. Inside was Mama's gold locket. I couldn't believe she was giving it to me.

"Oh, Mama, you're not . . ."

"Hush, Florrie. Yes, I am giving it to you. You're old enough not to let anything happen to it."

I lifted the locket out of the tissue paper, holding it in the palm of my hand. It was ornately carved around a raised, smooth center. Engraved on the smooth center were Mama's initials. *JML*, Julia Margaret Lee. On the back, in old English lettering, were her initials again. Grandfather Lee had given it to her when she was three years old, the year he died.

"I'll put your picture inside, Mama."

"When I get a good one made, you can."

She sat down at the table with me, and we sat looking at the locket. "Papa said when he gave it to me, 'this is for baby.' I don't remember it, I was too young. He bought it in Birmingham, and on the inside he had it engraved with the doctors' emblem. See, right here," she said, opening it. "He brought Mira Gray and Marcy a dress, but I was always glad he gave me the locket, because that's something you can keep forever. You can pass it down to your daughter, Florrie."

I wrapped the locket back up in the tissue paper.

"Promise me you'll take care of it, Florrie, and never lend it to anyone. If you do, you'll never get it back."

"I promise, Mama," I said, and went to my room.

I put the locket between the handkerchiefs folded in my top drawer. Then I got my school notebook off the top of my dresser and took out the present I had made for Mama in school.

It was red construction paper folded in the middle to make a

208

book; in each corner were green holly sprigs with red berries made out of construction paper. Pasted on the front was a picture of Whistler's Mother. Inside, we had copied the poem "Mother" in white ink.

I held it behind my back and went back to the kitchen. Mama was drinking a cup of coffee.

"Which hand?" I asked, trying not to laugh.

"Right, but what's so funny?"

"Nothing," I handed her the poem.

She held it carefully at the edges and read the poem, and when she finished she smiled. "That's a real sweet poem, Florrie."

"You really like it?" I asked.

"Yes," she said, and then the laughter came. "The only thing is, I wish you'd picked out a younger mother for the front."

"I thought you'd like that old mother." I laughed with her. "I'll give you one just like it for Mother's Day."

Mama pushed herself up from the table and, still holding the card, danced around the kitchen. "For a wrinkled old mother, I feel mighty spry today." She danced out of the kitchen, humming, her dress whirling around her like an open umbrella.

I finished eating breakfast, and thought about Daddy not getting any Christmas present at all. I felt sorry for him. He was out at the fields every morning in the cold thinning the oats. When I got dressed, I would go to wish him a Merry Christmas.

The bare branches of the hickory tree scraped against the kitchen window. I sighed, and longed for white clouds drifting in summer skies and hot days that sent me to the deep shade of the woods. I wished that there was no such thing as winter.

I decided that I would take a walk in my woods. I had not been there since late fall, and it was wrong for me to stay away so long, leaving my old friend to struggle alone in the cold grip of winter.

I went to find Mama. She was in her room, sitting on the side of her bed with her small cedar chest, open, beside her.

"What are you doing, Mama?" I asked, sitting down next to her.

"I was putting your Christmas card in with your other school papers, and got to looking at everything else. When you're an old married woman, I'll take your school papers out and look at them and wish I had you back with me, little again."

She had saved my school papers from the first grade on. I picked up a booklet from the bed. It was a weather booklet from first grade and the first page said "Weather." Inside there was a page for every day of the month of January 1929. I flipped through the pages and found only two days that said, "Today the sun is shining." I closed it, smiling at such childish occupation.

Mama was reading a letter. I leaned on her shoulder and saw that it was an old letter from Daddy, one that told her about their little white "B." She folded it to put it away.

"Let me read it, Mama."

She put it in its envelope. "Pshaw, Florrie, you've read these letters a hundred times. I don't know why I even keep them. Force of habit, I guess." She put the school papers and letters back in the cedar chest and I handed her my first-grade weather report.

"Mama, do you love Daddy at *all?*"

"What makes you ask questions like that, Florrie? Go ask Mr. Birdsong if he loves me. Besides, I haven't got time to worry about who I love today, I've got to get the cake out of the oven."

She put the cedar chest back on the shelf of her closet, and I followed her to the kitchen. I sat at the table and watched her

210

take the layers out of the oven and turn them upside down on the table to cool. Then she poured herself another cup of coffee and sat down with me at the table.

"The only time Toliver and I were really happy was the year we lived in Atlanta. That was a year I won't forget as long as I live. I talked him into leaving the farm in Tolbertville and going to school at Georgia Tech. He could go at government expense, you know. Grandfather Birdsong didn't like it, but we went anyway. In those days I could talk Toliver into doing most anything I wanted him to.

"Toliver went to school during the day and when he came home, late in the afternoon, we'd walk down Peachtree Street. We lived in a boarding house on Peachtree Street, and our landlady's name was Mrs. Petree. Toliver called her Mrs. Petree of Peachtree Street, and for some reason we thought that was real funny. We went to see the Cyclorama and to the picture show when we had a little extra money. And then Toliver got the flu. It was in nineteen-eighteen, and people were dying from it like flies. Mrs. Petree helped me take care of Toliver. She said he cheered her up and made her feel good. Can you imagine Toliver cheering up anybody?"

Mama went to the stove and poured another cup of coffee and got a cigarette from the drawer. She lit it and sat back down. "Mrs. Petree and I nursed him for two weeks before he started getting better, and I guess the Lord was with me and Mrs. Petree, because we never did catch it from him. Toliver talked out of his head when his fever was high. He kept talking about some girl named Nancy that he loved once over in Marietta."

The fire in the kitchen grate was red coals, so I got a pine log from the corner of the kitchen and put it on the coals. I poked at it until blue flames began to curl around the bottom and I knew it had caught and would burn. I sat down and pulled my bare feet up under my gown to get them warm. Mama drank her coffee and smoked the cigarette. I thought that the day didn't feel like Christmas, it felt like an ordinary winter day.

"Talking about love," Mama said, "I loved Toliver then. I knew I didn't want him to die, and I thought I'd done wrong pulling him off the farm like I had when he loved it so much. Sometimes I think it's the idea of farming he loves, not farming itself. Farming never has made him really happy, at least not the kind of happy I can understand."

Mama took a deep puff of the cigarette and blew the smoke straight out in front of her. "It took me a long time to realize my life was important, too, just as important as Toliver's is. Just because I'm a woman, it doesn't mean I don't have dreams, because I do. And I don't believe it's a wife's duty to follow her husband unless she wants to. Sauce for the goose is sauce for the gander, and when you're dead, you're a long time dead. When I get my hands on some money, I'm leaving farms behind forever, and it's 'hello, city' for me."

"Mama, I love the farm and the land like Daddy does. The only thing that ruins it for me is that you aren't happy."

"I know how you feel, Florrie, and that was a bitter pill for me to swallow. But I swallowed it, and you and Mr. Birdsong can swallow the way I feel about living in town. And I give you the same privilege I've given myself. Hurt me as it would, I wouldn't force you to go with me. I want you to know what I didn't. That you've got a choice. You have a choice, Florrie, and I would rather you knew that, than have you go with me."

We were quiet while Mama finished her coffee and her cigarette, and then she got up to put the cake together.

"I'm going out to walk, Mama. Come with me and we'll look for reindeer tracks."

"Reindeer tracks?"

"Santa Claus was supposed to come last night," I said.

212

Mama stopped stirring the white frosting. "Those were the happiest years of my life, getting ready for Santa Claus to come. I wish I could live those days over again."

I went to get dressed. I put on a pair of denim overalls and a sweat shirt Dink had given me. I thought about Dink as I pulled the shirt over my head. He was home for Christmas, because I had seen him in the car with Aunt Mira. But I had not talked to him.

I put on two pairs of socks and had to pull hard to get my old white sneakers over the double thickness. I put on my brown wool school coat and tied my red scarf around my head. That ought to warn hunters in the woods that I was not a deer.

I clumped through the kitchen and told Mama good-bye, running my finger through the icing on the cake. I went out the back door and down the steps, sucking in great lungfuls of cold air. The sun was bright, but the day was freezing. I rubbed my hand over the slick ice in the rain barrel, and then went across the road to the field.

Daddy had planted oats where there was corn last year. I climbed the fence and went to where he was kneeling in the oats. He looked up when I got close to him. "You're up early for a vacation day, Florrie."

"I came to wish you a Merry Christmas, and I'm going for a walk in the woods. How are the oats doing?"

"They're doing fine, fine. I'm going to have a big crop of oats this year. We'll have some money next spring if we can just hold out until then. I don't have a present for you, Florrie. I'm sorry. But next Christmas I will, and that's a promise."

"I don't want a present, Daddy. My goodness, I don't have one for you either. Don't worry about things like that. I just want spring to hurry up and come. I'm so sick of winter, I could scream."

Daddy's hands were blue with cold.

"Daddy, you better go back to the house and warm up. Your hands look like they're frostbit to me."

"I'm going in a minute, I'm just about through. What's your Mama having for Christmas dinner?"

"Japanese fruitcake, for one thing. I don't know what else."

I left him kneeling there, and walked carefully so as not to step on the oats. I went in the woods and walked on the fallen leaves, thinking how strange it was to be able to see so far and not be afraid of stepping on a snake.

I came to the barbed-wire fence that marked Charlie Swinburne's land. I leaned against the wood post of his gate and turned my face to the sun for warmth, but it was without strength; it could not bake the cold from my bones. The wind raced across the meadow where Charlie's cows grazed, feeding on the brown grass. I was cold in spite of all my clothes.

I climbed a tree to keep in practice. I was heavy and clumsy, but I made it to the top of a sycamore. I could see Daddy still kneeling in the field, and I could see the roof of our house with the smoke pouring from the chimney. I thought then that I would go home and get behind the stove and read for the rest of the afternoon.

I started home, my feet as numb as they had been when Mama and I walked to Huxley. When I crossed the field I waved to Daddy, but didn't stop to talk this time. When I was almost to our front gate, I saw Dink sitting on his bicycle at the back door. Mama stood in her bare sleeves on the steps, hugging herself against the cold.

"Dink was coming after you, Florrie. He says Mira Gray wants us to come eat Christmas dinner with them."

"How you been, Dink," I asked.

"Okay. You been okay?"

"Yes. How long you home?"

"Until the day after tomorrow. We don't get much time at Christmas," he said. "Will you come to eat dinner with us?"

"I don't believe so, Dink. I believe I'll stay home and read this afternoon. Do you want to go, Mama?"

"Tell Mira Gray, Dink, that I've already got dinner started here," Mama said. "But tell her thank you very much." Mama went in the house.

"Well, good-bye, Florrie," Dink said. "I hope you have a nice Christmas." He pushed the pedal up with the top of his foot and started to ride away.

Mama came out the back door carrying our cake with a bread wrapper spread across the top. "Wait, Dink, come back," she called.

"Mama, what are doing?"

"Hush, Florrie."

Dink came back.

"You take this home for you all's Christmas dinner, Dink. Christmas is the Lord's birthday and a time for sharing. Tell Mira Gray Merry Christmas for me."

I gave Mama the meanest look I could muster through my shock. We had walked eight miles in the snow and nearly gotten killed for that cake.

"I don't think it's right to take your cake, Aunt Julia. I don't think Mama would want me to take it."

"That's right, Mama," I said. "I don't think Aunt Mira would want Dink to take it."

Mama looked at me, but she was talking to Dink. "Take the cake, Dink, and tell Mira Gray I'm sorry we couldn't come to dinner."

Mama helped him settle the cake in his bicycle basket, and I stood wordless, watching him wobble through our front gate and across the road. "He'll never make it home with our cake.

He'll turn over and smash it. Do you realize that we walked eight miles for that cake, Mama, and nearly got knocked in the head besides?"

"I felt sorry for him, Florrie. And you don't treat him nice anymore. What happened? You all used to be good friends."

I shrugged. "I don't know. We just outgrew each other, I guess. Anyway, don't change the subject. What are we going to have for Christmas dinner?"

"Come on in the house," she said. "I'll make you some tea cakes. And you can eat them while they're still warm."

We went in the house, and after I had pulled off my scarf and coat, I crawled in the warm corner behind the stove with my book and watched her mix the batter and roll out the dough.

I slept, and when I woke up the tea cakes were stacked in a brown mound on a plate, sitting on the table. I crawled out from behind the stove. Mama was sitting at the table, working on her contest. "They're still warm, Florrie," she said without looking up. "You can eat some now, and we'll have dinner about four o'clock. There's some coffee on the back of the stove, if you want it."

I sat with Mama at the table and ate the tea cakes and listened to the wind whistle as it whipped around the corners of our house.

☨☨☨☨☨☨ 25

Aunt Mira sent the cake back the day after Christmas. Dink knocked on the back door at twilight, right after we had finished supper and gone to the living room to listen to the radio.

Mama and I went to the door, and Daddy turned the radio down so he could hear what went on in the kitchen. "I hope nothing's happened," Mama said.

She opened the door, and Dink stood there with the cake in his hands. He held it out to Mama, like an offering. It was covered with the same bread wrapper Mama had sent it in. "Mama said to tell you we can't keep the cake, Aunt Julia."

"Come on in, Dink," Mama said, "before you freeze to death."

He stepped into the light of the kitchen, and Mama took the cake from him and set it on the table. "Why did Mira Gray send it back, Dink?" she asked.

"Mama said you had no business spending money on a cake like that when you can't even pay the rent." His face flamed red.

"You go back and tell her we'll make any goddamned thing . . ."

"Florrie!" Mama said, turning on me, furiously.

"I don't care. I told you not to give them our cake. You see how mean she is, I hope you don't ever speak to her again."

"I'm sorry, Aunt Julia," Dink said.

"You can tell Mira Gray for me, Dink," Mama said, "that whatever I do for Christmas is my business. If she wants to send back my Christmas present, that's all right with me."

"There's a good Catholic Christian for you," Daddy said from the doorway.

"Get on back in there and read your paper, Mr. Birdsong. This is between my sister and me."

"She's sure not my sister," Daddy said. "And if she was, I wouldn't claim her." He went back to the living room.

"I'm sorry, Aunt Julia," Dink said again.

"You run on back home, Dink, and get out of the cold," Mama said. "You'll be sick if you stay out too long." Mama patted him on the shoulder as he went out the kitchen door. I saw him pass the kitchen window on his bicycle.

"Stick your lips back in, Florrie," Mama said. "I could sit on them and ride to town."

"Sit on them and ride then, I don't care. One of these days I'm going to tell dear old Aunt Mira exactly what I think of her."

Mama took the bread wrapper off the cake, and it looked just as pretty as it had yesterday when Dink took it away with him. "That cake's better traveled than most folks I know," Mama said, and I laughed.

"Get the knife and let's cut us a piece, Mama. I'm glad she sent it back. I didn't want her to have it in the first place."

Mama and I ate a piece of the cake, talking all the while about how good it was. Mama cut Daddy a piece when we were finished and took it to him in the living room. We pulled the porch rockers up close to the fire. Every winter we brought in the rockers when cold weather came. I rocked and watched Daddy as he sat up close to the lamp reading the paper, and I loved him. After all, didn't I have hands and feet just like his?

"Mama," I said, leaning close to her. "Do you know what Aunt Marcy told me when we were over there on Thanksgiving?"

"No telling," she said.

"She said Aunt Mira told her that she makes sure people in Gray's Chapel know that she's not blood kin to Daddy, tells them there are no farmers in you all's family. She lets them know that your kin people were all doctors and lawyers. Things like that."

"That's just some more of Marcy's talk, Florrie. She's giddy and gossipy, and you'd do well not to pay attention to everything she tells you. Why should people in Gray's Chapel look down on Toliver? They're farmers just like he is."

"To tell you the truth, Mama, I'm ashamed of Aunt Mira, the way she beats people out of their money. Talk to people around here and you'll find just about every one of them has had bad dealings with her."

Daddy rattled the paper as he folded it and put it on the floor beside him. "That's the truth, Florrie," he said. "Ask people around here what they think of her, and just about every one of them hate her God-damned guts."

"I hope you're satisfied, Florrie," Mama said. "Now you've got old man Birdsong started. There's nothing he likes better than to get started on Mira."

I rocked and watched the flames in the fireplace wrap around the hickory log and leap up the chimney. Mama and I had pulled those hickory logs from the woods after Daddy cut down the trees. I stretched my feet to their warmth. I wished I had my cat again. Spot died last winter from distemper, and I had buried her under the apple tree in back of the barn. I missed seeing her curled up on the hearth.

Daddy cleared his throat, getting ready to talk. Mama turned her chair so that her back was to him, humming as she rocked.

"Florrie," Daddy said, "you don't ever have to be ashamed of your people on your daddy's side. My people came over here after two hundred years in England. They migrated there from Poland. My Great-great-granddaddy John Birdsong got here in time to fight in the Revolution. He was a patriot. He settled in Virginia and had three sons.

"Great-granddaddy Nathan Birdsong was a third son and didn't inherit any of his daddy's property in Virginia. It all went to the first son and sometimes the second son, but never the third. When the government told the people of this country that they could have all the land they could run the Indians off of, Great-granddaddy Nathan Birdsong took his family to Georgia and fought the Cherokee Indians in Meriwether County. They ran the Indians off the land, but later the Indians came back and burned them out and scalped them. Granddaddy Hiram Birdsong was just ten years old at the time. The only reason he wasn't scalped, too, was because he was five miles down the road playing with a neighbor's boy. Nathan Birdsong's sister came over from Tolbertville and got Hiram and took him to live with her. Hiram grew up and got married there in Tolbertville. He built the old home place."

"It's a wonder to me," Mama said, "how you keep all those great-granddaddies straight. I must have heard that story since I've been married to you a thousand times."

"Madam," Daddy said, "just because you're not interested in history is no sign other people aren't. Mrs. Kirk, for all her big cars and money, can't trace her people back any further than Stillwater."

"That's all you know about it, Mister. My family was Scotch-Irish. Marcy's got our family tree anytime you'd care to see it. But as far as that goes, it doesn't amount to a row of pins tracing back your ancestors. It hasn't helped you any that I can see, Mr. Birdsong."

"Florrie's interested. She takes after the Birdsongs."

"She's the image of her Grandmother Lee," Mama said.

"I don't care so much about taking after either side, listening to you all talk," I said.

Mama stood up and looked at the clock on the mantel. "I'm going to work on my contest before I get too sleepy. Don't sit up past ten, Florrie."

"What time it it?" I asked.

"It's seven o'clock."

"The only way you'll ever make any money, Mrs. Birdsong," Daddy said, "is to work for it. Nobody's giving money away."

"Those puzzles are hard," Mama said. "I'm working for the money."

"Don't you know you're not going to win anything in that contest? Don't you know they've got it planned ahead of time who's going to win? It's just a way to get you to buy their cigarettes."

"I don't know any such thing," Mama said and left the room.

"Bah," Daddy said.

I turned and looked at him. "How can you be so cruel, Daddy? Do you get fun out of tearing her down?"

He picked up the paper and started to read again. I looked into the fire just as the log broke in the middle, sending sparks flying up the chimney. I took the poker and pushed at the end of the log, coaxing the embers into a blaze. It was too late in the evening to put on a fresh log. It would be time for bed before it started burning good.

Daddy tapped me on the shoulder. "I'll finish telling you now, Florrie, what I started telling you when your mother interrupted."

The ends of the log were burning good now, and I got up and turned off the lamp. "Is that all right with you?" I asked.

"That's fine. This reminds me of when I was a boy back home. We'd sit in the firelight after supper. There weren't any electric lights then, just kerosene lamps. Mama tried to be sparing of the kerosene, and pulled her chair close to the hearth to darn by firelight. You know, socks, and the knees of our pants where we'd worn them out."

I pulled my chair around sideways to the fire so I could see Daddy. He leaned forward in his rocking chair, his arms braced on his legs. In the firelight his face was eager and young, like in the pictures I had of him that were taken when he was in the Army. His hair was coal black then, and his cheeks round and filled-out.

"I was telling you about Granddaddy Hiram Birdsong building the old home place. Papa was born there, your granddaddy, and he lived there with Hiram when he got married. I was born there, and your Uncle Ernest and Aunt Fannie. It's a shame you never have been there. I'm going to take you with me over there one of these days to let you see it. It's good for a person to have a sense of place and know where he came from, where his roots are."

"Wasn't Granddaddy Birdsong's name Toliver, too?"

"That's right. I was the oldest boy, and I was named for Papa."

I closed my eyes, sleepy from watching the fire.

"Papa used to tell me the story of how he watched Granddaddy leave for the war," Daddy said. "Papa said he rode on the back of the horse with Granddaddy until they reached the woods in back of the house, then he made Papa climb down and go back home. Papa was thirteen years old, and he said he just wanted the war to last long enough so he could go, too. The war did last long enough, but he was the only boy, and Grandmother needed him at home with her.

"Papa said he'd walk down from the house to the road and watch the young boys from Tolbertville as they went by on their way to the war. Papa said he was so jealous, he just about couldn't stand it, having to go back to the house and chop stove wood when he could be going off to fight Yankees."

"He must've been crazy to want to go to war like that."

"No, that's the way Southern boys are. They like to fight. And they especially like to fight when it's for something they believe in. I've never known one yet to run from trouble."

"If it was slavery they were fighting for," I said, "then they were fighting for a bad thing."

"It wasn't just slavery, it was the God-damned Yankees trying to tell them what they had to do. No Southerner likes to be told what he has to do, Florrie."

"Then, I guess I'm a Southerner, because I understand not liking to be told what I have to do; still, I would have thought the South could see the wrong of what they were doing. Buying and selling human beings and separating mothers from children was a terrible thing."

We sat rocking, thinking of those far-away years that weren't really so far away from us after all. Daddy's grandfather had fought in the war, and Mama's father, going when he was only fifteen years old. The Civil War was real to me.

"It was more than slavery they wanted to destroy, Florrie. It was the Southern spirit, too. There's never been anything like it in the history of the world, the pride of a Southerner. They beat us in the war, and then they set out to bring us to our knees, kill our pride. But they didn't. It's still intact, and I wouldn't give you one Southerner for all the Yankees you could stack in this room."

"I believe the war was fought to do away with an evil, and I read in a book I checked out of the library that deep down inside, the South was glad that it lost the war and the slaves were freed. The book said 'a master cannot respect his slave and a slave cannot love his master.' "

"That book was written by a Yankee. They write things the way they wish they were, not the way they were. John Birdsong in Virginia had slaves, and it came down through the family how they loved him. When school's out next summer, I'll take you over to Georgia to see some good old Georgia red dirt."

I yawned, giving a long moan. "I'm going to bed, Daddy. I'm so sleepy I can't hold my head up."

I went to the kitchen, my eyes half closed, and kissed Mama good night. She told me to be sure to wipe the soot off my feet before I got in the bed. "If you'd just wear shoes, you'd help me keep the beds cleaner, Florrie. It's hard, washing in the winter, you know that."

Sometimes, when Mama was washing in the big iron pot outdoors, her hands got so cold that she came and sat down in the kitchen, crying. She rubbed her hands and held them over the stove until they were warm again.

"I sure will be glad when spring comes, Mama."

Daddy was still sitting in the rocker. "You usually beat me to bed, Daddy. Aren't you sleepy?"

"No, not yet, Florrie. I'm going to sit here in front of the fire for a while. You stirred up a good blaze there. I'll wait until it dies down and then bank it so I won't have to get up and start a fresh fire in the morning."

I wanted to kiss him good night, but I knew it would embarrass him. I went to bed and left him sitting by the fire, the shadows moving on his face.

We ate hog jowl and black-eyed peas for New Year's dinner; Daddy sat in front of the fire most of the day, still weaving his white oak baskets. "I let the boll weevil scare me," he said. "Next summer I'll plant cotton and poison the bolls to kill the weevils."

"Where're you going to get all that money, Mr. Birdsong?" Mama asked.

"Work for it in the oat patch, Mrs. Birdsong. Work for it in the oat patch," Daddy answered.

After dinner Daddy took my arm and led me to the field. We stood in the muddy rows, and Daddy made his plans. "I'll plant at least two acres, Florrie. I ought to get at least a bale of cotton to the acre. Do you know how much money that is? That's two hundred dollars. Two hundred dollars!"

He was a lot more excited than Birdsongs usually got, and the wind swooped down and rattled the brittle corn stalks; I couldn't imagine it getting hot enough to grow cotton. I left him standing there huddled in his old gray overcoat, mentally walking off the size of his cotton field. I went back home to sit in front of the fire.

Christmas vacation was over the next day, and I went back to school. January slid by in rain and mud, and then it was February. Winter loosened its hold enough to let a few warm days slip by. Mama came in from the yard one morning, smiling.

"Well, I never would have believed it, but there's a robin sitting out in the yard. Either he's crazy or we're going to have an early spring this year."

I ran to look, but it had flown away.

The second of February, the ground hog saw his shadow and

Mama got a letter from her contest. The ground hog went back in his hole for six more weeks of winter, and Mama and I went to the kitchen table to read her letter.

"Bring me my glasses off the mantel, Florrie."

I brought her glasses, and she adjusted them on her nose. She turned the letter on both sides, looking at it, and it was all I could do to keep from screaming: *Open it, open it!* "Mama, go on and open the letter, please."

"Give me time, Florrie, give me time," she said. She ran her finger under the flap and opened the letter, oh, so gently. She took out a folded sheet of paper, her lips moving silently as she read. "Hot dog!" she said, and handed the letter to me, smiling.

I read:

Dear Mrs. Birdsong,

We are happy to tell you that you are a finalist in our Old Gold contest. If you correctly solve the enclosed ten puzzles, you will be one of our major Prize Winners. They should be completed and mailed to us no later than March 30, 1939. Please enclose two Old Gold wrappers along with the puzzles.

Congratulations! I hope that we will have the pleasure of notifying you that you are our Grand Prize Winner.

Sincerely,
Thomas J. Ohrbachs, Advertising Manager.

When I finished reading, Mama was looking at me. "I can't believe it, Florrie. I can't believe that I'm this close to winning. Just wait until I tell Toliver. This time next year, we'll be living in town, that's what I'll tell him. And you'll be taking piano, and Lord only knows what else we'll be doing!"

On February twentieth I celebrated my birthday. When I came home from school in the afternoon, Mama had baked me a birthday cake; she had colored the layers pink. A deep snow

226

lay on the ground, and the afternoon paper said that if more snow fell that night, the schools would be closed the next day. I devoutly wished for more snow.

When we finished eating supper, Mama lit all sixteen candles on my cake and turned off the light in the kitchen. She sang happy birthday to me, and Daddy said I was getting to be a real old lady. That's what he said every year on my birthday.

"I wish I had been born in the hot summer," I said.

Mama got up from the table and went out to the back porch. She took a bowl with her and gathered the clean snow that lay heaped on the bannisters and brought it into the kitchen. She sprinkled it with sugar and vanilla and we took spoons and ate it out of the bowl.

"Children born in the hot summer," Mama said, "don't get snow ice cream for their birthday."

🌲🌲🌲🌲🌲🌲 26

March came in like a lion, and the wind blew day and night for a week and more; then it stopped blowing, and the sun came out warm. The daffodils bloomed bright yellow in the lane and along fences, and I gathered as many as I could carry and put them on Goo-Goo's grave.

The black mud dried in the fields and turned gray. Tiny cracks appeared, running in every direction like lines on a road map. Swollen places on the tree limbs burst open, and ruffled new-green leaves were born.

I rushed in the house after school, threw down my books, and rushed back outside to sit under a tree and look at spring. I whispered to myself the words from Solomon: "For, lo, the winter is past, the rain is over and gone; the flowers appear on the earth, the time of the singing of birds is come, and the voice of the turtle is heard in our land."

I felt like I was getting well from a long sickness. I looked out the window in history class. When Miss Crenshaw called on me, I hadn't heard her question.

"Ma'am, Miss Crenshaw?" I said, and she looked at me for a long time. Then she stood halfway up from her desk and looked out the window, straining her neck. "I declare if I see what's so interesting out that window, Florrie. Maybe you'd like to share your interest with the class?"

The girls and boys turned in their seats to look at me. They were smiling. I can't blame them, I thought, because anything that breaks the boredom of the class is meat to pounce on and savor. I would have done the same thing.

"Florrie?" said Miss Crenshaw, "Are you ready to tell us what you see out the window? Stand by your desk, please."

I stood up by my desk, and my face turned red. I hated Miss Crenshaw so much, I could feel my fingers closing around the soft, wrinkled flesh of her throat.

"Florrie, you have one more chance. Either you answer my question or go to see the principal. Right now."

"I was looking at spring."

The class burst into laughter.

"You were looking at spring?" she asked sarcastically. "I don't understand, Florrie. How can you look at spring?"

"You can look at the sunshine and look at the leaves that have grown big enough to speckle the shade. You can wish you were out there instead of in school."

The class tittered and shuffled their feet, and I felt them all still staring at me. But I wasn't embarrassed any more, and I wasn't afraid of Miss Crenshaw.

"You don't enjoy my history class, Florrie?"

"No, Ma'am, I despise your history class. It's the most boring class I've ever been in."

The truth exulted inside me, and my face broke into a smile of happiness. The class was so quiet, you could hear the twittering of the birds outside.

Miss Crenshaw stood up, and now it was her face that was red. "Florrie, come with me to the office. The rest of the class will read from page one hundred fourteen to one twenty-five and be prepared to take a test when I come back to the room."

I followed her from the room and down the hall. Students looked up, curious, from their desks as we passed their rooms.

Miss Crenshaw marched along the wooden floor, her large, pointed breasts keeping time with her feet. A yellow pencil stuck from her hair, resting behind her ear; her face wore a look of determination and purpose.

We passed the gym. Boys played basketball in blue satin uniforms and high-top tennis shoes. I followed her around the corner and up the stairs.

She had threatened me with the principal's office if I did not answer her question. I answered her, and I got the principal's office anyway.

We went into the school office, and Miss Crenshaw told the thin, black-haired woman behind the counter in the outer office that she wanted to see Mr. Langtree. The woman went into his office, then came out and told us to go in. We went in, and when we stepped inside his door, Mr. Langtree stood up.

He was a tall, broad-shouldered man with a head of thick gray hair. He wore gold-rimmed glasses, and vests with his suits. I thought he was handsome, but I had never been so close to him before. Miss Crenshaw came only to his shoulder; her head tilted back as she spoke to him.

"Mr. Langtree," said Miss Crenshaw, "Florrie Birdsong has been rude and impudent to me, she . . ."

"Come in, Miss Crenshaw, Florrie," Mr. Langtree said. He pulled two straight chairs close to his desk. "Sit down and we'll talk, get the matter straightened out."

We sat down, and I clasped my hands in my lap to stop their trembling. Mr. Langtree sat behind his desk, took a pencil from his holder, and pulled a sheet of paper in front of him. He was ready to write down my transgressions.

"Florrie Birdsong," said Miss Crenshaw once again, "spent her time in my class this morning looking out the window. And when I asked her to enlighten the class and to enlighten me on what was so interesting out the window, she said it was because she despised my history class, that she found it to be boring beyond endurance."

Mr. Langtree nodded his head and wrote on the paper. "Miss Crenshaw," he said, "if you'll leave Florrie here with me, I'll talk to her. We'll straighten the matter out and then I'll send her back to class."

Miss Crenshaw stood up and smoothed her hair, and the air in the small office smelled like sweat. "There'll be extra homework for you tonight, Florrie," she said as she left.

Mr. Langtree sat with his head bowed, writing on the paper, and I watched him, wondering what he would say to me. I wondered if they would send me home, as they had last year when I played hookey.

Mr. Langtree looked up and smiled. "What happened, Florrie? I heard what Miss Crenshaw said, now let me hear you tell what happened."

I shrugged. "What she told was true about me looking out the window. She asked me what I saw and I told her spring.

"Spring?"

"Yes."

He smiled. "What then, Florrie?"

"She asked me if I didn't enjoy her history class, and all of a sudden I felt like telling the truth. It's not often a feeling like that hits me, but it did in her history class this morning. I told her that not only did I not enjoy it, that I despised it and that it was boring."

He shook his head. "That may be the first time in the history of the school that the complete truth has been told, by either teachers or students. I'm going to tell the truth, too, Florrie. I've visited Miss Crenshaw's room, and you're right. It is boring almost beyond belief."

"It sure is," I said.

"But you are not to take what I've said and construe it to mean that I approve of what you did. The complete truth is too shocking."

"She was making fun of me, Mr. Langtree, and she got mad when I fought back. She had no right to make fun of me in front of the class that way. It's not a sin to love springtime."

"No, it's not," he said. "Did you know that Miss Crenshaw takes care of her old father, that her father is completely bedridden? She doesn't make enough money teaching school to hire any help, and sometimes she stays up with him all night. She never married, after her mother died, so she could keep house for him. Her neighbor next door looks after him during the day, while she's at school."

I thought about Miss Crenshaw taking care of her old father, and I felt sorry for her. I had never thought about her having a life outside the school; I had thought of her as part of the school equipment.

"I'm sorry she's having a hard time, Mr. Langtree, but still I don't think that excuses her for making fun of me."

"No, it doesn't excuse her, and I wasn't trying to make you think it did. Sometimes, though, when you understand why people do things, it makes you not so mad at them."

"I'm not mad any more," I said. "I'll even apologize to her if you want me to."

"I'd apologize to her if I were you, Florrie, more for you to think well of yourself than to help her feelings. I'll still have to mete out punishment for you, though."

"Yes," I said, and thought that I would be sent home and that Mama would have to come to school with me the next day.

"Florrie, you're to leave school right now," he said, handing me the paper he'd been writing on. "Spend the rest of the day celebrating spring."

I looked at the paper he gave me. It was a pass out of the building.

"You're kidding."

"No, I'm not kidding, Florrie. I'll tell Miss Crenshaw I sent you home, but I won't tell her what for. That is, unless you decide to tell her tomorrow."

"No, I won't tell her."

I stood up to leave, offering him my hand to shake. He stood up and shook my hand.

"What will you do this afternoon, Florrie?"

"Go to the woods. I haven't been in the woods since Christmas. I'll take my lunch that I brought to school, and my book, and I won't go home until it's time for school to be out."

"Goodbye, Florrie."

"Goodbye, Mr. Langtree. Thank you."

He waved his hand for me to leave, and when I got to the door, I looked back. He was standing with his hands in his pockets, staring out the window.

✝✝✝✝✝✝ 27

The letter came the middle of April, two weeks after Mama had mailed the last of her puzzles. The postman honked down on the road one Saturday morning after he put our mail in the box. The last mail we'd had was a week ago, from Aunt Fannie. She said she was going to visit us this summer.

Mama sent me down to the box and stood on the front steps, waiting for me to come back. I took the letter out of the box, and when I saw it was from the Old Gold people, I ran all the way back, shouting and waving the letter. "It's here, Mama," I yelled, "the letter's here."

She ran down the steps and met me at the front gate, grabbing the letter out of my hand.

"Open it, open it, open it, Mama," I begged, but she went on in the house and sat down at the kitchen table. She held it away from her, at arm's length, reading the envelope, and I tried to grab it and read it for her.

"Stop it, Florrie," she laughed. "Hand me my glasses off the mantel." I went to the living room and brought back her glasses, and she put them on and ripped open the envelope. She pulled out the folded letter, and a slip of paper fluttered to the table.

She unfolded the letter and smoothed the creases. I leaned over her shoulder, trying to see what it said.

"For goodness sake, Florrie, let me read it first, then you can read it," Mama said.

I sat down on the chair next to her and tried to read what the letter said from her face. Her lips moved, but her face was blank, without expression. I thought the slip of paper that fell on the table must be a check, and I wondered how much it was for. Mama's lips stopped moving; she sat with her elbows resting on the table, holding the letter in front of her.

I reached over and took the letter from her hands. She didn't say anything. I read:

Dear Contest Winner:
    Congratulations!
    We are happy to inform you that, although you are not a Grand Prize Winner, you are indeed a winner of one of our minor prizes. The coupon enclosed entitles you to a free giant size jar of Lady Esther Face Cream. We know you will enjoy this fine face cream, and we thank you for your interest in our contest.
    Let us at Old Gold assure you that you were a fine contestant. We only regret that all our contestants could not be Grand Prize Winners. Grand Prize Winners will be announced in your local newspaper on April 30. We will be offering other contests in the future, and we hope that you will enter them also.
    We hope the fun of working these puzzles has gotten you

in the habit of enjoying our fine cigarettes, and we wish you many hours of smoking pleasure.

Sincerely,

Thomas J. Ohrbachs, Advertising Manager.

I picked up the coupon and looked at it. It did indeed entitle Mama to a free jar of Lady Esther Face Cream. She only had to pay the tax.

"I'm sorry, Mama. I know you got all those last puzzles right. I don't understand what happened."

"It'll make Toliver happy, anyway," she said. "He said I wasn't going to win any money," and she lay her head on the table and cried.

I leaned over and put my arm around her shoulders, and I cried too. "I wanted you to win, Mama." I lay my head on the table next to hers, and we cried for a long time. Far away, a dog barked, and a mockingbird sang as it built its nest in the April sun. I heard Daddy pass the window with Beautiful Eyes, the bell around her neck clanking as she walked. I studied the red and blue flowered pattern of Mama's dress.

"Everything will be all right, Mama. Please don't cry."

"Hand me that dishrag, Florrie," she said, lifting her head. I handed it to her, and she dried her face.

"Here, wipe your eyes, too," she said. "Hush crying before you make yourself sick."

I wiped my eyes and hung the dishrag on the nail by the window. I sat back down at the table, and Mama held out her hands for me to see. "Look at them, cracked open from hanging wet clothes out in the freezing cold," she said. She picked up my hands, and tears ran down her face again. "Look at your knuckles, getting big from ironing with those heavy flat irons. Your beautiful hands. And Toliver hump-shouldered before his time, pushing that plow."

I looked surprised.

"Oh yes, I notice him too, whether he notices me or not. Dixie's right eye is gone from that cataract. Next summer he'll be pushing that plow without a mule to help. The land will kill us all before it's through."

"Look out the window, Mama. Look at spring and see how beautiful the land is."

"No," she said. "I don't understand you and I don't understand Toliver. I don't see that watching something grow up out of the ground is anything to die for. The land won't treat us any better than it has anybody else. Grandfather Birdsong died dirt poor, and Toliver will, too. Have you seen that picture of Grandmother Birdsong he keeps in his drawer? She died at thirty-five, all her teeth gone and her eyes all haunted. She looked like an old woman."

Somebody knocked on the front door, but neither one of us got up to see who it was. We just sat there, listening, until the knocking stopped.

"Mama, the land is like somebody," I said, looking into her face. "I love it because of the way the sun slants over the cornfield on a summer afternoon, and for the way the ground smells after the rain. I love the grassy shade and the fields and the woods. Daddy calls it being next to nature."

Mama looked at me. "The city, Florrie, is like loving somebody, too. I love the way the sun sets over the streetcar tracks, because those tracks mean you can get out and go without having to walk there, or wait all day long for the bus. I love the way city sidewalks smell after the rain, and I love the bank, because that's where you put all the money you make, living in the city. And I call that being next to heaven."

"Daddy says he's planting cotton in a week or two," I told her, "and he says this year, he'll make some money."

236

"And of course you believe what Daddy says," Mama stood up from the table and smiled. "I don't believe what Toliver says. We'll be poor as long as we stay here. Trees are just trees, and corn is something you cook for dinner. There's nothing romantic about dirt farming, Florrie. You'll find that out if you marry a poor farmer and stay on the land. Life is a lot more than roaming the woods and picking blackberries. I hope you never find it out the way I have."

She took the letter and tore it up, letting the little pieces flutter into the trash sack by the stove. "I haven't given up, Florrie. Just because I didn't win in the contest doesn't mean I've given up. I'm a long way yonder from being beaten." She went to the pantry and brought back a can of syrup and set it on the table.

"What's that?" I asked.

"What does it look like? It's a can of syrup. But it's not just an ordinary can of syrup," she said, tapping the can with her finger.

"What's different about it?"

"When you and I went to Pitilla's to get the coconut at Christmas, Mr. Pitilla and I got to talking. He had a whole stack of this syrup by the counter. He said a woman that lived right over there in Huxley started making it several years ago, and he helped her sell it. She sold it at first in jars, with nothing but a gummed label on the front.

"He said it wasn't long before he could sell every jar she brought him in a day or two, and not long after that, she sold the recipe to some syrup company in Birmingham and got rich. Off just the recipe, mind you."

We sat there, looking with awe at the can of syrup. On the front was a picture of an old-timey lady, dressed in a long black dress and wearing a white cap and white apron. Her face was long and weather-beaten, and she stared sternly straight ahead, as if she dared you not to like her syrup. Across her apron were the words "Old Tyme Cane Syrup."

"That's when I got the idea," Mama said.

"What idea is that?" I asked.

"The idea for making preserves. I decided then that if I lost the contest, instead of putting up jelly and preserves for us this summer, I'd make it to sell. You know what good jelly I make, Florrie, everybody says so. Mr. Pitilla said he'd let me have the jars and tops on credit, and that he'd help me sell it like he did the syrup lady."

"Mama, you know you hate making jelly. That'll keep you indoors most of the summer."

"I don't hate anything that makes money. There's money in that fruit we've been letting lie out there on the ground and rot."

We didn't say anything for a moment. Then Mama nodded to herself. "Go on out in the yard, Florrie, and let me clean up the kitchen," she said. "I want to track down all my jars and see how many I've got, then go ahead and wash them. I'll boil them when I start making the jelly."

I got up and went out on the back porch, and Mama came to the door and looked at me through the screen. "Florrie, if you'll help me gather the fruit this summer, I'll dance at your wedding."

"I'll help you, Mama," I said, and headed for the woods to see what wildflowers were blooming there.

🌲🌲🌲🌲🌲🌲 28

A storm was coming up. It was dusk, and Mama stood on the porch, watching the jagged streaks of lightning pierce the black clouds. They hung directly over the oat field, after moving in slowly from the southwest all afternoon. The wind blew the afternoon paper all around the living room, and then it calmed.

A loud clap of thunder came with the lightning.

"That does it," Mama said. "Come on, Florrie, we're going to Mira Gray's. Tell Toliver."

I went in the living room. Daddy had gathered up the paper and was reading it, sitting close to the lamp.

"Come on, Daddy, we're going to Aunt Mira's."

He lowered the paper. "I'm not going to Mira's or any place else. Tell your mother to come on in the house and cut out her foolishness. I've worked hard today getting the oats ready for the threshers tomorrow, and I'll be damned if I run from a little thundercloud."

I went back to the front porch. "Daddy says he's not coming, Mama. He says for you to come on in the house, that it's just a little thundercloud."

"Come on, Florrie, before it hits," Mama said, and she grabbed my hand. We ran down the front steps and out of the yard. Just as we crossed the road and headed down the lane, lightning struck in the field next to us. A blue ball of fire mushroomed where it struck, and we heard it sizzle as it ran along the ground.

"Lord save us, it's a cyclone, Florrie," Mama said, and the first drops of rain began to fall.

It turned black as midnight in the lane, and the wind roared through the woods. We ran holding hands, and Mama's voice rose over the sound of the wind as she prayed. I was scared, and thought we would be blown away before we reached Aunt Mira's house.

"Sweet Jesus, help us in the hour of our need," Mama prayed as we rounded the last curve and started down the hill.

The wind was not blowing so hard now, but the rain was pouring, and it was cold, unlike the warm rains of summer. Then we were in Aunt Mira's yard, and when we ran up on the porch, we were drenching wet.

Mama pulled at her wet dress. It clung, following the curves of her body. "We left the house too late, Florrie," she said. "We went through the worst of the storm in the lane."

We stood on the porch, and I looked at her. "You look like you just jumped in the river with your clothes on, Mama. Do I look as drowned as you do?"

"You sure do. We both look like something the cat dragged out. In all my years of running from storms, I never got caught in one before. It's a shame I've spoiled my record."

We laughed as we stood there, looking at each other, and then the front door opened. "Is that you, Julia?" Ralph Junior asked.

"It's me and Florrie," she said.

Aunt Mira stood behind Ralph Junior, looking over his

shoulder. She opened the door wider. "The storm's over now," she said. "If you'd just waited at home a few minutes longer, you could have saved yourself the trouble of getting wet, Julia."

"Damn," I said under my breath. "We missed our holy water."

"What did you say, Florrie?" she asked.

"Nothing," I answered.

Mama stood first on one leg and then the other, taking off her shoes. I had come barefoot.

"Come in and dry off," Aunt Mira said. "Ralph Junior can drive you back home." They stood back from the door, and we went into the living room.

"Julia," Aunt Mira said, "you and Florrie go and sit by the fireplace in the dining room. You look vulgar in front of Ralph Junior, the way your clothes are sticking to you."

Ralph Junior looked away from us, and Mama and I went to sit by the fire in the dining room until we looked fit for Ralph Junior to drive us home. The radio was playing in the living room, and I heard Aunt Mira ask Ralph Junior which station he wanted.

Mama pulled a straight chair up close to the fire and took down her hair, shook it, and leaned forward, holding the wet strands close to the flames to dry. I stood on the hearth and turned myself around and around, drying my clothes.

"Florrie," Mama said, "you ain't game if we don't spend the night, now that we're here. Toliver didn't build a fire in the living room today, and the house is going to be cold from the storm."

"We could take a warm bath, too," I said.

"We could. Go tell Mira that Ralph won't have to drive us home, that, if it's no trouble, we'll stay the night."

I went to the living room. Aunt Mira and Ralph Junior had

pulled the brocade chairs close to the radio. The Philco console sat on the floor; it looked like a miniature cathedral. They were listening to a man talk about the Catholic religion.

When Ralph Junior saw me standing there, he turned down the radio. "What is it, Florrie? Are you ready to go home?" he asked.

Aunt Mira adjusted her pince-nez.

"Mama said we'll just spend the night and save Ralph Junior from taking us home, Aunt Mira."

"It's no trouble to take you all home, Florrie," he said.

"Tell Julia," Aunt Mira said, "that Dorothy didn't come today and the beds aren't made up. I've been all the way to Huxley collecting rent, and I'm too tired to fool with getting out sheets and pillow cases. Tell her it's not convenient tonight."

I turned away from them. I felt put-down, embarrassed. I went back to the dining room, furious. Mama's legs were stretched out in front of her, her hands folded across her stomach. She was looking into the fire.

"Mama," I said, my voice trembling, "Aunt Mira says we can't stay, that it's not convenient. The beds aren't made up."

Mama sat up straight, and pulled her hair into a bun, fastening it with the hairpins. "Come on, Florrie," she said, standing up. "Let's go home."

We went into the living room. Aunt Mira and Ralph Junior still sat in their chairs. I thought they looked married, because Ralph Junior didn't look any younger than Aunt Mira. He stood up, but Mama and I kept going to the front door.

"Wait, Julia," Ralph Junior called. "I'll drive you home."

We went on out the front door to the porch. Aunt Mira followed us, and Ralph Junior looked at us from inside the screen door. Aunt Mira took me by the arm. "Wait, and Ralph Junior can drive you all home, Florrie."

242

Mama jerked my arm loose from Aunt Mira's hand. "Take your filthy hands off my girl, you old Catholic."

"What's the matter with you, Julia?" Aunt Mira asked, stepping back.

"There's not anything the matter with me. What's the matter with you?" Mama asked.

We stood there looking at each other, and the screen door squeaked as Ralph Junior came out to stand with us. "Aunt Julia, I'd like to drive you all home," he said.

"No," Mama said, "that's all right, Ralph. Florrie and I will walk home, and we'll sleep in our own beds. I don't have to take favors from you or Mira Gray."

I looked at him, at his balding head and paunch, and it was hard to believe that he owned a still in the woods.

"Go on in the house, son," Aunt Mira said. "It's cold and damp out here. There's nothing wrong with Julia except that she's having a mad spell, like she used to when she was little. If things don't go to suit Julia, she gets mad and has a tantrum." Ralph Junior went in the house.

"It's a sin," Mama said, "what you've done to that boy. You've kept him here to take Ralph Senior's place for a husband. One of these days, he might get fed up and murder you in your bed."

"How can you talk to me like that, after all I've done for you, Julia? I've helped you when nobody else would."

"No, you haven't, Mira Gray. You haven't helped me. But I tell you one thing, I don't love you. I never have had any sisterly love for you, and it made me feel guilty. But not any more. There would have to be something wrong with me to love a person like you."

Hooray for you, Mama, I thought.

"You're a taker, Julia," Aunt Mira said. "You think because

you're the youngest in the family, that Marcy and I owe you something. I don't have to support you and your husband. I've been telling you for years to get off my place, and then maybe Mr. Birdsong would get a job. But you don't have enough pride to leave."

I put my arm through Mama's and stood with her, facing Aunt Mira. "Don't you talk to my mother like that. She's good, and I hate your guts, Aunt Mira."

"Florrie, what in the world am I going to do with you?" Mama said. She took my hand and pulled me to the steps. The storm was over, but the night air was cold, and I shivered.

"Goodbye, Mira Gray," Mama said. "I'll never set foot in this house again as long as I live, so help me God."

Mama and I walked down the steps and away from her. The moon was behind the clouds, and I was scared to walk through that dark lane, but I didn't tell Mama. I put my arm around her waist as we walked.

We climbed the hill and I closed my eyes as we walked past the woods; and then we were between the fields, the wind sighing as it blew through the oats. I was freezing, but too tired to run.

Finally, we came to the gates and crossed the road. The house was dark, no light left on to welcome us home from the storm. We climbed the steps and went into the house. I followed Mama into the kitchen and we turned on the light, pulling our chairs close to the still-warm stove. I huddled there with Mama for a few minutes, and then I kissed her and went to bed.

When I woke up the next morning, I thought from the brightness of the room that it was late.

I tried to think if it was Saturday, and my mind finally settled on Wednesday. A school day. Then why was I still lying in bed, with the sun high enough to shine in my window?

I got out of bed. A tiny flame of alarm licked in my stomach as I opened the door to the kitchen. The table had not been set for breakfast, and the light was off. The stove was cold when I touched it. The kitchen screen was still latched. I shivered, and called to Mama. There was no answer.

I left the kitchen and went to her room. The shade was down, and her room was almost dark, but I could see her in bed. I tiptoed over and looked down at her. The covers were pulled up close under her chin.

"What's the matter, Mama?" I asked.

She opened her eyes and looked at me and then closed them again.

"Mama, are you sick?"

"Yes."

I felt her forehead. It was hot and dry. I smoothed her hair back from her face and didn't know what to do.

"What hurts, Mama?"

"Don't talk to me, Florrie. I don't want to talk. I want to sleep." She turned over onto her side.

I went to the window and let up the shade. Morning sun came in. Then I looked at Mama. She was breathing hard, her breath coming in puffs.

I left her then, going to look at the clock on the living room mantel. It was a quarter after nine. I went on the front porch and looked toward the fields. The threshers were here already, the men perched atop the orange machines, the oats falling before the whirling blades. The threshers would be paid one third of whatever money Daddy got from the oats.

I went down the steps and out of the yard. The men were calling back and forth to one another with happy voices. I crossed the road to tell Daddy that Mama was sick. One of the men waved to me as he rode past, and I waved back. Any other day, I would have been excited for the threshers to be in the field. They would be finished by early afternoon.

I stepped over the ditch and stood at the fence, motioning for Daddy. He pushed through the oats and came up to the fence. "What's the matter, Florrie? Why aren't you at school? I saw the school bus pass more than an hour ago."

"Mama's sick, Daddy. She didn't get up this morning, and when I woke up and went to her room, she was still asleep. I'm scared it's her heart."

"Ah, Florrie," he said. "Don't let your imagination run wild. She'll be all right. She probably just took a little cold."

"She's burning up with fever, Daddy. Come back to the house with me and see what you think."

He looked around at the two men riding the threshers back and forth across the field. "I guess they'll do it right without me here to watch them. Our cotton is riding on this oat crop, Florrie. I can't buy seed, or fertilizer either, without the money from the oats. So I've got to stay with it. I'll go see what's the matter, but you know it'll just make her mad if I say anything."

Daddy went around and came through the gate and I waited for him across the road. When he caught up with me, we walked together toward the house.

"Daddy, Mama finally told Aunt Mira last night what she thought of her. We got wet in the rain, and Aunt Mira wouldn't let us spend the night with her, said it wasn't convenient."

"Everybody has a pay day for the things they do, Florrie. Hers is coming one of these days. She'll have her pay day, just like everybody else."

"She told Mama that she didn't have any pride, to keep on living in her house."

We walked up the front steps, and Daddy said under his breath, "The son of a bitch."

I walked ahead of him into the living room. Mama was coughing, and when I opened her door, she was sitting up in the middle of the bed. Her hair was coming down from its pins, and I thought she must have felt bad last night if she had left her hair up.

I went to the bed and Daddy followed me. I pulled loose the hairpins, and her hair fell around her shoulders. Mama lay back down and closed her eyes. I could see her shaking under the covers.

"Are you cold, Mama?" I asked.

"I'm freezing. I don't think I'll ever be warm again."

"Do you hurt somewhere?"

"My chest hurts."

It was her heart. I turned to look at Daddy, and he motioned me to follow him from the room. "She's got a chest cold, Florrie," Daddy said, outside her door. "The weather changes this time of year and people take colds all the time. Your Mama doesn't take well to being sick. You know how you can hear her moaning all over the house when she's got an upset stomach."

"I know it, and that's what scares me. She's not making any noise at all, except when she coughs. That's not like Mama, to lie there so still."

Daddy started for the kitchen. "Come on and let's have a cup of coffee. I've been up since five o'clock and I need a cup."

"There's no fire in the stove, Daddy."

"I'll have one started in no time, Florrie. You get the pot ready, and I'll build the fire."

We went in the kitchen and there was something strange; the room was too light. I went to the window. The hickory tree lay on the ground, great clumps of dirt hanging from its roots. There was a deep hole where it had grown, and its branches, full with half-grown leaves, pointed toward the cemetery.

I looked at the huge, invulnerable tree and the tears came. "What happened, Daddy? What happened to our hickory tree?" I said, still looking out the window.

"It wasn't more than five minutes after you and your mama left last night that the goddamndest roar I ever heard in my life came through here. I thought the house was going. I tell you, I lorrie, I wished I'd gone with you all to Mrs. Kirk's, but it was over in a minute and I didn't think any more about it. I didn't know the tree was blown down until this morning, on my way to the field."

I dried my eyes, and Daddy started the fire in the stove. I got the coffee pot and the coffee and then went to the well on the back porch and drew fresh water. Mama said coffee was better made with fresh water.

Daddy had the fire going, but the stove wasn't hot yet. I set the pot on the cold stove and went to sit at the table. Daddy stood by the window, looking at the tree. "Well, your Mama finally got her cyclone. She won't even be surprised when she sees the tree. I won't ever hear the end of it, either."

"When Mama was little, she remembers seeing a cyclone, Daddy. She said she stood in the back door and watched their barn at Stillwater blow away, and then the horse and buggy after it. They found the buggy later, sitting straight up in a field, not hurt at all, but the horse was dead."

"There's no denying that things like that affect you the rest of your life," he said. "Your Mama has an abnormal fear of storms."

"It looks like she was right, Daddy. She was right to be afraid."

The coffee began to percolate, and it smelled so good, I thought I would ask Mama if she wanted a cup. It might make her feel better.

I went to her room and looked in the door, but she was sleeping and I didn't want to wake her up. I went back to the kitchen and got cups for Daddy and me, and the sugar from the pantry.

Daddy sat down at the table and I poured the coffee. It

248

looked pale and weak, but Daddy said it was fine, so I poured mine too, and sat down with him.

"It's funny without Mama," I said. "She loves her morning coffee so much that I hate to drink it without her."

"That's not the way to be, Florrie. Everybody gets sick sometimes, and she's no different from anybody else."

I sipped the coffee. It tasted like hot sugar-water, it was so weak, but I drank it anyway. I would have a stronger cup later.

It was going to be one of those perfect days that come after a storm. The sun would shine, but not too warm, the wind would blow, but not too hard; the wildflowers were back in the fields and woods, and the white bloom was on the blackberry vine. It was a day to break your heart with happiness.

And I was sick with worry about Mama.

"Daddy, after you finish your coffee, I want you to walk to Huxley and get Dr. Fairfax. Don't you dare to ask for a ride with the Kirks." I sounded like Mama.

"I need to get back to the field, Florrie. I don't think there's a bit of use in the world going after Dr. Fairfax this morning. She'll be a hundred per cent better when she wakes up."

"Daddy, I want you to go this morning. If it was you or me sick, Mama would see to us. I want you to go as soon as you finish your coffee."

He didn't say anything, but when he finished his coffee, he rolled down his shirt sleeves and got his hat, hanging from a nail on the kitchen wall. "I'll be back in a little while, sugar pie. You keep your eye on the threshers to let them know somebody's watching them."

I went to the front porch and watched him march down the road, his left arm swinging in time to the drill sergeant's silent count.

🌲🌲🌲🌲🌲🌲 29

Dr. Fairfax stayed in Mama's room a long time. When he came out he was frowning and looking at the floor, and I knew for sure there was something bad wrong with Mama.

It was afternoon before he got here. Daddy saw his car in front of the house and came in from the field to sit with me in the living room.

"It's serious, I won't try to make it sound less serious than it is," Dr. Fairfax said. "Julia never was a strong woman, and the trouble with her heart last fall just makes this worse. She has pneumonia in both her lungs. I don't know whether she'll make it or not."

Cold, electric fear ran through me, and I was surprised that I could sit there and look at him and nod my head. Last night Mama and I had run holding hands down the lane to Aunt Mira's; this afternoon Dr. Fairfax was saying that she might die. I pressed my fingers into my eyes and thought, no, I mustn't think that word.

Daddy cleared his throat and crossed his legs. Dr. Fairfax and I looked at him to see what he was going to say, but he didn't say anything. He looked down at the floor, with his chin jutting out.

"Dr. Fairfax," I asked, "is there a chance she can live?" And the feeling came over me that this was a crazy conversation I was having with Dr. Fairfax about my mother.

"Yes. There's a chance, Florrie. All we can do with pneumonia is wait and see. If she makes it through the next few days, she'll be all right."

I walked him to the door.

"Make her drink water every chance you get, and two aspirin every three hours. It doesn't matter how hard you have to shake her to wake her up when it's time for the aspirin."

I held open the screen door for him and watched until he drove away. I sat back down beside Daddy.

"Do you think Mama's going to die, Daddy?"

"No. She'll be up and around again in no time. She's a strong woman."

"Dr. Fairfax said she wasn't strong, Daddy. He said she's never been strong."

"He doesn't know her like I do, Florrie," Daddy said. "She'll be all right. I called your Aunt Marcy to come and help, because tomorrow I'll be gathering oats. I've got to stay in the fields, now, and get those oats harvested."

"I wish you hadn't called Aunt Marcy, Daddy. I'm going to take care of Mama, myself."

"I want you in school tomorrow, Florrie. It's not often I tell you something to do, but I want you in school, getting your education."

I knew I didn't have to go if I didn't want to, that I didn't have to do what he said. Daddy set a great store by education, but I did not think that schools were places that educated you. They were jails that imprisoned you for a certain number of hours every day, making you the whipping boy of any teacher in ill humor. I did not have much respect for the low intelligence of most of the teachers I knew. As soon as it was in my power, I would quit school and go about the business of educating myself.

"If Mama's better by tomorrow, I'll go, Daddy."

"That's fair," he said. "She'll be better by tomorrow."

I went to Mama's room and looked at her. I thought she was breathing easier, and as I looked at her, I felt young and strong. I closed my eyes and whispered, my strength is flowing into Mama, my strength is flowing into Mama. I felt weak, trembly.

I kissed her lightly on the hair; she stirred and settled into sleep again. I tiptoed from the room.

Daddy was gone. I smelled bacon frying and knew he was cooking the last of the bacon that Mama had been saving, making it last as long as she could. It was a long time between now and hog-killing time. But the weather had turned so warm that it wouldn't keep, and I thought it was good that he was cooking it.

Mama was coughing, deep wracking coughs, and I went back in her room. She was lying on her back. I smiled and lay the palm of my hand on her forehead. It was still hot.

"How're you feeling, Mama?"

She turned her head and looked at me. Her eyes were bright, her flushed cheeks making them look bluer than they were. "Is it time to go to bed, Florrie?"

"No, Mama. Look, see the sun coming in your window?"

She turned her head, looking upward to the window. "I see," and she closed her eyes.

I took her hand and held it in mine. I stood next to her bed until she went back to sleep, then walked away softly on my bare feet. When I reached the door, she called: "Florrie, don't leave me."

I went back and took her hand again.

"I'm scared to die, Florrie," she said.

"You're not going to die, Mama. You ought to be ashamed of yourself, talking like that. Dr. Fairfax said you have a chest cold."

"Has he been here?"

"Don't you remember? He came a little while ago. Aunt Marcy's coming to help out so I won't miss so much school."

"Chicken."

"What, Mama?"

"There'll be chicken, Florrie. Chicken."

I started to laugh, and felt the tears instead. Mama slept again, but I stayed for a long time. I laid her hand on the cover and waited, but she didn't wake up. I went to the back porch, leaned against the wall, and let the tears come.

The crab apple tree in back of the barn was in bloom, and I could smell its spicy perfume from here. I looked at the blurred, pink blossoms, and thought I would take some to Mama. The back screen door opened, and Daddy came onto the porch. I turned my head away, wiping at the tears because I did not want him to see me crying.

His hair was freshly combed, and smelled of tonic. It was cruel of him to smell of tonic when Mama was so sick. He wore field clothes, his blue workshirt sleeves rolled halfway up his arms, over the sleeves of his long underwear. Summer was not here, because Daddy still wore his long underwear.

"Mama told me she's scared to die," I said.

"Ah, that's just some of your Mama's hysterical talk, Florrie. You know she's always thought she was dying when she had an upset stomach."

I put my hands over my face and knew that I could not live without Mama. "What would we do without Mama, Daddy, what in the world would we do without Mama?"

253

I felt his arms around me; he had not put his arms around me since I was a little girl. I put my head on his shoulder, and he was lean and bony and unfamiliar. I was embarrassed and pulled away from him. It had been too long, too many years since we had found comfort in each other's touch.

I got the bucket and dropped it down the deep, dark hole of the well. The handle that pulled the rope unwound itself backwards, and in a second I heard the hollow splash of the water. I left the bucket long enough to fill, and then cranked the wheel and drew the water.

I poured fresh water in the washpan and splashed my face and washed my hands. I took the bucket and set it on top of the stone well. I heard Daddy rattling dishes in the kitchen.

I went to the table, and there were scrambled eggs and bacon on my plate, and a cup of coffee beside it. My stomach curled in distaste at the sight of the food, but I sat down and ate a few bites so I wouldn't hurt his feelings. He sat down at the table with me.

"I've got your basket finished for cotton picking this summer, Florrie."

I didn't look up or answer, and he didn't say anything else. I was mad at him and didn't know why and was ashamed for treating him shabbily. I ate a little of the food and drank a half cup of the strong coffee.

"I enjoyed it, Daddy. Thank you for cooking it for me." It was his turn not to answer, so I went to see about Mama.

The clock on the mantel said one o'clock. It was time for Mama's aspirin. If I were at school today, I'd just be on my way to lunch, but the thought didn't seem real. School was a long time ago, and the dishwater smell of the lunch room.

I got a glass of water from the kitchen. Daddy had gone back to the fields and left the dishes on the table. Steam still rose

254

from my half-filled coffee cup. The table set for two people, and the dishes unwashed in the afternoon, was sad. I wanted to run out the back door to the woods. When I came back home Mama would be up and cooking supper; we would talk about making jelly to sell.

Jelly to sell. I had paid little attention when she told me about it. Inside, I had known that wouldn't work for her either, that it was only another one of her schemes to make money, that it would fail like all her other schemes. And I knew that not only would it fail, I wanted it to fail. I closed my eyes, and the guilt I felt made me wish that I could run away from the terrible person that was myself.

I hurried to Mama's room to tell her I was sorry. I could hear her breathing when I was still far away and I was scared.

"Mama," I said.

She opened her eyes and looked at me, but without recognition.

"Mama, it's Florrie," and the tears ran down my face. "Mama, I want to tell you I'm sorry. I'm sorry for every mean thing I've ever said to you, and I'll never curse again, either."

But she closed her eyes, and didn't answer. I pulled the rocking chair close to her bed and sat there watching her for a long time. She'll be all right when the fever breaks, I thought. This time tomorrow, I bet, she'll be a whole lot better.

I held her hand gently in mine and rubbed my finger over the smooth gold band Daddy had given her when they were married. Inside were Mama's initials and his, and an engraving of an orange blossom. Mama had told me the ring would be mine when I got married.

Somebody was knocking on the front door. I went to see who it was, and there was Mrs. Goggins, shading her eyes and peering in through our screen door.

"Hey, Mrs. Goggins," I said.

"I saw Dr. Fairfax leave here a while ago. Is somebody sick?" she asked hopefully.

"Mama's sick."

Mrs. Goggins pulled at the door; I was glad that I had latched it.

"You can't come in Mrs. Goggins. Mama's asleep. She'll be up in a day or two. Dr. Fairfax said she has a chest cold."

"Is that all?" she asked.

"Yes," I said and she left. But when she got to the bottom of the steps, she stopped and looked up at me.

"Po' old Mrs. Birdsong. She's had a hard time."

She clapped her hands to the dogs that were whining for her against the fence. She talked to them all the way out our front gate and down the road, telling them that they were her sweet lambs and precious loves.

✝✝✝✝✝✝ 30

Aunt Marcy seemed always to come with the night. Just at dusk, Uncle Joel's Packard stopped in front of the house and Aunt Marcy came to the front steps with her suitcase. I brought it into the house for her, but since Uncle

Joel didn't come in, I didn't go out to speak to him, either. I was tired of trying to make him love me again.

Aunt Marcy hugged me and kissed me and pulled off her brown leghorn hat and lay it on the chair. "I didn't know I'd be back for a visit so soon, sugar," she said.

We stood in the door and watched Uncle Joel drive away. Then I led Aunt Marcy to Mama's bed.

"Do you know who this is, Julia?" she asked, leaning over Mama.

"Get out of here, Mira," Mama said. Her eyes were wild and frantic as I pushed her back down on the pillows.

"It's Aunt Marcy, Mama, come to help 'til you're well again."

Mama put both arms around my neck. "Don't leave me, Florrie. I'm scared, and when I go to sleep, I dream of hell, and they won't let me into heaven to see Mama."

I sat on the side of her bed and stroked her hair back from her forehead. Aunt Marcy sat in the rocker.

"Brush my hair, Florrie," Mama said. "That'll make me go to sleep."

I got Mama's tortoise-shell brush off her dresser. I pulled her hair from under her shoulders and spread it on top of the cover, pulling the bristles over the dark red strands. My left hand followed the path of the brush. Her hair was smooth and cool. She went to sleep.

Aunt Marcy crooked her finger at me and I followed her from the room, leaving Mama's brush on the dresser.

Aunt Marcy sat down on the wicker love seat, and I told her what Dr. Fairfax had said. She cried as I talked, pressing her handkerchief against her lips. I watched her coldly, despising her for crying.

"When you cry, Aunt Marcy, it's because you think Mama's going to die. If you think that, then you ought not to be around her, because she'll know how you feel. Mama's good at catching what other people are feeling."

Aunt Marcy wiped her eyes. "She's my little sister, Florrie. It breaks my heart to see her sick like that, on top of the hard time she's had."

"We are having a hard time, Aunt Marcy. Everybody in this country is having a hard time but you and Aunt Mira. Every day in the paper it's about the Depression and the bread lines and people committing suicide. You and Aunt Mira come around here and try to make Mama and Daddy believe there's something wrong with them for being poor. You've convinced Mama with your big house and your blue velvet evening dress that you wear to your women's club that she's a failure and Daddy's a failure. But you're wrong, there's nothing the matter with Mama and Daddy, it's you and Aunt Mira and Uncle Wilbur and the whole damn Lee family, if you ask me. Except Mama. Somehow she escaped being like the rest of you."

Aunt Marcy laughed, but without joy. "You've got Lee blood. Don't forget when you talk about the Lees, you're talking about yourself."

All at once, I was tired, weary to the bone. I wished that I could go to sleep, someone would wake me when the trouble was all over and Mama well again. "You can get up now, Florrie. Everything's all right," they'd say.

"I'm sorry, Aunt Marcy," I said. "It was wrong of me to talk to you that way. You've always come when Mama needed you."

Aunt Marcy smiled and called me a little old monkey, and we went to the kitchen to see about supper. She had brought with her some canned vegetable soup and a bakery chocolate cake. When the soup was hot, I called Daddy, and we all sat in silence eating our supper. Nobody ate any cake. I thought how funny that was, because only yesterday, that cake wouldn't have lasted two hours between Mama and me.

Daddy left the table and said he was going to talk to Charlie Swinburne for a while, but I knew he'd be drunk and coming home late. Aunt Marcy and I went and sat with Mama, me on the bed and her in the rocker. We didn't talk, and there was no sound but Mama's heavy breathing. A car passed along the road now and then, and I wondered who it was and where they were going. In another two weeks there would be the sound of the tree frogs at night, and you'd know that summer was here to stay.

I dozed and nearly fell off the bed. I kissed Mama's forehead and whispered, "I love you, Mama."

I went to bed in my clothes and dreamed that Mama was well. We were walking across the grass to catch the bus and ride to town with Frank Sadler. I was so happy I danced along beside her, and spring was bright green all around us. Mama spread her arms wide.

"Everything's *beautiful*," she said. "I wonder why I never noticed it before."

"See, Mama, I told you we'd be happy once spring was here."

✝✝✝✝✝ 31

I went back to school because it worried Mama to see me home. She thought I had been expelled and that she would have to go to school with me like she had last year.

"Florrie, what am I going to do with you, playing hookey," Mama said. "It's embarrassing to have to go to the school because your daughter has played hookey."

So Friday morning I got dressed and kissed her good-bye, and she smiled at me and was happy. I sat in my desk at school and thought about Mama and was scared, my heart beating hard, when someone came in and gave a note to the teacher. I thought the note would say that Mama was dead and for me to come home right away. But the note was for someone else, and I relaxed until the next time.

It was the first day of May, and the weather was warm as summer. Daddy said the fields were ready for spring plowing, and at school there was a May festival. Mary Anderson was May queen. At auditorium period on Friday, the whole school went to the baseball field to see the seniors dance around the Maypole.

The girls wore crowns of daisies, and Mary sat on the grass in a long white dress, reigning over her court and the festival. I forgot about Mama for a while as I watched the girls wind the colored streamers around the pole and lay an armful of flowers at the feet of the queen.

Friday night Dr. Fairfax came, and Mama called him "Papa."

"Hush, Julia," Aunt Marcy said. "Dr. Fairfax isn't old enough to be your papa. She doesn't know what she's saying, Dr. Fairfax."

Mama talked about living in Georgia, and once she thought she was a child again back in Stillwater. She was hitching Molly to the buggy for Grandpa Lee to make a night call. She raised her arms to put the bridle on and said, "Whoa, Molly."

"Julia never did hitch up Molly," Aunt Marcy said. "I guess she remembers seeing Wilbur do it."

Dr. Fairfax shook his head when he left on Friday night. Mama was no better, he said. But on Saturday morning when he came, her fever was down, and he said there wasn't so much congestion in her lungs.

"She's not out of the woods yet, but there's hope now, where I'd just about given up yesterday."

I hugged Aunt Marcy and ran flying to the fields to tell Daddy. "Dr. Fairfax says Mama's better, Daddy," I said, out of breath.

"See there, I knew she'd be all right. You worry too much, Florrie."

A crow flew over, cawing and swooping, and we looked at the sky, watching until the crow disappeared over the trees.

"I'm glad I'm not planting corn this year. I won't have to worry about the damn crows anyway. It made me so mad last year to see them in the corn. I'd have wrung their necks if I

261

could've caught one. A few months from now, all you're looking at, Florrie, will be white with cotton. Can you see it?"

"Yes, I can see it." I left him in the field, clearing away the last of the oats.

Mama wasn't talking out of her head anymore, but she looked weak. I told Aunt Marcy I was worried because Mama looked so pale and tired.

"It's because you're used to seeing her face flushed from fever," she said, and I thought that she was right.

I stayed with Mama all day Saturday, even though on Saturdays I seldom stayed in the house. I asked Mama if she remembered me asking her forgiveness for all the mean things I'd ever said.

"No, I don't remember. But I do. Forgive you, I mean. That is, if you'll forgive me." We laughed, and I was so happy, I felt like shouting or running around the room. I was glad it was this time today and not this time yesterday.

"Get the brush and brush my hair for me, Florrie." She moved until her hair was hanging off the bed. It almost touched the floor. "Be careful of my mole," she said. She had a tiny mole on her hairline in the middle of her forehead. I brushed and smoothed and brushed and smoothed, and Mama closed her eyes.

"I remember getting awful mad at Mama once," she said. "Mama wanted me to help her with some darning. She brought me a chair from the dining room into her bedroom, where she kept her sewing machine. I didn't want to sew, I wanted to play, and I snatched the chair from her and slammed it down on the floor. She told me I'd never forget doing that, and I never have."

I brushed until she said she was tired. Then I told her to wait a minute before she moved. I went to my dresser and got a blue satin ribbon out of the drawer, one I'd been saving. Aunt

Marcy had given it to me the last time she was here. I pulled Mama's hair back into a long swatch that hung down her back, and tied it with the blue ribbon.

"How does it look?" she asked.

"Pretty. Only your's is bonnie red hair."

"I don't understand," Mama said.

"You know, the song 'Johnny's So Long at the Fair?' 'He promised he'd buy me a bunch of blue ribbons to tie up my bonnie brown hair.' "

Mama smiled. "You like music don't you, Florrie?"

"Yes. I like to sing. That's the only thing that's any fun at school, when we go to the music room and sing. Sometimes we sing 'Johnny's So Long at the Fair.' I sing in the woods when I know no one can hear me."

"Why don't you want anyone to hear you? I'd like to hear you sing."

"Mrs. Gary wouldn't let me in the Glee Club. Only me and two other girls and a few boys didn't make it. I can tell from that, that I can't sing. If I could, I'd have gotten in the Glee Club."

"Who's Mrs. Gary?" Mama demanded.

"She's the music teacher, Mama."

"Well, she ought not to be if she kept you out of the Glee Club. Why didn't you tell me before?"

"Because I was ashamed. I thought it was terribly important to be in the Glee Club, but I don't any more."

"Why not?" Mama asked.

"Because I can have more fun in the woods singing by myself. I just don't care anymore, and I don't know when I stopped caring, I just did. I'm not even embarrassed anymore when I'm one of the three girls left sitting in the room while the others go to Glee Club. We have to do extra math."

"You'll be in the Glee Club when we move to the city, Florrie. These country people don't know a good voice when they hear one."

She lay back on her pillows and soon was sleeping again. I left and sat on the front porch steps. It was late afternoon and I watched Daddy for a while in the field, not wanting to help Aunt Marcy with supper. I stretched and yawned, contented because Mama was almost well. I knew I would have to help her more than I had in the past, but the three days gone by were nightmares, to be forgotten. Aunt Mira's car drove through the gates, but she didn't turn toward Huxley. I sat straight and watched to see where she was going. She came up the side road to our house.

"Hellfire and damnation, what does she want," I wondered.

She parked her car and got out. I didn't stand up. She came to the foot of the steps and looked up at me.

"Is Julia sick?" she asked.

"Yes."

"Why wasn't I called?"

"Because Mama didn't want you. Aunt Marcy's here to help look after Mama."

"I know Marcy's here. I called her, and Joel said she was here."

She came up the steps and pushed past me. I followed her to the kitchen.

"Marcy, how come you didn't call me and tell me Julia was sick?"

Aunt Marcy dried her hands on her apron and smiled as though Aunt Mira had come for a social visit. "Come on in and sit down, Mira," she said.

"I don't have time to sit down, Marcy. Answer my question."

"I've already told her why, Aunt Marcy," I said. "I told her Mama didn't want her, that's why."

264

"Julia was out of her head, Mira. She told me to get out of the room, and called me Mira."

Aunt Mira pulled off her glasses and rubbed the red spots on her nose with her thumb and index finger. "I came to tell Julia I'm sorry for what happened the night of the storm," she said. "I've already been to confession."

Aunt Marcy looked puzzled.

"Mama and Aunt Mira had a fuss the night of the storm that pulled up our hickory tree, Aunt Marcy. We went down the lane to Aunt Mira's and got caught in the rain, and Mama wanted to stay the night with Aunt Mira because she was so cold. But Aunt Mira told her it wasn't convenient, and Mama and I walked home in the cold wind. That's what gave her pneumonia." Let her conscience gnaw on that on a cold winter's night.

Aunt Mira set the glasses back on her nose. "I'll send Father O'Bannon by to see her," she said.

"No, you don't, Aunt Mira. Mama's not a Catholic, you are. Leave her alone and stay out of there with your holy water, too."

Aunt Mira left without saying good-bye. Aunt Marcy and I stood in the middle of the kitchen, looking at each other, and then I got the plates from the pantry and began to set the table. I walked around the table with the plates. When I looked up, Mama was standing in the kitchen door. She was holding her gown off the floor with one hand, and bracing against the door frame with the other. I ran to her, still holding the plates.

"Mama, you're not supposed to be up," I said.

"I feel real good," she said. "As a matter of fact, I feel so good, I decided to get up and make tea cakes. I don't make tea cakes nearly enough, the way you like them."

I felt her forehead and it was cool. I looked at Aunt Marcy.

"Julia, you ought not to be up, sugar," she said. "I'm going

265

to beat you up if you don't get back in the bed," and she folded her hands into playful fists.

Mama pushed between us and sat down at the table. "When I make up my mind to do something, I do it," she said.

Aunt Marcy nodded to me, and I brought Mama her yellow mixing bowl and a wooden spoon. I set the flour and sugar and vanilla in front of her. On the back porch I pulled up the bucket that held the butter and eggs in the well. There was a whole cake of butter, and six eggs. But there was no milk. I was glad; now she couldn't make the tea cakes, and would go back to bed. I took her the butter and eggs.

"Mama, there's not any milk."

"Tea cakes have to be made with milk. Go bring Beautiful Eyes down and I'll milk enough for the tea cakes."

I was scared of the cow. "Mama, you ought not to . . ."

"Florrie, if you don't go get the cow, I will," she said.

The sun was going down as I went in the barn to get Beautiful Eyes. She looked over the stall at me and mooed. I jumped back and thought, how unfriendly she was. I got the rope off the hook inside the door and tied it around her neck before I unhooked the door to the stall.

I pulled the rope as far as it would go before I tugged on it, urging her to come out the door. Beautiful Eyes mooed again and walked out of the stall, pushing open the door. I walked the full length of the rope in front of her, looking back all the time to make sure she didn't have her head lowered to butt me.

"Mama, here's Beautiful Eyes," I called.

She came through the back door, leaning on Aunt Marcy's arm, and sat down on the steps. She pulled her gown close around her legs, her bare feet on the ground. "It's good to be outside," she smiled.

"You can't stay too long, sugar," Aunt Marcy said, and sat on the step next to her.

"Be quiet, Marcy, I'll stay as long as I want to." She took a deep breath and looked toward the barn at the crab apples in bloom.

"When we move to town, Florrie," Mama said, "I'm going to have a crab apple tree outside the kitchen window, where I can look at it and smell it while I'm washing dishes."

"That'll be good," I said and Beautiful Eyes mooed and pulled on the rope, straining for the grass just out of her reach.

"Mama, you better go ahead and milk her before she butts me trying to get the grass."

"Push her up close to the steps, Florrie," she said.

I pushed Beautiful Eyes, and she stepped sideways until Mama could reach her. She rested her head on the cow's side, holding the cup under her tit. She squeezed and pulled, squeezed and pulled, the milk hissing on the side of the cup. When it was full, she said, "That's enough," and took the cup away.

I took Beautiful Eyes to the barn, and when I went back to the house, the first stars were out. Venus shone brightly to the south, over the oat field. Daddy was coming through the front gate, but I didn't wait for him.

In the kitchen, Mama was stirring the batter in the yellow bowl, and Aunt Marcy was flouring the rolling board. Daddy came up on the porch, stamping his feet to get the mud off. He poured water into the pan, and there was splashing and blowing as he washed his face.

"Well," he smiled as he opened the screen door. "It looks natural to see you in here, Mrs. Birdsong."

Mama didn't look up from stirring. "I'm feeling weak, Mr. Birdsong," she said. "As soon as I get these tea cakes in the oven to bake, I'm going back to bed."

Mama wouldn't let Aunt Marcy or me finish them for her. She stood at the table and rolled them out, taking a drinking glass to cut them out. She spaced them neatly on the pan, and watched me when I put them in the oven.

"I'm going to rest now," she said, and I helped her back to bed.

ⵣⵣⵣⵣⵣ 32

Mama and I talked until midnight. I sat in the rocker, and she told me stories. After supper I brought her some tea cakes, but she wasn't hungry, so I set them on her sewing machine. She said she would eat them later.

Mama had been quiet for a long time, and I sat drowsing in the chair, warm and contented.

"When I sixteen, just your age, Florrie, I loved a boy named Bud. I haven't thought of him for a long time."

"I've never heard you mention him before, Mama."

"Wilbur wouldn't let me go out with him, so the only time I saw him was at church. There was a Valentine's party, and Bud asked me to go with him. Wilbur wouldn't let me, so I waited until he and Ruby were in bed Valentine's night, and then I climbed out the window and didn't come home until late.

"I slipped back in the window about eleven o'clock, thinking he didn't know I'd left the house. After I got in bed, he came to my room with a long switch. He pulled back the cover and whipped me, and that green switch cut all the way through my gown. 'I'll beat the sin out of you' he told me.

"I cried and begged him to stop, but he wouldn't until I promised him I'd never slip away again. He sat next to me on the bed and cried and started to kiss the cuts on my legs where the blood seeped through my gown. I crawled under the covers and told him to leave me alone or I'd tell Ruby. I still hate him, Florrie, and I don't care if it's a sin to speak ill of the dead."

I kissed her and told her I would see her in the morning. I looked back when I got to the door, and she smiled at me.

"You're a good girl, Florrie. I know I've got one person in the world that loves me."

I went back to the bed and kissed her again and turned out her light. Aunt Marcy was already asleep in my bed. I was glad that soon she would go home and I would have my bed to myself again.

Aunt Marcy shook me awake at daybreak. I sat up in bed, my heart pounding, with Aunt Marcy's face close to mine. Tears were streaming down her face.

"I think Julia's dead, Florrie. I just went to her bed to see about her and I couldn't hear her breathing," she sobbed. "Go get Mr. Birdsong, because I shook her and shook her and I can't wake her up."

I jumped out of bed and ran out of the house. I ran toward the cemetery, away from Aunt Marcy's voice calling to me. I stopped in horror. Not the cemetery. I didn't want to go to the cemetery. I ran across the yard and through the grass. I crossed the road and ran through the oat field and into the woods.

It was near dark in the woods, the birds making their first tentative sounds of morning. I sat down under my tree and rubbed my cheek on the bark. The pain felt good. I prayed, dear heavenly father please let Mama be living when I get back home, I love her so much. Amen.

I lay back on the grass and looked up through the leaves to the sky. I would wait a long time before I went home, and when I did everything would be all right. Aunt Marcy would laugh and say she was sorry to have scared me. Daddy would tell me I was going to have to learn to control myself. Mama would call from her room to see what all the fuss was about.

I smiled, certain that was the way it was going to be. I had sat with Mama until midnight last night. I had thought, Sunday already. Nothing so terrible as death could have happened to Mama between midnight and dawn. Oh God, I thought, what if she tried to call us and we didn't come, but I put the thought quickly away. Mama was living. I must learn to control myself.

I lay under the tree for a long time, until the sun rose high enough to send slender shafts of light through the trees. It was like the light in the picture of Jesus that hung in the church, the one where the light streamed onto Jesus' face. I thought the heavenly light was God's sign to me that Mama was not dead, so I left the woods.

When I get home, I thought, Mama will be drinking a cup of coffee with Aunt Marcy and Daddy, wondering where I've been. I hurried so as not to worry her. I had gotten almost to the fence when I saw the cars parked in front of our house. Ralph Junior's car was there, and Dr. Fairfax's. There was a cream-colored ambulance with its back doors standing open.

So it was true. Mama was dead. I ran and I was floating, my legs taking me home so slowly I hardly moved at all. A grasshopper jumped from the fallen oats, soaring in a graceful arc in front of me; he was moving as slowly as I. A car crept along the road, and I could see the feathers in the wings of a humming-

270

bird, poised over a white flower. The world had run down, like Mr. Saxon's Victrola.

I climbed through the fence and then I was on the front porch, pushing through the people who had gathered there, Mrs. Goggins, and Ralph Junior with a sad face.

Aunt Marcy and Aunt Mira were in the living room talking with Dr. Fairfax.

"Aunt Marcy, is my mother dead?"

Dr. Fairfax came and put his hand on my arm, but I jerked away from him.

"Aunt Marcy, I said 'is my mother dead?' "

"She's with the Lord, sugar."

I went and stood by Mama's bed. She looked no different than when I sat by her and she was sleeping; no different except that now there was no sound of her breathing. The tea cakes I had taken her last night were still on her sewing machine, and her hair, tied with the blue ribbon, lay long over her shoulder.

Her arms were on top of the cover. I took the square thumbs she was so ashamed of and tucked them under her fingers. Then I went to the back yard.

I sat on the trunk of the fallen hickory tree; its leaves were still fresh and crisp, living on stored moisture. The tree looked healthy, as if it only needed raising and some kind hand to place the dirt back tenderly over the torn roots.

But in a few days the moisture would be gone and death would blow his breath and wither the bright leaves, for even now he was among the branches, waiting.

✝✝✝✝✝✝ 33

Mama lay in the casket over her grave. It was covered over with a blanket of pink roses. She had lain in the Methodist church all morning, and then they had brought her here. Early afternoon sun shone on the roses, and on the mourners gathered at her grave.

This morning I had sat in the living room and talked politely to people when they came, pouring them coffee and answering their questions.

No, I wasn't going back to school.

Yes, if there was a heaven I thought Mama was there, and no, I didn't know that people thought her peculiar but sweet. She was just Mama.

Brother Gridley came and said that he would pray for her. "I don't think it's necessary to go to church to get to heaven," he said, "but it helps, it helps."

Aunt Mira lit a candle for Mama at Mass and brought Dink home from school for the funeral. I was glad to see him, and he sat now in the chair next to me. Yesterday afternoon we walked in the woods and talked about Mama, remembering funny things she'd done. It was like opening the sluice gates to talk to Dink about Mama, because nobody else would. They didn't want to make me sad.

Aunt Marcy got her preacher from the big Baptist church in Birmingham to come for the service. "Julia couldn't stand that Brother Gridley," she said, fresh tears flowing.

Aunt Mira picked the spot where Mama would be buried, because it was her cemetery. It was a place near the fence, under an oak tree. Daddy had fifty dollars left from selling his oats and paying the threshers, and had walked to Huxley and caught a bus into Birmingham the day Mama died. He tried to buy a place for Mama in the big cemetery, but when he came home, he said there were none there for that price. He went to Charlie Swinburne's and didn't come home until the funeral.

Aunt Mira came to talk to Daddy, but when she learned he wasn't home, she talked to me.

"You all will have to move, Florrie. The only reason I ever let Mr. Birdsong live here was because of Julia. She's blood, and you are, but he's not. Now that Julia's gone, he'll have to go. I'll support you, but I won't support him any longer."

"We won't stay a day longer than we have to, Aunt Mira."

She started to leave, but turned back. "Come and spend the night with me, Florrie. I never got to tell Julia I was sorry for the fuss we had."

"No, I don't want to spend the night with you, Aunt Mira."

She left; I didn't see her again until today.

The preacher from Birmingham wore a black suit and held his small Bible. The wind blew through his thick gray hair, and it blew through the crab apple trees, sending showers of pink blossoms to the ground. There was a large crowd around the grave. Aunt Mira and Aunt Marcy wore black crepe dresses and black hats and black shoes. Uncle Joel was dressed in black, and Dink wore his school uniform. Daddy wore his wedding suit, and I wore my blue Sunday chambray dress with the white collar and cuffs, and under it, my pink brassiere.

The preacher raised his arms in the manner of Brother Gridley and prayed: "Dearly beloved, we have come to bury this noble woman, this wife and mother and sister. Her years were short on this earth, but she will have life eternal in thy paradise . . ."

I stopped listening to his words and looked at Mama's casket. I didn't believe that she was in there. When I went home she would be sitting at the kitchen table, smoking a cigarette, waiting to hear how the family was taking it. The sun glinted on the silvery ends of the casket; I closed my eyes.

The preacher was reading from the Bible, "In my house are many mansions, if it were not so I would have told you, I go to prepare a place for you . . ."

Dear Lord, I begged, please let Mama's mansion be blazing with lights when she gets there.

The men stepped forward and dropped ferns on Mama's casket. Effie Johnson left the circle of mourners and went back to the church. Aunt Marcy sobbed and tapped me on the shoulder. "Cry, Florrie, you'll feel better if you cry." I turned my head away from her.

Daddy, sitting on the other side of me, looked steadily into his lap. His hands were clasped, the knotty fingers wound around one another. What was it about hands? Hands were honest, they told about you. Faces lied with smiles and words, but never hands. They told you what a person was really like. I put my hand over his, because I loved him.

Mr. Lowery took the roses off Mama's casket, and began to turn the handle that lowered her into the ground. I left, because I never stayed when the dirt was shoveled back into the grave.

I walked across the grass, and the warm day swam in front of my eyes. I kicked a rock, and when I looked at our kitchen window, I thought that Mama was watching for me. I was at the cemetery gate when Frank Sadler called to me. I stopped and waited for him. When he got close, I could see his eyes were red from crying.

"I wanted to tell you," he said, "that I loved your mother. I never told her I did, but I hope she knew it."

I didn't say anything.

"She's one of the kindest people I ever knew, and she loved to have fun. I'm not going to be able to look at this place when I pass by. Times when she went to town by herself, she and I would have ourselves a time talking. I used to pass up people waiting for the bus so we could be on there by ourselves and talk."

I was glad that Frank Sadler loved my mother, glad she'd had a pleasure I hadn't known about.

"Mama and I had a good time when we went to town," I said. "If we weren't sick from eating when we got home, we hadn't had a good time."

Frank smiled. "Julia sure loved you. She used to talk about the things she was going to do for you when you all got moved to town."

We stood there for another minute not talking, everything quiet except for the organ music coming from the church windows.

"Well, I better be going," Frank said. He held out his hand and I shook it.

"I'll be seeing you," I said.

"Goodby, Florrie," he said, and he put on his hat and walked toward the road.

I went home. I stood in the middle of the kitchen; it was

clean and cool. "Mama," I called, and waited. There was nothing except the sound of the cars pulling away from the side of the road. I went to her room.

Mama's bed was neatly made with the blue hobnail bedspread, her sewing machine by the window covered with a white doily. Her good shoes sat on the sewing machine pedal. I picked them up and ran my hand along the smooth black leather. They had new shoestrings with tassels on the ends. I put my hand inside the right shoe and felt the ridges that her toes had made. I turned them over and looked at the soles; they were hardly worn at all. The sole was still clean up next to the heel.

I put them back on the pedal and went to her dresser. I picked up her brush. There were auburn strands of hair caught in the bristles. I laid it down and sat in the rocker. I sang,

"Lead kindly light, amid th' encircling gloom,
Lead Thou me on; the night is dark, and I am far
    from home . . ."

I went to her closet and opened the door. I put my arms around her clothes and buried my face among them. They smelled musty.

"I wondered where you were, Florrie," Aunt Marcy said from the door. "Come and eat, the neighbors brought us food."

She put her arm around my shoulder as we walked to the kitchen, and told me I was a brave soldier. We sat around Mama's table. There were bowls of potato salad and macaroni and cheese and fried chicken. I sat down next to Dink.

I listened to Aunt Marcy tell Uncle Joel about Mama. "I woke up at dawn and went to see about her, Daddy. At first I thought she was just deep asleep when I called her from the door, but when I got closer I knew she was dead. Her eyes were closed, so she must have died in her sleep."

I closed my eyes.

"None of this food," Dink said to us all, "is as good as Aunt Julia's salmon croquettes."

Nobody said anything.

✟✟✟✟✟✟ 34

Aunt Mira went home early in the afternoon, and Ralph Junior and Dink followed her in Ralph Junior's car. Aunt Marcy called me into the living room. She sat on the wicker love seat next to Uncle Joel. Daddy sat in the rocker, looking down at the floor, his legs crossed.

The room swam with somber, late-afternoon glow. It was too early to turn on the light, and yet it was hard to see their faces in the shadows. And I was lonely. No, it felt more like homesickness, the way I felt when I was a little girl and had been away from Mama too long. Only this time, it could never be relieved by going home.

"Sit down, Florrie," Aunt Marcy said. "We have something to talk over with you."

I sat down in the rocking chair next to the fireplace.

"Joel and I want you to come and live with us, don't we, Daddy?" Aunt Marcy looked at him for approval.

Uncle Joel smiled and pulled at his shirt collar. "Yes, that's right, Florrie," he said.

This was one of those crazy conversations that went on so much these last few days. All the talk about Mama dying and where she was going to be buried, and now, Aunt Marcy asking me to come live with her. I didn't believe that Mama was dead and I was sitting in this gloomy room talking about where I would live.

"Well, Florrie?" Aunt Marcy asked.

"I don't know," I said, and I closed my eyes and saw Mr. Barfield walking down our steps and fading into the night. This time last week, what were we doing? We were most likely finishing up supper, and I tried to remember the night Mama and I last ate together. Our last supper, and neither of us knew it. And when was Mama's last cup of coffee? I thought back and realized it was only last Tuesday. And Saturday night she was living her last night and I had treated her as if she had ten thousand more. Oh, if I had only known, I would not have left her. I would have spent the last hours telling her how much I loved her.

"Florrie," Daddy said, "Are you all right?"

"Yes," I said.

"Florrie," Aunt Marcy said, "do you want to come live with Joel and me, sugar?"

"Daddy, what do you want me to do?"

"I want you where it's best for you. I'm busted except for the fifty dollars I got for the oats. Mrs. Kirk says she has people waiting to move into this house that can pay rent. She says if I can't provide for you, she'll have you put in a Catholic orphanage until you're of age."

"She won't put me any place," I said.

"Florrie, if I can't take care of you, she can take me to court and have you taken away from me. All the work I've done on her land and keeping up the cemetery for her doesn't count for a thing as far as she's concerned. She'll get even with me for marrying your mother, if she can."

"Florrie," Aunt Marcy said, "Joel and I have been so lonesome since little Janie died. If you'll come live with us, I'll have the best time sewing for you and we'll go to the picture show every Saturday. You know how when you were little, you always made me take you to the picture show when you came to visit? Mr. Birdsong can come to see you anytime he wants."

I was tired of them. I would not talk to them any longer. "I don't know. I don't know what I'll do," I said and stood up. "Good-bye, Aunt Marcy, Uncle Joel. Daddy, I'm going for a walk. I'll be home in a little while."

I went to the back yard to the crab apple trees and broke off limbs with fresh-looking blooms, then to the cemetery and kneeled by Mama's grave. I pushed away the blanket of pink roses and lay the crab apple blossoms in their place. But I didn't believe she was there under those flowers. Not my mother with the long red hair and square thumbs.

I started slowly back home and I heard the front screen slam. Aunt Marcy and Uncle Joel walked down the path to the black Packard. In their black clothes, they looked like a tall and a short black bird.

The house was dark when I got there; no lights had been turned on. Daddy was sitting on the front porch, and I sat on the steps to keep him company. Cars came and went along the road, as if Mama hadn't been buried today, and Mrs. Goggins's dogs barked when a young boy ran past their fence. Crickets began their lonesome singing as dark crept cross the field. I stood up.

"I'm going in, Daddy, I'm too tired to stay up any longer."

"Good night, Florrie."

I went in Mama's room and closed the door. I sat on the side of her bed and brushed the dirt off the bottoms of my feet before I lay down and put my head on her pillow. The room was dark. I cried for the first time since she died.

I cried because she would never live in town and because she had had to work so hard and wear men's clothes. I cried because she wouldn't see summer, and because she would lie forever in the dark that she hated. I cried because I would never see her again, and because I missed her so much.

Then I felt her next to me. I raised my head. "Mama?"

"Hush," she said. "Lie down and go to sleep, Florrie, you'll make yourself sick."

I turned over on my side and she lay her arm across my shoulder and fit her body to mine. I slept. When I woke in the morning, she was gone.

"Mama?" I said, but there was nothing.

I lay there tired and heavy. After a while I got up and went to the kitchen and built a fire in the stove. I cooked breakfast for Daddy and me and washed the dishes. I looked out the window and watched the school bus go by and couldn't remember that it ever had anything to do with me.

Daddy went to the fields, because habit was too strong or because he didn't have anything else to do. I looked for Mama everywhere, and I walked through the house and looked at things I had paid no attention to before. I touched the hem in the curtains she made, and watered the flowers that were coming up in her window box.

Daddy and I knew we had to leave here, but neither of us made any move to get ready to go. The days passed in a dream. Daddy was as grouchy with me as he'd been with Mama when meals weren't ready on time. He went almost every night to Charlie Swinburne's, and I lay on Mama's bed and listened to him bump his door when he came in.

Last week I picked the wild red roses that grew on the cemetery fence and put them on Mama's grave. As I knelt there, the feeling came over me that I had to leave here, get away from Gray's Chapel. Daddy was talking now about staying, talking about living in somebody else's tenant house, and I saw the years go by; I was his devoted old-maid daughter, keeping house for him. And even if I wanted to stay, Aunt Mira wouldn't let me. She'd put me in the Catholic home. I was scared.

"Mama, I'm going. I'm leaving Gray's Chapel whether Daddy goes with me or not." I went to the field where Daddy had hitched up poor, blind Dixie and was plowing.

"Daddy, it's no use plowing," I said. "We've got to leave here."

He fussed at me and argued with me, but when I told him I'd go without him, his shoulders slumped and he unhitched Dixie from the plow and followed me to the house.

We started packing that afternoon. I gave all of Mama's dresses to Dorothy, and her coat with the fur collar and her shoes. I gave her the sheets and the bedspreads and Mama's dishes. Dorothy's husband, Mitchell, came at dark in his wagon and hauled it away. But I kept Mama's blue eyelet dress, because it looked so much like her. And I kept her tortoise-shell hair brush, and the Whitman's candy box with a five-dollar bill in it.

I looked in the drawer of the work table in the kitchen. Mama's contest was still there, and the scratch paper where she'd figured the puzzles, and two pencils, sharpened with the kitchen knife. I kept the contest papers and her small cedar chest with my school papers and her letters from Daddy. I kept Grandpa Lee's surgeon's kit. All the thing's of Mama's that I kept fit in a small cardboard box.

When I finished packing, I walked down the lane to Aunt Mira's. I called Aunt Marcy and told her we were leaving; she said that Uncle Joel would pick us up at the bus station in Birmingham tomorrow afternoon. I told Aunt Mira she could have all the furniture for the rent except Mama's dining room table and chairs and her sewing machine.

I walked back up the lane, and when I got home I told Daddy to go and hire Peachtree and tell him to bring his wagon and move our dining room table and sewing machine to Aunt Marcy's.

Then I cooked supper, and went to bed at dark to sleep in Mama's bed for the last time.

🌲🌲🌲🌲🌲🌲 35

Daddy and I sat on our suitcases under the tree by the road and waited for the bus. My cardboard box was next to me. I looked at the house; it didn't look empty from the outside. But it was. When Daddy and I left and I slammed the front door, the sound echoed through the rooms.

Aunt Mira sent a man with a truck early this morning to take away our furniture. The sign on the side of the truck said "Apex Used Furniture," so I suppose she sold it all to him. There wasn't much, just our beds and dressers and the wicker love seat and chairs. And the porch rockers. Ralph Junior came and led Dixie and Beautiful Eyes away down the lane. He took Daddy's plow, too.

"I believe this is the hottest May we've had for a long time," Daddy said, and took out his handkerchief and wiped his neck and forehead.

I squinted my eyes down the road but the bus was not in sight. Daddy and I were going to stay with Aunt Marcy until we found a place to live and Daddy got a job. But I knew that Daddy wouldn't stay in Birmingham long enough to find a job, because already he was talking about going back to Georgia. He'd go to Georgia and find himself a piece of land to farm on somebody's place, and I'd have to decide whether I would go with him or stay with Aunt Marcy. After all, it was like Mama said, I had a choice.

"Florrie," Daddy said pointing to the field, "last year this time the corn was already coming up. Remember, I got the seed in the ground the first of April, and by this time it was a foot high. If the drouth hadn't come, that would have been the best corn I ever had."

"You can make things grow, Daddy. It was the weather. You can't do anything about the weather."

Far down the road I saw the bus coming.

"Come on Daddy, I see the bus," and I picked up my suitcase.

He stood up and looked toward the house, his face bitter. "This is a sorry day to go away and leave Julia in that woman's cemetery. And after seventeen years of hard work, what do I have? Fifty dollars and a suitcase full of field clothes."

I took his arm, pulling him to the road. "Don't talk about the past, Daddy. Let's just go on and see what happens. You can't plan anything."

The bus pulled over to the side of the road and stopped. Daddy climbed on with our suitcases, and I went back to get my box. I looked across the grass at the house where I was born, and I felt my roots torn loose from the earth. The voices from the past called to me, and it was more than I could bear to leave.

"Florrie," Daddy called, leaning from the door of the bus. "Come on."

I picked up my box and walked to the bus.

"Afternoon, Frank," I said as I climbed the steps.

"Afternoon, Florrie," he answered, and jumped up to take my box. "I declare, you get prettier every time I see you. There won't be a boy around, before long, without a broken heart."

I smiled at him, and he set my box on the floor by the driver's seat. I sat down next to an open window. Daddy sat behind Frank. They began to talk as the bus pulled away from the side of the road.

"Good-bye, house," I whispered, and through the afternoon haze I thought I saw Mama hoeing in the garden and that she waved to me.

As we passed the cemetery, I strained to see Mama's grave, but it was too far from the road. Frank shifted gears, and the bus whined as it picked up speed. We passed the church and rounded the curve, and after the Fowlers' house there was nothing but woods.

I sat back in my seat and let the fresh May air blow on me and watched the blurred green of the trees flashing by.